# The
# Error of Our
# Ways

ALSO BY DAVID CARKEET

*Double Negative*

*The Greatest Slump of All Time*

*I Been There Before*

*The Full Catastrophe*


FOR YOUNG READERS

*The Silent Treatment*

*Quiver River*

# The
# Error of Our
# Ways

A NOVEL

## DAVID CARKEET

HENRY HOLT AND COMPANY
NEW YORK

Henry Holt and Company, Inc.
*Publishers since 1866*
115 West 18th Street
New York, New York 10011

Henry Holt® is a registered
trademark of Henry Holt and Company, Inc.

Published in Canada by Fitzhenry & Whiteside Ltd.,
195 Allstate Parkway, Markham, Ontario L3R 4T8.

Work on this novel was supported by a Fellowship from
the University of Missouri Weldon Spring Fund.

Library of Congress Cataloging-in-Publication Data
Carkeet, David.
The error of our ways: a novel   /   David Carkeet. — 1st ed.
p.     cm.
I. Title.
PS3553.A688E77   1997                              96-16510
813'.54—dc20                                          CIP

ISBN 0-8050-7114-8

Henry Holt books are available for special promotions and
premiums. For details contact: Director, Special Markets.

First Edition—1997

DESIGNED BY KELLY SOONG

Printed in the United States of America
All first editions are printed on acid-free paper. ∞

3   5   7   9   10   8   6   4   2

*For Harold and Edith Lubin*

# The
# Error of Our
# Ways

# 1

"Sesame."

"Buckle your high chair first."

"Sesame."

"It's coming on right now. See? They're thanking viewers like you, so just buckle."

"Cheerios."

"I've got 'em. Can I buckle you?"

"*No!*"

"Then you buckle."

"I buckle."

"Good. Great. Good job. Here's your breakfast."

"Potty."

Ben's shoulders slumped. Negotiating with Molly was as taxing as dealing with his suppliers and customers. More taxing, actually. Adult rules remained constant, but Molly's changed from week to week.

He slid the high-chair tray out, squeezed open the plastic

buckle, and lifted his daughter out. In the kitchen, he pulled down her pajama bottoms and eased her onto the blue-and-white potty stool. She immediately produced great quantities of fluid. This moment was still a miracle to him, for she was only a month out of diapers. The transition had been sloppy, and just when he and Susan were concluding that they had rushed her, Molly turned a corner and entered the sunny valley of sphincter control. It had gone faster than he remembered for his other daughters, insofar as he could remember anything about their early development. Molly didn't even wear a diaper at night now. In the crib, her unconscious would scream at her for ten hours to *hold it!* Then, on rising, she might dawdle for an hour before saluting the new day. She, at two and a half, had a stronger bladder than he, at forty-four.

"Wipe in front," Ben said.

She took the toilet paper he had given her and pressed it against the side of one buttock. "Here?"

"No. Wipe in front."

She switched hands and pressed the paper against her other buttock. "Here?"

"No. In front."

Back to the first buttock. "Here?" This was her great dawn comic routine.

"Shall I do it?"

She immediately wiped in front, rose, and pulled up her pajama bottoms. Ben put her back in the high chair and stood in her line of sight to the TV. She buckled. He gave her a fresh helping of cereal, then rinsed out her potty bowl in the toilet.

Now, with luck, he could eat his breakfast and read the paper. He grabbed a box of Just Right from the pantry shelf. From the feel of it, there was enough for only one serving. He put it back and searched the shelves, rejecting the several boxes of Chex cereals because Ralston was too big in town already. He finally settled down at the table with a bowlful of Shredded Wheat. After two bites he looked down. It had been years since he had eaten Shredded Wheat. It was like chewing a bird's nest. He imagined tiny beaks poking up from it. Who invented this stuff? How in the hell had it been a success?

Karen, their fourth-grader, came into the kitchen, dropped her backpack on the floor, put an English muffin into the toaster, and asked where the funnies were. By this time, Ben was deep in an "Ask the Doctor" column, trying to determine if the tendonitis described there was what shot through his right elbow every time he picked Molly up. The funnies were in the section of the paper he was reading, but he gave it to Karen and told himself he would return to the column later.

"Can we get a bunny?" she asked.

"No."

"I'd take care of it."

"You have a hamster."

"Yeah, and I take good care of him. I'd take good care of the bunny, too."

"No."

In his experience, no one could take care of a bunny. They were effluent machines. He remembered how Andrea's bunny had nipped his knuckles whenever he changed the soggy newspaper in its cage. He remembered the sound of the pellets dropping onto the fresh paper before he was halfway up the basement stairs.

Karen abandoned the subject, mainly because Pam, rounding the corner from the bottom of the stairs, tripped over her back-pack and snapped at her. Molly, drawn to all discord, shouted nonsense from the den.

"Every morning," Pam complained. "Every morning I trip over that butt-ugly backpack."

"So you should have learned by now," Karen said coolly. She took a dainty bite of her English muffin.

3

Pam poured Just Right into a bowl and left the empty box on the counter instead of throwing it away. She sat down across from her father. When she saw that Karen had the funnies, she writhed in protest. "*Every* time," she said. Without looking at her father, she said, "Can I sleep over at Jennifer's tonight?"

Ben couldn't think of a good reason to say no. "What else do you have planned?"

"Why?" Pam snapped. "Don't you trust me?"

Karen made a noise in her throat that could have been caused by a fragment of muffin. Pam ignored it.

"Just remember the new rules," Ben said.

"Yeah, yeah."

Pam and her tight circle of five eighth-grade friends had lately redefined "sleepover" in bold new terms—so bold that the parents of the circle had had to meet on a recent Saturday morning to establish rules. Ben was the only man there. After too many cups of coffee and far too many anecdotes from the women about their own teen years, they hammered out this code: one sleepover per weekend, on Fridays only (Saturday sleepovers left the kids still groggy on Monday); no getting into a car unless a parent was the driver; no staying out past midnight; no sneaking out of the house after curfew and roaming from one end of Aberdeen to the other; and no male visitors dropping in through basement windows or old coal chutes.

For every stipulation there had been a violation, each catching Ben slack-jawed. His innocence had confounded him. Shouldn't he, with an older daughter—a senior, now coming quietly into the kitchen—have known this was possible? But Andrea had never had sleepovers patterned after Mardi Gras. She had never mixed Scotch and grape Kool-Aid over the laundry room sink. She had never run wild with older boys late at night on the grounds of Concordia Seminary. Instead, Ben remembered quiet

4

visits by demure friends, one or two at a time, with a few giggles and, at worst, spilled hot chocolate. Andrea had long black hair and a narrow, almost gaunt face. He watched her taking her large vitamins and wished she smiled more.

Molly shouted in the den, but she was just interacting with the TV, well ahead of the new entertainment curve. Andrea joined them at the table, and Karen looked up from the funnies.

"What was your bunny's name?" she said.

"Alfred."

"What happened to him?"

"Dad made me give him to a day-care center." Andrea reached for the front section of the paper and gave him a look.

The truth was worse than she knew. Alfred had died in transit. Ben's surprise had been monumental as he had opened the van gate and beheld the bunny, immobile, lying on his side on fresh newspaper he had managed to soil on this, his ultimate journey. Andrea was sitting in the front seat. She was in seventh grade at the time and had agreed to the donation without much of a battle. Biting his lip, Ben asked her if she had said good-bye. She said yes, but she said it again, over her shoulder. "Good-bye, Alfred." She could see only the top of the cage. Ben scooped the cage up, shielding the corpse from her view with his body, and took it to the entrance, luckily situated around the corner of the cinder-block building. Here he faced a new challenge. The day-care center was open, the eager kiddies inside. He could hardly go forward with the transfer of ownership he had so carefully set up. He kept walking to the rear of the building, where, with a "Good night, sweet prince," he heaved the entire load into an open Dumpster. He lurked there for an appropriate interval, then returned to the van with a full report on the apple-cheeked joy of the youngsters.

He looked across the table at Andrea. She had checked out, as she often did. Her face was flooded with emotion from a private

5

world. He felt a shock of worry for the way she was turning out. The odd thing was, he didn't know how she *was* turning out.

"What are you thinking about?" he asked, determined to get to the bottom of her.

Her face cleared. "I smelled ammonia when I walked by a chem class yesterday. It made me sad and I couldn't figure out why. Now I know. It reminded me of Alfred—the ammonia in his pee." She looked closely at her father. "Hey, I agreed to give him away. I wasn't enjoying him anymore. All he did was scratch me."

Ben managed a smile. "How are the essays coming?"

Andrea shrugged. "I'm done with Amherst's. Mrs. Sloak is looking at my Swarthmore one. That leaves five. One of them is a bunch of large theories about life that we have to deal with. I hate that. The one for Bryn Mawr has to be about some woman I admire—someone I know."

"Do Roberta," Pam mumbled over her cereal. Karen laughed. Ben gave them his frowning smile—his standard expression for the many occasions when they were bad but funny. Roberta was yet another female in Ben's life—his secretary, as painfully loyal as she was excruciatingly asexual. She had been with him from the beginning, from the day eighteen years ago when he had surveyed the St. Louis economy and declared, "What this metropolitan area needs is a nut dealer." Roberta had just begun a promising career in the lower rungs of middle management at Southwestern Bell when she dropped into Ben's lap, an orientation destined to remain figurative for two reasons: Ben's nearly unblemished loyalty to Susan and, sufficient all by itself, Roberta's personality, which Andrea once labeled "extraterrestrial."

When he hired Roberta, Ben was less nervous about her social skills than he was about her aspirations. Why was she willing to shift down to an executive secretary position? As it turned out, she proved to be perfect, an under-salaried partner in essence. He tried to make up the monetary inequity with bonuses and surprise

6

vacations (she traveled abroad frequently with a female cousin living in Indianapolis), and also more personally, with frequent invitations to join the family for dinner, where her behavior provoked deep wonder. Roberta's speech was blandly polite, becoming peppy only when she produced folksy clichés that gave Ben the feeling she was much older than he, when in fact she was younger. ("Dancing in the hog trough" was one of her favorites; Ben had no idea what it meant.) And Roberta responded to speech with an unnatural delay. Ben had watched each of his children be frustrated by this quirk into puzzled silence, and he had explained it to them afterward, so that they wouldn't blame themselves.

"So," Ben said, "sounds like seven applications now."

"Yeah," said Andrea. "Another fee. Sorry."

"That's all right. What school have you added?"

"Williams. I'm obsessed with New England lately. Probably because of the play."

Ben nodded, though his understanding was imperfect. Andrea was directing a student production of *Our Town*, scheduled for an early December performance. He had thought it was set in Kansas.

Karen looked up from the funnies with a peaceful smile. "I love Calvin," she said. Andrea gave Ben a small smile, a parent's smile, as if they were both raising her.

Pam shoved her chair back, gathered some of her dishes, and carried them to the sink. She went to the drawer where Ben kept his wallet. "I need twenty dollars," she said—not to him, but to the world in which she was forced to dwell.

"Ooh," said Karen. "That reminds me. I need a check. Picture day."

"It's on the counter," said Ben. "It's stapled to the form." He looked at Pam. "What's the twenty dollars for?"

"Jennifer's birthday."

"I can't contribute twenty dollars for all your friends on their birthdays. I just can't."

"It's not for *all* my friends. I never said it was for *all* my friends. I said it was for *Jennifer*."

"I'm good for ten." This seemed both overgenerous and stingy to him.

Pam snatched a bill angrily from his wallet. "All you've got is twenties. I'll owe you." She slammed the drawer closed. "Where's my brown sweater?"

Andrea said, "Mom brought some cleaning home yesterday. It's in the hall closet."

Pam left the kitchen and began thrashing in the nearby closet. Then she stomped up the stairs. Ben expected to hear the jet-engine roar of her hair dryer next. Instead, her shoes clomped on the bare wooden steps going up to the third-floor study. Susan was about to be interrupted.

Susan wrote books for children. She had published one book five years earlier—a "young adult" novel for readers twelve and up, but not too far up. It was a strikingly quiet event—two or three reviews, small sales, and no apparent impact on the youth of today. Since then she had written two rejected manuscripts for that same age group. Her failure, which she acknowledged more openly than Ben ever would have, had led to some changes in her writing.

First, her current manuscript, whose subject she kept secret from Ben so that he could be surprised when he read it (he had a secret too: he was growing increasingly nervous about reading it), would be for younger children, kids from eight to twelve. Second, she had studied several books about writing, and one of these effectively removed her from the breakfast table. The book recommended that the writer go directly from bed to desk because the writer freshly released from sleep was a pure writer, uncorrupted by humdrum reality—high-chair buckles, bunny grudges, and the like. When Susan summarized the theory for Ben and said she would like to try it, he agreed.

The regimen was about four months old now. Susan would slip out of bed every morning at five-thirty, go right to her study, and emerge three hours later wearing the dreamy smile of postcoitus. As for Ben, he looked back wistfully on the eighteen-year era when Susan rose ahead of him and did almost all of the morning labor. And he couldn't help envying her for having work that was free of economic pressure. He bore sole financial responsibility for six people. He knew he wasn't alone in the world in this regard, but sometimes, as a pure idea, it floored him.

In the den, *Sesame Street's* Eastern European enumerator was going at it. Molly yelled "Count!" Karen, hunched over the funnies, imitated the count's peculiar laugh.

Pam clomped back down the stairs and stormed the closet again. "Oh, excellent!" she yelled. "Excellent!" Ben quietly noted the wisdom of Susan's shift from writing books for and about people like Pam to writing books for and about people like Karen.

Andrea stood up and took her dishes to the sink, then went to his wallet drawer. "You've got two fives here. Can I take them for field hockey snacks?"

"Sure," said Ben. So Pam had lied. He would take it up with her later. As Andrea returned his thinning wallet to the drawer, he had a sudden fancy that his pockets were full of little birds, constantly flying out with a noisy flurry. Each flight made him flinch. But he would pat his pockets and think, "There are plenty of birds left."

"Ten minutes," Andrea announced. Karen automatically rose, reading the funnies, and continued to read them as she headed up the stairs. Ben would have to learn about his possible tendonitis later. Andrea put all the dishes in the dishwasher and wiped the counter clean. In the hall, she said to Pam, "Train leaves in ten minutes," to which Pam replied, "That's such a Dad sentence. What are you, an old man?"

Ben went into the den to check on Molly. She was watching an old Kermit the Frog sketch. *Sesame Street* these days was a mix of old and new skits. A rap song with quick cuts might be followed by a gentle narrative he had watched with Andrea fifteen years earlier—like this one, in which Kermit was interviewing Jack of Jack and Jill.

Ben wanted to call out to Andrea to see if she remembered the skit. It might bring a rare smile to her face. He would ask Karen, too, and he might even ask Pam, just to see if she was capable of speech that didn't flame from her mouth. But the girls were in a hurry. He heard their footsteps in the front hall, two of the three called out good-bye to him and Molly, the front door closed, and they were off to their three separate schools. In the sudden quiet, the house seemed to settle a bit.

Molly was almost done with her cereal, so Ben stood up to make her some toast. One of her rules was one course at a time on her tray. He was itching to get to work. He listened at the bottom of the stairs for a sign that Susan might be wrapping it up. As second best, he grabbed the wall phone and punched the buttons that would take him to his voice mail. Roberta often left messages there on the days he left work before she did, as he had done yesterday. There was one brief message about a cable from India.

Ben smiled. The cable would be from Nathan Ravindranathan, cashew processor par excellence. Ben had gotten his name from the International Tree-Nut Dealers Directory and had sent him three identical letters, figuring at least one would reach him despite India's notorious mail system. The cable was a good sign. A bit old-fashioned, but Ben was used to that in his dealings with third-world suppliers. Ben was on a quest for a cheap cashew, inspired by the comparative bulk prices in the local supermarket: cashews, $5.99 per pound; peanuts, $2.39 per pound. Between those extremes was a land waiting for him to plant his flag. People loved cashews. The kidney-shaped nuggets were like a drug. Ben believed with strange certainty that some untried route existed, some undiscovered passage that would bring a cost-effective, quality cashew to America. The route would begin on the Indian subcontinent, perhaps with Nathan Ravindranathan.

He spied Karen's picture-day check and form, forgotten on the counter. He would drop them off on his way to work. He didn't mind. Karen might see him in the hall, and she would say, "Hey, Dad, what's up? It's weird seeing you here." As he imagined this, he realized with a pang of loss that he was basing the little drama on an actual moment with Pam in grade school. If he showed up in Pam's middle school now, she would spit on the floor.

Susan came down the stairs and into the kitchen.

"Pam interrupt you?"

"No," she said spacily. Her eyes hadn't yet come to rest on anything. "I mean yes, but I was done. I had a good morning."

"Good."

"I moved some stuff from one chapter to another, and then I took part of what I moved and moved it back to its original chapter."

"Uh-huh."

"It changed everything."

"Good."

Susan stared out the window over the sink. These comments were typical of her daily report. Ben had no idea what the hell she was talking about.

"Roberta won't be here for dinner," he said.

Those words brought Susan back into the world. "What is that, the third turndown? Does she have a life all of a sudden?"

"I hope not," said Ben. "I like her the way she is."

Susan smiled vaguely. "I need to take a shower. Ten more minutes?"

Ben agreed, though Susan's "ten" meant twenty. He remembered why he had come into the kitchen and put a slice of bread in the toaster. When it popped out with a clatter, Molly automatically yelled, "Toast!"

"That's right."

"Toast!"

"Coming at you."

As he lightly buttered the slice, Ben thought of the picture book he had read to Molly the night before. To her surprise, he had read it twice, but the second time was really for himself. In it a kind-faced farmer dressed in overalls rocked his baby to sleep on the front porch. (The farmer's wife was already asleep upstairs.) Once the baby had fallen asleep, the farmer held his dog in his arms and rocked it. Then he rocked his hen, his sheep, and his pig. With farm equipment he rocked his cow and his horse. He rocked the whole farm to sleep. He worked hard, this farmer, tending every creature.

# 2

"I don't hope for a perfect world, Jeremy," said Duckwall. "That would be asking for too much."

"Right."

"People will always trip over their feet, get a fellow's name wrong, misspeak."

"That they will." Cook glanced around for their waiter. If he brought the check, it might bring Duckwall to the main point.

"What I hope for," Duckwall went on, "indeed, what the institute hopes for, is *major error avoidance*." He leaned forward, and Cook watched his starched white shirt edge over the lip of his lunch plate into a pool of gravy. "Just to show you what's possible in this realm, I personally haven't committed a major error in more than eighteen months."

Cook was all astonishment, even though he figured he could make the same claim about himself. Why was he here, flattering this rigidly proper man with agreement and pretending to be what he was not? Why does one ever flatter, agree, and pretend? For a job, of course. But what job? Duckwall wasn't telling. All Cook knew was that the man ran an institute devoted to the study of error and that he was bonkers on the subject.

Cook was a linguist, and while error analysis was a neat little corner of the field, it wasn't clear to him how the prospective job involved linguistics, even though Duckwall had said Cook was "peculiarly well equipped" for the position—had said it twice, once in his surprising letter of the week before and again over lunch. Cook had reviewed some linguistics literature for the interview and had even memorized examples of the four kinds of spoonerisms, but thus far Duckwall had dominated. He had pretty much lost himself in a review of the institute's research on classic boners from history: the charge of the Light Brigade; the sinking of the *Titanic*; Wrong Way Corrigan; the Cerro Tololo pulsar; and the Australian cane toad and its American counterpart, the kudzu vine.

With pursed lips, Duckwall set his tea bag in his spoon and wrapped the string around it, trying to squeeze a third cup from it. His upper forehead was bald, giving his face, Cook now noticed, the exact shape of a narrow oval. Cook finally spotted their waiter, but it was a discouraging sighting. He was passing by on the other side of the plate glass window in his street clothes, lighting a cigarette. Cook resolved to take over the agenda.

"I can see why you might be interested in someone like me," he said.

Duckwall blinked. It was a hard blink to read.

"Many errors have a linguistic component," Cook went on, drawing on extremely recent reading. "Schiaparelli's 'canali,' for example. He was an Italian astronomer, and he used the word 'canali' for what he saw on Mars through his telescope. It means 'grooves' or 'channels,' but it got translated as 'canals.' The English word implies intelligent construction, which made many earthlings believe in Martians. It's a classic case of words making us believe something false. Linguistics and error—there's a natural connection."

"I would like to finish telling you about the institute." Duckwall gave each word exactly equal weight. The effect was chilling.

"Sorry," said Cook.

Duckwall fussed with his tea bag. His top button was tight around his neck, although he wore no tie. Cook wanted to reach out and violently undo it. "Six years ago," Duckwall went on, "my wife drowned in a swimming pool, right under the eyes of a lifeguard. She had a heart attack in the water, but the cause of her death was drowning. She might have been saved, but no one was watching the area where she was stricken. There was prior miscommunication among the lifeguards—a routine jurisdiction error. Originally, I had no intention of taking legal action. Then I changed my mind, and here's why. I wanted to learn why such things happen. I committed myself to establishing an organization devoted to error—to understanding it, classifying it, and conquering it. I threatened to sue, we settled out of court, and with the money I founded the Error Institute."

"Ah," said Cook.

Duckwall leaned forward and folded his hands on the table. He seemed to signal a new phase in the meeting. "I'm glad we've come back to the question of financing. You seemed concerned earlier about the funding."

"The money dried up at the last two places where I worked. That's why."

Duckwall nodded. "Insolvency always lurks. I'm constantly on the prowl for funds. Riley was my first employee, the victim of an exploding oven. Her personal injury award gave her a lovely dowry for the institute. There have been others, right along, who

15

have earned fortunes the hard way, you might say, and who look with favor on our mission. I hire them, and their injury awards keep us afloat. But we're ready for a new infusion of capital. I've got a prospect in Toronto that I'm presently wooing. He's suing the pants off Air Canada."

Cook felt he could risk raising the question again. "Where do I fit in?"

Duckwall laughed strangely, then checked himself. "Do you have to ask?"

"Of course I do."

"Well, to be frank, although you've made a nice impression on me today, the initial attraction was naturally your testicles."

Cook felt a slight retraction in that region. "*What?*"

"Your testicles. They're very important to us. I'm sure they're important to you too, but that's water under the bridge, isn't it?"

"Are you talking about my guts? My . . . balls?"

"Them too. It takes balls to do what you're doing." Duckwall banged a fist on the table, making his spoon dance. "Personal injury litigation is not for the faint of heart."

"I'm afraid I—"

"On a one-to-one basis, it means nothing to me. It's the human condition. Hell's bells, man, we're all wounded in some sense." Duckwall leaned across the table. "You seem uncomfortable talking about it. I assumed from your lawsuit that the subject was fair game."

"What lawsuit?"

Duckwall flinched and leaned back. "You're not going to let them cut your nuts off and get away with it, are you?"

"Look, I don't know what you're talking about. I have two balls. Two tangible, hairy balls. Are you talking about them or something else?"

Duckwall blinked several times. "Your testicles weren't surgically removed by mistake?"

Cook winced. "No. What a horrible thought."

"Last January? In Dallas?"

"My testicles have never been to Texas."

Duckwall pursed his lips. "Your name *is* Jeremy Cook, isn't it? Jeremy Jacob Cook?"

"Yes."

"Don't tell me there are two of you." Duckwall made a peevish noise. "I gave 'Jeremy Cook' to Peoplefinders, and they found over a hundred matches in the country. I went back and did more research on the surgery, and one of the newspaper stories reproduced the hospital admissions sheet. It showed the poor devil's full name. His occupation too—a travel photographer. I took the full name to Peoplefinders and got just one match this time, right in my own backyard: Jeremy Jacob Cook of St. Louis, Missouri. Age: thirty-four. Unemployed."

"And uncastrated."

"Good for you, bad for me. I had hoped to get deep into the pockets of St. Anthony of Dallas. My man must have left the country. Or died. Who knows? A pox on him. Oh, I shouldn't wish him ill on top of everything else, but . . ."

Duckwall's voice trailed off, leaving Cook free to contemplate his true status in his eyes: not a linguist with promise, but a nutless financial wonder. "Peculiarly well equipped" indeed.

Cook scooted his chair back from the table. "You made a mistake," he said coldly. "I'd call it a major mistake. Your perfect record is shot to hell."

"Yes," Duckwall said philosophically. "The right-in-my-own-backyard element seduced me. A classic serendipity error. Ah well."

"I came here with hope," Cook said, rising. He had wanted to be strong, but his voice cracked.

"Sorry," Duckwall said crisply. "I'll make it up to you." A bright smile flashed across his oval face. "I'll get lunch. How's that?"

Cook did something he had never done socially before. He was already standing and facing Duckwall, so it was easy. With a widespread hand he reached down and clutched himself right where it counted, right there where the initial attraction was.

⁓

As Cook crossed the Buford University quadrangle, the autumn leaves blowing at his feet whispered today's theme to him: "The initial attraction was naturally your testicles." You could wake up and greet the day with high hopes for a fresh start, and all the while a sentence like that was lying in wait for you. It showed how foolish it was to have any hopes at all.

Gothic towers stabbed the sky on all sides of him. Because Buford was a mediocre place, its architecture made Cook think not of grand European universities but of the quality of life in the Middle Ages—of pain, plague, and ignorance. But Buford had a good library, and that was his destination.

Universities could be as anonymous as large cities. Cook was certainly a man without a face in this one. Paula had been teaching here for a month. He had met several of her colleagues, but they had failed, or pretended to fail, to recognize him on subsequent encounters in the two buildings where he lurked, the library and the campus bookstore. He thought of himself as the Shadow. But all he really was, he knew, was a faculty spouse.

He stepped into an empty elevator and pushed the button for the top floor. Just before the doors closed completely, a meaty hand reached in and shoved them apart. A bearded buffalo of a man stepped in and grunted when he saw that the top button was already lit. Cook briefly speculated how meager his chance of surviving would be if the man chose to kill him with his bare hands.

The elevator chugged to a start. The man snapped his fingers and pointed at Cook. "You're Paula Nouvelles's husband. We met at a faculty party. I'm Ted Chambers. Phonetics."

Cook relaxed a little. "Jeremy Cook. Syntax."

They shook hands. Besides being larger than Cook, Ted seemed a little older; or he could have been the same age and just dissipated. He cocked his head sideways and beamed through his beard. "I'm still smarting from the drubbing Paula gave me yesterday," he said.

"Drubbing?" said Cook.

"Her net game is flawless."

"Ah." Cook found it hard to picture Ted playing tennis. Or doing phonetics, for that matter. In Cook's experience, phoneticians were little people.

"Off to the P's, are you?" Ted said, referring to the call-number range for linguistics.

"Right. *The Journal of Child Language*."

"An exciting domain. Messy, just like the little buggers themselves, but exciting. Are you and Paula coming to the picnic this afternoon?"

"Just Paula."

"It's quite an event." The elevator doors opened. They stepped out and walked toward the stacks. Ted bumped into a book cart and sent it careening. "Chairman Sam has this place in the country, and a strange magic takes over out there. All the rules get suspended, if you take my meaning."

"Do people get drunk and make passes at each other?"

"Good man! You've cut right to it." Ted lacked a library voice. Half the students studying at tables were looking up at them.

Softly, Cook said, "Isn't that a little disruptive to workplace harmony?"

"Oddly enough, no. When Monday comes, we all sort of say,

'Well, we've shown our dark sides, now let's get back to work.' Does that make any sense?"

Cook didn't answer this question on principle. He had heard it before and not liked it. In his world, you either made sense or you didn't, and it was up to you to know which. But Ted's size made the question tolerable, almost endearing. It struck Cook that big people and little people had very different constraints on their behavior. He slowed in his walk, for they had reached his row.

Ted didn't seem to want to let him go. "Are you working on anything in particular?"

"Just keeping up with the literature on language acquisition. I don't have any informants right now."

"You sound sad about it. I have a niece in town, a two-year-old, with some interesting things. She has partial reduplication for plurals. 'Box-ox' is her plural of 'box.'"

Cook was impressed. "Is it productive?"

"Don't know. Cute girl. Molly. My sister's daughter. I'll give her a call and see if I can wangle a get-together."

"I don't know—"

"Oh, come on. You don't want to be in here. You need to get out there and taste life."

"I think I'll pass, actually."

"No, no. I'll set it up."

"No. Really."

"I'll give you a call. It's what you want." Ted gave him a grin and disappeared down an aisle.

Cook watched him go with the firm belief that he wasn't serious. How could he be in the face of such clear rejection?

Cook tracked down his journal, grabbed the most recent volume from the shelf, and carried it off to an isolated table. He read it, then stayed there in the P's, browsing and reading for five hours in all. He spent the last two of them researching reduplication as a spontaneous grammatical marker in child language. He knew of languages that duplicated part or all of a word to signal plurality (in Malay, *kapal* meant "ship"; *kapalkapal* meant "ships"), but he had never heard of an English speaker, young or old, doing so. Judging from his reading, neither had anyone else. Something new, perhaps.

As he stared out the window, he sensed a shift in the light and looked at his watch. He packed up his notes and headed for home. He walked south across the campus into a residential neighborhood lying in the east end of Aberdeen, a near-suburb of St. Louis. Six blocks deep into this neighborhood, the narrow, tree-lined street opened to reveal the expansive grounds of Concordia Seminary to the right and small brick apartment buildings to the left. Cook and Paula lived in a two-bedroom corner apartment, which sat atop an antiques store operated by their landlord.

Cook trudged up the outside wooden steps. He went directly to his "study"—a designated corner of the living room. (As the only salaried member of the marriage, Paula had claimed the extra bedroom as her study with surprisingly little discussion.) He set his briefcase down on his desk—actually a hollow-core door on cinder blocks. (As the only salaried member of the marriage, Paula had claimed their one true desk for herself with surprisingly little discussion.) He took off his sweater, folded it, and set it on a shelf in the hall closet. (As the only salaried member of the marriage, Paula had claimed the one closet in the bedroom with surprisingly little discussion.)

He went into the kitchen and turned on the overhead light, a fluorescent ring suitable for illuminating cult mutilations. He took a bowl of yesterday's spaghetti out of the refrigerator. The answering machine blinked at him on the counter: two messages. He set the bowl down and pressed the button. Duckwall's voice invaded the apartment.

"Mr. Cook, it's eleven-twenty A.M., and I'm calling to confirm our luncheon appointment, but I suppose you must be on your way there now." There was a pause. "But perhaps you're in the bathroom. If so, I'll wait." A long pause. Cook stared at the machine. "But I don't want to rush you. Take your time in there." Another pause. "In the meantime, I'll say this much: I hope we can move forward quickly toward a mutually beneficial agreement. Also, on a personal note, let me say that I believe manhood can take many forms, and the absence of its corporeal manifestation must count for very little in a humane and progressive social order. Enough said."

Cook closed his eyes and waited for the second message.

"Hi hi! What a party. Wish you were here. Am I slurring my words?" She was. "You can always tell, you sober thing. Anyway, we're at Chairman Sam's, and then we're going to Debbie's—I think Debbie's. Hang on." She yelled a question to someone. Cook heard laughter, then some shouts. It sounded like a John Cheever party. "Never mind. We should end up at Ted's. Call me there to tell me about your interview. At Ted's. Did I say that? He said he saw you today. He thinks you don't like him. I told him you like everybody. Listen, I don't have his number, so, umm, I'll call you, okay? I'll call you. From Ted's. Shut up." She giggled. "That wasn't for you. Listen, that man you were going to meet called just after you left. I was in the shower. I saved the message, but for the life of me—*Wait! I'm coming!* Gotta go."

Cook killed both messages and threw the bowl of spaghetti into the microwave. He stared out the kitchen window. The Asian couple in the apartment across the side street were eating dinner. In the growing dark, their kitchen was lit like a small balcony in a stage play. They were young, probably Buford U. graduate students. The man reached his chopsticks across the table and fed a little something to his wife. She did the same for him. Cook turned to the microwave and watched the plastic wrap puff up over his bowl.

He left the bowl there and went into the living room, where he put on some Karl Ditters von Dittersdorf. He plopped on the couch with his earphones, powerless to do anything else. All reading he did, even leisure reading, was work related, and since he didn't feel like working, he didn't feel like reading. His mind was like a union shop, where one shutdown led to many.

⌐⌐

Some time later, Cook was awakened by a painful pressure on his head. He had rolled over on his earphones in his sleep. He yanked them off, sat up on the couch, and peered at the wall clock. One-ten in the morning. He went to the front window. Paula's car was in its usual spot. She was safely home, in bed.

As he was about to turn away, he saw someone in a car parked across the street holding a hand to his head and jerking. For a moment, Cook thought the man might have been shot. Then he saw that he was just holding a car phone to his ear. For Cook, this reclassified him from victim to victimizer. The car, he now saw, was a Saab. What the hell kind of deal could the yupster be closing at this hour?

"Shoot him," Cook called out to the darkness. "Someone shoot the sonofabitch." He flopped back onto the couch and returned to sleep.

# 3

Ben held his car phone to his ear and peered through his window at the sloping lawn of Concordia Seminary. He wore a leather jacket over his bare chest and jeans over his pajama bottoms. He was searching for his daughter.

He waited for Susan to answer, hoping she hadn't fallen asleep. Twenty minutes earlier, the two of them had just turned off a movie on the bedroom VCR when the phone had rung. Ben answered, knowing that the call would be about Pam. Jennifer's mother told him she had just gone into the back bedroom to check on the girls and found it empty. They had left by the fire escape. Did Ben or Susan have any idea where they were?

They did not. In truth, at that moment they had only one idea, which in good conscience they could not now carry out. Jennifer's mother said she figured the girls were either at Concordia or at the apartment of Terri's father, who was out of town. She had phoned that apartment and gotten no answer, which could mean anything. Terri's mother, she said, could not be reached for an opinion. Ben wouldn't have valued it in any case. It was Terri's mother who, on a previous sleepover, had permitted Pam's eighth-grade gang to watch *The Lover*, a movie in which a golden-bunned thirty-two-year-old steered a pouty teenager all over his apartment floor. It was this movie that Ben and Susan had just turned off, shocked, in order to pursue its central subject on their own.

Ben had said the only thing he could say: Jennifer's mother should stay there at her apartment in case the girls returned, and he would go out and look for them. He had pulled on his jeans, pocketed his erection, and driven to Terri's father's apartment. In front, he saw none of the cars belonging to the sophomore boys the gang hung out with. When he listened at the apartment door, all was quiet. The girls were habitually clumsy sneaks, given to giggling and hushing that always betrayed their positions. It was a safe bet they weren't there.

Now his eyes scanned the dark hillside while he waited for Susan. It took four rings, but she sounded alert. He gave her an update, then asked if she had been awake.

"Molly," she said. "She had to pee. I just settled her down. No more apple juice after eight o'clock. We can control *her* behavior, at least."

Ben wasn't too sure about that. "I need to call the other parents."

"I'll get the Buzzbook." Susan went away but came back surprisingly fast. Pam must have left the directory in plain view atop the devastation of her bedroom. Susan tracked down the five phone numbers and read them to him. He told her to go back to sleep.

"You think she's okay?" she said.

"Yes. But someday she's not going to be if she keeps experimenting like this."

25

"I hope that's all it is. Experimenting. I hope this isn't who she is."

"Nah."

"How can you be sure?"

He shrugged in the darkness. "Listen, when's that movie due back?"

"Tomorrow at seven."

"Let's pay a late fee." He could sense her smile. "Turn your ringer off and go to sleep. I'm on the job."

"What if Pam calls? What if she's stranded somewhere?"

"She won't. She's not. Andrea'll be home soon. She can answer the phone. Go to sleep."

Ben looked at the clock in the dash. One-twenty. He would call Ginny's house first, because it would be the worst. Ginny's mother and father were rubberneckers at the accident scene of their daughter's adolescence. When called to action, they wrung their hands. Their primary parenting act was to give voice to their helplessness.

Ben woke them out of profound sleep. The conversation was even more sigh-filled than usual. "I just don't know what to do with her," the mother said. She put her husband on. "Ginger's mother and I are very concerned," he said.

Ben called Fawn's parents next. He got the father, who was not only wide awake but ready for fun. He wanted to schmooze. He wanted to laugh it off. "Kids," he said. "We did the same thing when we were young, Ben."

"But we got punished. Last weekend we all met and decided to tighten up."

"Who met?"

"The parents. All the parents of the girls."

"I was out of town, Ben."

"But Kathy was there."

26

"She didn't mention it. She's out of town now."

Out of town seemed to be the place to be. Ben called Dawn's parents next. Dawn was Pam's oldest friend, from their former neighborhood. Ben knew her full name—Dawn Michelle Oliver—because he heard it a lot in those early days. Her mother would yell out the door, "Dawn Michelle Oliver, get out of that mud!" "Dawn Michelle Oliver, get in the house right now!" In Ben's experience, parents who used long versions of their kids' names always had the least control over them. Dawn's parents liked to "crack down" and "lay down the law." On this night, they declared Dawn's sneaking out "the absolute last straw."

They gave Ben more than bluster, though. They gave him a name. A new girl was in the picture, one Brigitte Duvray. It was their impression that all the girls were spending the night at Brigitte's house. Ben had never heard of her. Dawn's parents weren't able to help him with a phone number. In one of their punitive rampages they had wrested their daughter's Buzzbook from her and burned it.

That left Terri's mom, who was divorced and possibly had the hots for Ben. She was full of information. The girls were indeed at Brigitte Duvray's. The plan was for Brigitte's mother to pick them up at Jennifer's just before midnight and take them to Brigitte's for the night. Brigitte's mother had called her the night before to set it up.

Ben shook his head, trying to clear it. "She called *you?* But Jennifer's mom says they sneaked out. They took the fire escape."

"Oh, they just like those stairs, Ben. I don't think they sneaked out."

"She says they did. They were supposed to spend the night with her, and suddenly they were all gone."

"Jennifer must have forgotten to tell her. The girls are terrible about communicating things."

This was true. It galled Ben how they played that defect to their advantage. They claimed carelessness precisely when they had been most calculating. But sometimes they were just plain careless.

He asked for Brigitte Duvray's phone number. Terri's mother went off in search of the Buzzbook. He scratched his bare chest under his jacket and peered at the dark hill.

"Brigitte's new to school," she said when she came back to the phone. "She's not listed."

"They send updates with the Monday newsletter. Do you have those handy?"

She laughed. "I'm a single mother, Ben." He was clearly asking for too high a level of organization. "I'm sure it's fine. I spoke with the girl's mother, okay?"

Ben suddenly felt pushy. "You're probably right. I'm sorry I woke you up."

"No problem. I think it's important to stay on top of these things. But they're fine tonight."

Ben pulled into the street as soon as he hung up. But then he pulled over again. Terri's mother, after all, was the one who had let the gang watch *The Lover*. He grabbed the phone and called Jennifer's mother. She had been waiting for his call. She strongly contradicted everything Terri's mother had said. The girls had definitely sneaked out. The name Brigitte Duvray meant nothing to her.

Ben looked at the dashboard clock and called home again. Andrea answered right away, as he had hoped she would.

"Andrea, listen, can you do me a favor, and—oh, how was your date?"

"Okay," Andrea said a little dully. Ben realized he had no idea whom she had gone out with. "I was just going to bed. Where are you?"

"At Concordia. Pam's on the loose. She's supposedly at some girl's named Brigitte Duvray. You know her?"

Andrea was silent for a moment. "No."

"She's not in the Buzzbook. Can you check the updates in the kitchen drawer? They're under the phone book."

After another pause, Andrea set down the phone. She came back to it right away.

"There is no Brigitte Duvray."

"Did you look? In the kitchen?"

"There is no Brigitte Duvray."

"But you couldn't have checked."

"I'll say it again. There is no Brigitte Duvray."

"What do you mean? Her mother talked to Terri's mother."

Andrea said nothing.

"Come on. Give me the story."

"I hate this."

"Tell me."

"She's such a little bitch."

"Come on."

"Brigitte Duvray is a phantom student. Last year she was the name everyone used to back up a lie about something, and then it became a joke. I mean, it became a joke real fast. I guess it trickled down to eighth grade. I can't believe they're still using it. It's so *old*."

"What about the mother on the phone?"

Andrea laughed. "You remember the girl you saw in *Damn Yankees* last year? The one who played Lola?"

"She was terrific."

"She's a sociopath. Her name's Linda Lindner. They call her Linda Linda. She wanted to be in my play this year, and I said no way. It would have been the worst mistake of my life. She can do a real good motherly voice on the phone. She hires herself out for stuff like this, or to call the attendance office."

Ben struggled against a feeling of helplessness, a feeling that he was a chump, that however he saw things, it was wrong, and something entirely different was going on. He heard a call-waiting click at her end. "Take it," he said. "It might be Pam. But come right back."

Andrea went away. Ben ran his eyes over the grounds of the seminary. He wanted to see a silhouette against the night sky at the top of the hill. He wanted it to be his daughter, walking toward him. He wanted to open the door for her and take her home.

Andrea was back. "It's some guy from India. Nathan with a big last name."

"Jesus. Is he still on? Find out when he's in. We've missed each other all day."

"He's kind of hard to understand."

"Do your best."

She went away again. He wanted to go too. He would much rather chase cashews in India than adolescents in America.

"He'll be in his office for the next hour," Andrea said. "He said it's a different number than the one you called. I *think* he said that." She gave it to him and he jotted it down. "What time is it there?" she said.

"About twelve hours later. Midday. It's odd he'd call here, actually. He must know how late it is."

"Yeah, well, he's gone now, and I'm real sad I can't take it up with him."

Ben smiled. "Okay. Now, where's Pam?"

Andrea groaned. "There's a big, empty apartment building in the Moorlands. It's a new hangout."

"Jesus Christ." Ben switched to the speakerphone and took off. "Where is it exactly?"

"On Byron. It's across from this place called the Corey Building, so people call it 'the Corey,' even though it's not actually the Corey Building."

"How do you know she's there?"

"They were talking about it tonight in the basement. I was in the laundry room."

"She'll know you told me."

"Do I care? As Molly would say, 'Fuck her.'"

Ben turned onto Clayton Road. "You can go to bed now. Oh, how was your date?"

"Okay," she said. The dullness in her voice reminded him he had already asked her this. "Scott says his dad's going to interview you for the *Business Journal* next week."

"Oh. Yeah. I forgot about that." So she had gone out with Scott Marlin—a classmate she had dated when she was a freshman or sophomore. Scott was something of a dim bulb. Ben wondered what the attraction was. "Well, sleep tight," he said. "Thanks for ratting on Pam."

"Any time."

Ben hung up and turned off the phone with a sense of unease. Scott Marlin, he thought.

An ambulance approached from behind, and he pulled over to let it pass. It turned up a side street across Big Bend. A half mile farther to the west, emergency vehicles of a different sort helped him locate "the Corey." Two Aberdeen police cars sat in front of it, one on each side of the street. A cop leaned casually against the roof of one of them, talking to another cop behind the wheel.

Ben saw no sign of the gang near the cars—or in them, thank God. He slowed and came to a stop. "Have you seen any kids around here?" he said. "I'm looking for my daughter. She's thirteen."

"Thirteen?" the cop in the car said. "Her curfew is midnight. That's a city ordinance."

"I know," Ben said tiredly. "I'm trying. I'm doing the best I can. Did you get a complaint? Is that why you're here?"

The cop in the car looked away indifferently. The other one was more helpful. He told Ben that a neighbor had called about fifteen minutes earlier to complain of trespassers in the vacant apartment building, but that it was empty when they arrived. Ben thanked him and drove on.

The Moorlands was a sloping rectangle of half a dozen long streets and three short cross streets. When Ben reached the downhill end, he formed a plan, based on his reconstruction of what had probably happened. He imagined Pam and the others holed up in that building (what did they do there?), and then dispersing in a panic when the cops drove up. The chaos meant they were probably on foot instead of in a sophomore's car. They would be slinking to the uphill end of the Moorlands, in the direction that would ultimately bring them to Jennifer's mother's apartment, where they no doubt hoped to return undetected. The Moorlands fed into the adjacent neighborhood via just one street. He would park there and wait for them to walk into his lap.

Twenty minutes later, cold and tired, he lost all faith in his plan. They should have reached him by now. He would give it ten more minutes and then drive to Jennifer's mother's apartment and wait there in his car.

Nathan Ravindranathan. Ben rolled the name on his tongue like an oily cashew. He fingered the phone number in his jacket pocket, then read it under the dash light. He punched the buttons that would take him to Mangalore, India.

Someone answered the phone and said a lot of things.

"Nathan Ravindranathan, please," Ben said, tossing his English out like a stone down a well. "U.S.A. calling. Missouri. Ben Hudnut, from Crunch." This was the name of his business.

The party at the other end burst into a staccato laugh, then went away. Ben waited. A minute passed. Two minutes. Something moved in front of the house across the street, but it was not his daughter. It was an opossum, waddling toward the front door of a house as if returning home from work.

Suddenly a tight voice pinged to him off a satellite. "This is Nathan. That is Benjamin?"

"Yes," said Ben. "How are you?"

"You have a dame from mystery."

"Pardon?"

"You have a name from history. I am thinking of your Benjamin Franklin. Did he not say that time is money?"

"Yes, I think he did say that." Compared with the Indian's high, compressed voice, Ben's seemed to boom uncivilly in his own ears.

"I myself am named after your Nathan Hale."

"Really? That's interesting."

"My father attended Northwest Oklahoma State University."

"Well, now. Listen, I'm calling about cashews."

"How many chicken do you have?"

Ben leaned forward, straining. "Can you say that again, please?"

"How many children do you have?"

"Four. Four daughters."

"And I have had the pleasure of addressing one of them."

"Yes."

"No sons?"

"No."

"I myself have five sons."

"Very nice."

"You call in rough-ins to car shoes."

Ben strained in the darkness. "Pardon?"

"You call in reference to cashews."

"Yes. Yes."

"You indicate in your letter an unhappiness with the pricing structure."

"Well, I'm trying to understand it. I thought you could help me. You're right in the middle of the process—a grower, an importer, a processor, an exporter."

"Not so much an importer, Benjamin. Not so much. The Mozambiquans have their own equipment now. India weeps."

"Pardon?"

"India weeps. For the lost market."

Ben relaxed a little. He was getting used to Nathan's accent.

"Twenty-five years ago," Nathan continued, "two-thirds of my father's nuts came from Africa. We lost Mozambique. Very sad. Then we gained the Tanzanian market. Very good. But now Vietnam challenges us. Vietnam and India are Fate Brothers in the cashew trade. You are familiar with the concept?"

Ben saw more delay coming. "Somewhat, yes. Listen, I'm interested in your break points—"

"There is a story, Benjamin, of two starving mendicants who are traveling toward each other. They see a mango tree by the road. It has one large mango on it—only one. They hurry to it and arrive together. They struggle for it, and they crush it between them. They realize they are Fate Brothers—that they have come together and will change each other's life, for good or ill they do not know, and it is very frightening. They vow to go away from each other in precisely opposite directions. They walk for days, for weeks, for months. But then they have the same thought, which is this: 'Some say the world is round, and if that is true, we will meet again.' To prevent this, they turn to the north. They walk for many more days. It grows colder, so they think— again at the same time—'I should turn and go back to my point of starting. If I do, I will walk in the same direction as my Fate Brother, and he is far, far ahead of me. We shall never meet.' Thus, in error, they turn and walk precisely toward each other."

"And they meet?" said Ben. Cashews, man, cashews.

"Ha! You are ahead of me. Yes, they meet, but not as you think. One foggy night, they take an unfortunate step—again at the same time—and fall over a cliff into a river. The two rivers flow together to become one large river. *There* they meet, and their limbs . . . how do you say, entwine, intertwine. Embracing, they flow into the sea together. Fate Brothers. It gives one goose chills, does it not?"

"Yes, indeed." Ben wasn't entirely clear on the outcome. Were they dead? They must have been.

"Vietnam, with its Vinalimex corporation, is India's Fate Brother in the cashew trade. All is uncertainty, Benjamin. In the world of commerce, all is flux."

"I know what you mean." Ben, lulled by the Asian tale, took a moment to respond to what he now saw: the long flame of a cigarette lighter. It was flaring behind a bush at the corner. He sat up. Three girls, cigarettes aglow, emerged from behind the bush and began walking down the middle of the street, right toward him. He slouched and peered through the gap between the steering wheel and the dash.

"What do you like, Benjamin? Wholes, splits, pieces, or baby bits?"

"Wholes," Ben managed to say. The one in the middle was Pam. He could read her thoughts as she saw the Saab, read the personalized license plate ("4 GIRLZ"), said "Omigod," and took off running back into the Moorlands. Ben put Nathan on the speakerphone, started the car, and turned his lights right on the two other girls. They screamed and ran after Pam.

"If you want wholes, then you want the Indian cashew, Benjamin."

"Why is that?" Ben said. He drove into the Moorlands. The two girls shot into the side yard of a house. Pam was ahead, sprinting down the middle of the street.

"The African nut spits."

"Spits?"

"Splits. But the two halves of the Indian nut cling like lovers in the Kama Sutra. You are familiar with the Kama Sutra?"

Christ, Ben thought. "Yes. Completely familiar." He watched Pam dart up a side yard. It was the house of a former friend of Pam's, a girl named Melanie who dropped out of Pam's life in seventh grade when Pam decided she was a nerd. She was a nice girl, and Ben missed her. What was a nerd? Someone whose father didn't have to chase her at two A.M.?

Melanie's yard connected at the rear with Meg Wilner's, an interior decorator friend of Susan's. Ben zoomed ahead to the cross street and swung around onto the Wilners' street. He immediately pulled over and shut off his lights. He tuned back in to Nathan, who had been talking for some time.

"—my country, the cracking of cashews is done by hand. The liquid is . . . what is the word, *caustic*, very painful. The nutcrackers squat on the floor and crack the nuts with a mallet, and the liquid splashes on their hands. They dip their hands into ashes to protect them, but it does not always work. I saw this as a boy, and I see this today. The work is done by women. Why in such a world would one want a child who is not a son? The Kama Sutra, as you know, does not teach us how to have sons. But there are other treatises. I am thinking of the verses of Dattaka. I am thinking of the fragments of the *Nandikesvara*. You cannot know these."

Ben spotted Pam skulking out of Meg's front yard. She thought she was being clever.

"One wants to have sons, Benjamin. Correct?"

"I suppose," Ben said distractedly. Pam looked up and down the street, then streaked across it into the new Moorlands School playground—which Susan, as chair of the PTO facilities committee, had worked hard to bring to completion the year before. Ben started his car and pulled up next to the playground fence. He saw Pam's white sneakers disappear into the bottom of a tube slide. She was trapped.

"I will send you this literature, Benjamin, when I send you some samples of our price list, which will offer my special rate, because I have so much enjoyed talking to you. The literature will teach you how to have sons. May I fax you?"

"Certainly." Ben, his eyes fixed on the tube slide, gave him his fax number.

"There is no danger the papers will fall into the wrong hands?"

"You mean a competitor's hands? No. No danger."

"I mean the hands of a child. The treatises are not for green minds."

The hard orange plastic of the tube slide suddenly glowed like a jack-o'-lantern. Smoke 'em if you got 'em, even if you're lying at a forty-five-degree angle.

"It is a question of preserving the innocence of the children, Benjamin."

Ben sighed. "I'm doing the best I can," he said.

# 4

Cook burped up the salty savor of bacon and expressed it into the morning air over the grounds of Concordia Seminary. He was taking a shortcut home from the IHOP, where he had made a discovery that gave his step unwonted lightness. The discovery related to his new project—his only one, actually—an essay that would reveal the soul of political conservatives based on the language they habitually used. Its working title was "A Lexicon of Hatred."

His data bank before this morning had had just two deposits, both of them from the radio interview he had been listening to while shaving two days earlier, when the idea had first struck him: "thug," as in "that thug Castro," and "throw money at," as in "we're not going to solve that problem by throwing money at it." Every time conservatives spoke about foreign policy they said "thug," and every time they spoke about domestic policy they said "throw money at." To Cook both expressions seemed inherently swollen with hatred, and he had definitely sensed hostile intonation when he had heard them on the radio. But he knew he would need something to quantify his impressions, along with many more examples.

Thanks to the robust-voiced diner who had sat next to him at the IHOP counter, he had another one: "happen to." While talking to the poor devil on the other side of him, the loud one had said it twice: "I happen to believe in a citizen's right to bear arms," and "I happen to believe we should run government like a business." Why "happen to"? There had to be a reason for it, and the reason was probably connected with conservative habits of thought.

"I happen to believe in a Supreme Being," Cook said aloud, just to experience the sentence from within. His words produced an angelic smile from a fair-faced fellow whose path crossed his at that moment. Cook suppressed the urge to make a loud public retraction.

He crossed the street and headed for the stairs to his apartment, but he slowed when he saw Arthur Delong, his landlord, unlocking the door of his antiques and jewelry store. It was presently eight forty-five. Delong kept odd hours bearing no consistent relation to the hours promised on the sign in front, eleven A.M. to three P.M. For the past month, Cook had heard the same discussions drifting up through his open window: "It's locked." "But the sign says it's open." "I'm telling you it's locked." "Try again."

Cook hurried toward him, reaching for his wallet, where he always carried a few spare checks. "Mr. Delong, I'd like to give you our rent. Tomorrow's the first of the month."

Delong, gray-haired and elegant in his usual coat and tie, turned with contrived difficulty and pretended to require a moment to place Cook. "This isn't the best time," he said.

"I don't need a receipt or anything. I'll just dash this off." Cook

39

unfolded a check and pressed it against the front window to write on it. He wanted to avoid seeing Delong for another month if he could, and he especially wanted to avoid walking all the way through the store to the office at the rear, where Delong holed up and listened to jazz. The mass of headboards, armoires, coatracks, lamps, vases, watch cases, gold cases, and jewelry cases agitated Cook, filling him with the urge to yell what Socrates, overwhelmed, was reported to have exclaimed in the marketplace: "Oh, the many things I do not want!"

Cook heard an impatient sigh as he filled out the check. Every transaction with Delong was a power struggle. Cook didn't understand why. Delong, as landlord, had the power in the relationship. Cook was willing to grant him that. But it never seemed to be enough.

Delong took the check, raised his half-glasses from the chain around his neck, and vetted the document for errors. He looked at the window behind Cook. "I just had that washed."

With a tissue, Cook erased a smudge where he had pressed his hand. His eye fell on the Royal Bayreuth Three-Color Rose Pitcher ($379) displayed behind the glass. He said, "Do you have any Mamie Eisenhower dishes—you know, with her picture on them?"

Delong shuddered visibly. The action involved a headshake as well, and this apparently would serve as the answer. It was Delong's practice to use as few words as possible with Cook. He pocketed the check and went inside the store.

Cook trotted up the outside stairs. He hoped to find Paula still in bed. Her favorite time to make love was first thing in the morning, when he, unfortunately, was congested and groggy from sleep. He liked it best late at night, when she, alas, was wire-tense from the day's events. Now, because he had been out and about, he had worked through his morning torpor and could meet her on her turf. In anticipation, he felt little stirrings as he climbed the steps.

But the clang of tennis-ball cans from the bedroom told him she was booked. He called out a hello and put on a pot of coffee. She came into the living room carrying her tennis gear.

"When did you get home?" Cook said. He threw open the kitchen window. The apartment felt stuffy.

"Eleven or so. You seemed comfortable on the couch, so I didn't wake you."

Another lost opportunity, thought Cook. Her end-of-day tension eased when she drank, so she sometimes met him on *his* turf. He hadn't touched liquor in years, and making love amid her fumes gave him complex pleasure.

Paula smacked her racket strings against the heel of one hand and listened to the vibrations like a violinist. "I had a great time," she said. "It was like a retreat. We're a lot closer now, the entire department. I might even end up liking it here." Paula had a distinguished publication record for such a fresh Ph.D. Unfortunately, recent openings for linguists were not as glorious as her credentials. After a yearlong search, she had had to sigh deeply and settle for Buford.

"Everyone asked about you yesterday," she said. "You've said you wanted more friends. Especially a male friend. You're not going to meet him at home, you know."

Cook leaned against the kitchen counter. "What I said was I didn't have any male friends. I never said I was pining for one."

She frowned. "Do you have any female friends?"

"I have you."

He couldn't tell if the frown he now saw was continuous or newly dedicated. Paula said, "So, tell me about your lunch meeting. Is it what you thought it was? A think tank devoted to error?"

"How long do you have?"

"Ted's coming to pick me up in a minute."

"A minute's not enough," Cook said. It was long enough to tell the story, but not long enough for sympathy. Sympathy was important to him.

"I didn't mean exactly one minute. You know that."

He shrugged. "It's just that the last several times I've tried to talk to you, something has come up."

"That's because you call me at the office. It's a madhouse there. Was there a job?"

"No."

"What happened?"

"As soon as I start telling you, you'll have to go."

"The longer you delay, the greater the likelihood of that."

A horn honked. "See?" she said. She looked out the window and waved. She was wearing her white tennis shorts, which fit her ass in a way that nothing else did. "Well, whatever happened, I'm sorry." She picked up her gear. "By the way, Ted told me he's got a two-year-old informant for you. He called his sister from Chairman Sam's country house and set up a dinner date for Friday, either next week or the week after. I'll check."

"He set it up? I told him not to."

"The guy—Ted's brother-in-law—is some big shot in the nut business. 'The Nut King of St. Louis.' That's what Ted called him."

"He's a businessman?"

"Jeremy, lots of people are businessmen. The world is full of them. He won't bite you. Just shake his hand and move on to the little girl."

"A *successful* businessman," Cook muttered. "They're the worst."

"How many do you actually know?" It was a fair question. The horn honked again. Paula walked to the door. "You'll just have to suppress your hostility to money. It'll be hard, but I have faith in you." She laughed lightly and was gone.

42

Cook remained leaning against the kitchen counter for a while after she was gone. The coffee machine beeped, and he poured a cup and took it to his desk. He wrote down the two sentences with "happen to" that he had heard at the restaurant. As he stared at them, bursts of jazz from Delong's store tickled his feet under the floorboards. He could never hear enough of the tunes to identify them. But wasn't that after all one of the conventions of the grotesque form—disguising tunes? Playing peek-a-boo with them? What kind of musical nonsense was that anyway?

He thought about the way Paula had frowned when he had said she was his friend. It could have meant anything, but it unsettled him. The harsh truth was that he was alone in the world except for Paula. He had lost touch with his old coworkers from the Wabash Institute. His parents were dead. His sister, whom he had once been close to, now lived in Scotland. When he met people, usually through Paula, it never worked. In theory he wanted to be a pal, a card player, a joke teller, a back slapper. But he was most Jeremy Cook when he was alone.

Being alone was lonely. In its pure form it was maddening. He had lived that way for a full year, and day by day he had felt himself losing touch, losing the knack. Self-speech became his only kind. Then Paula had come along, and with some effort he had convinced her to join her life to his. As he saw it, she had rescued him from the nuthouse threshold. Now he was proud to say that he never talked to himself.

"Fuckin' A," he said, making a little closed-fist gesture of solid mental health.

Then he thought about money. He hated it and wished he had lots more than he did. He remembered reading about an official in the Reagan administration who was blunt with superiors because his personal financial resources meant he could walk away from the job at any time. The guy had a special name for these resources. "I happen to have fuck-you money," Cook said aloud, just to see what it was like. He felt like a little boy shooting off a 10-gauge shotgun.

Cook suddenly had a thought so delightful that it made him sit up in his chair. The best source of data for an article on conservatives was—conservatives! The Nut King and his wife were guaranteed reactionaries. He could hear them now, spouting verbal trash across their elegant living room: "Dear, I *happen to* believe we should stop *throwing money at* social problems and punish foreign *thugs!*" "Me too, honey!"

"Ha!" Cook said aloud. "Lemme at 'em."

# 5

"Knock knock."

"Who's there?"

"Daryl."

"Daryl who?"

"Daryl never be another you."

"Good one, Roberta. Listen, which Nutpak was Willie talking about?"

"The Supreme. He wants two hundred. Knock knock."

Ben forced his eyes away from the inventory record displayed on his desk monitor and looked at his secretary. In some sort of delayed blossoming, at the age of forty-two she had discovered knock-knock jokes.

"Who's there?" he said.

"Al."

His eyes drifted back to the screen. "Al who?"

"Al leave if you're not nice to me."

"Willie Knudsen, right? In Seattle? He's never ordered that many before."

Roberta's silence made him look up. Her plain, low-slung face drooped even more than usual.

"Sorry," Ben said. "What was it again?"

"Al leave if you're not nice to me."

"That's a good one. They're all good. You should share them with Karen the next time you're at the house." Or Molly, for Christ's sake.

"Ooh!" said Roberta. "Pardon me."

"For what?"

"My tummy. A little rumble." She fluttered her fingers across her stomach. She was wearing her Monday outfit: the tight-waisted floral aqua dress with the strange little frill around the knees.

"Your sins are forgiven," Ben said, and she laughed in her musical tinkle. "So this is the only weekend surprise?" he said. "No faxes?"

"I don't think so. I'll check the machine." As she turned to go, she went "Ooh!" again, this time in surprise. At the door connecting her office with Ben's stood George Marlin, reporter and fellow citizen of Aberdeen. Whenever Ben saw George, his mouth went as dry as sunbaked sand.

"Yo, Ben. You got time for me, big guy?"

"Always time for you, George." Ben stood up. "You know Roberta."

"Yes, and I'll want to talk to her too. We all know it's the secretaries who keep a half-assed business like this afloat."

Although George favored her with his best standard grin, Roberta hurried back to her office with barely an acknowledgment. This puzzled Ben, but only briefly—not because he solved the problem but because he never thought about Roberta at length.

"I don't get up this way much, Ben," George said. "What the hell town are we in?"

"Bigelow Hills." Crunch was in northwest St. Louis County, which consisted of a hundred or so municipalities. George, acting more heavy than he was, sagged into the leather armchair across from Ben's desk with a groan. Ben hadn't seen him in a while, since early in the year, when they got together with two other friends to divvy up Cardinals season tickets. This yearly event had been the extent of his contact with George for some time.

"How's the family, Ben? Wendy said she saw Susan at the Galleria last week. Spending your hard-earned money."

Ben smiled and said everyone was fine. George's jokes were as uniform as socket-wrench sizes. George's wife, Wendy, was less predictable.

"Have you been following the series in the *Journal*, Ben?"

"Some, yeah."

"'The Mature Business.' That's what you've got, believe it or not." George looked around the office. "Nice prints." He was looking at the huge, finely detailed photographs of nuts—almonds, creamy Brazils, curvaceous filberts.

"Roberta brought those back from her travels one summer. They're by some Pole. She really is good, George. It would be nice if you could say something about her. She's been with me from the start."

"Yeah, I'll work it in. Lemme whip out the tools of the trade." George pulled an old-fashioned stenographic notebook from his briefcase. Ben felt a wave of pity for him. How long had he been doing exactly this—interviewing entrepreneurs for the *St. Louis Business Journal*? For as long as Ben had known him, at least—nineteen years. Not a bad job, exactly, but shouldn't it have been a stepping-stone to something else?

"Let's talk a bit about the early days, Ben. The name, first. Most guys would have called it Gateway Nuts or what have you. Where'd you get 'Crunch'?"

"From Susan. It was her idea."

"I knew she was the brains of the outfit." George laughed at his own joke, but unconvincingly. Sometimes even he lost interest in himself.

"I wanted something catchy," Ben said, "but I also liked the way it captures the whole experience of eating nuts—not just the crunch of the meat, but the crunching of the shell in the nut-cracker, which should be seen as something pleasurable, not as a nuisance." Ben watched George soberly writing this down, and Wendy swam into focus, her breasts glistening with Meramec River water. Eleven years ago. He and Susan had just bought the Voyager minivan to accommodate their growing brood. That always helped him date it. Five times. Five times in a four-week period eleven years ago.

"How about your initial capitalization, Ben?"

"I had a couple buildings in the Central West End that had shot up in value."

George nodded and jotted. "I forgot you were in real estate."

"Not for long. It's too crazy for me. But I borrowed against the buildings. It was enough—barely. Those were scary times. Actually, it was scary for a long time, because we kept trying one new thing on top of another."

"That's what we're looking at in the series. When did the scary period end?"

Right around the time when I slept with your wife, George. No, he wouldn't say that. Clearly George didn't know, and neither did Susan, and both marriages had stayed in their grooves. His own had, at least. As for George and Wendy's, all he knew for sure was that they were still together. The two families had drifted apart, as they had had to.

"What's unique about Crunch, Ben? Besides the name."

"Well, the packaging, for one thing." The shapes of the Nut-paks had been Susan's idea too. Shape them like nuts, she said—like huge nuts. It had taken a while to perfect, and Ben had begun to panic at the money he was piddling away on designs, but then they came up with one, a light wooden box shaped like a big al-mond, hinged at the wide end and opening to reveal individual groups of assorted nuts, each nestled in a plastic half shell in the shape of the nut it contained. The customer paid a lot for the look of it, but the cost actually slowed down the eating. It made the whole thing a delicacy, and that was the way Ben liked it. He didn't want people to confuse his product with a bag of Planter's you gobbled during the Super Bowl.

He watched George write all this—watched his heavy hand la-bor across the stenographic pad—and remembered the first of the five times. It was not on the heels of a drunken New Year's Eve party, but rather on a cloudless afternoon during a family camping trip. George and Wendy had fraternal twins exactly Andrea's age (seven then), a boy and a girl, and they had a daughter a year older than Pam, so the two families got together fairly often, and a weekend on the Meramec had become an annual event. It was August in Missouri, a lazy day on the river. The kids wanted to ride horses at the nearby stable. Susan and George took them. Ben and Wendy hung out at the campsite until Ben, suddenly self-conscious at their isolation, suggested they go for a swim at the river beach. They took two air mattresses and drifted down-stream on them. To stay together, they hung on to the front cor-ners of each other's air mattress. That was the beginning, really—hanging on to each other's air mattress like that. They landed on a sandbar, and there, without a word, they went after each other behind some willow bushes. Ben later marveled at the way he had been able to act without any thought whatsoever.

49

"Let's talk about your fall catalog, Ben," George said. "The pictures of you and Susan and the kids make a real nice impression, family-values-wise."

Ben managed a smile. The family pictures had evolved naturally, beginning with a candid photo of Ben and Susan putting together Nutpaks themselves. The next year they used a somewhat haunting picture of baby Andrea sticking out of a barrel of macadamias. As the business grew, they moved on to more dignified (and costlier) studio and on-location photographs.

The pictures suited the way Ben ran the business—personally, with lots of friendly phone contact. He was comfortable with people on the phone. He was a good schmoozer. (He told George all this, but not boastfully. He knew how to present himself to good advantage.) He remembered little things from previous phone calls, spontaneously. He might be talking up his line with a client, when he'd suddenly say, "You ever get that leaky roof fixed, or is it gonna take a slip-and-fall case to make you do it?" He surprised them all the time, and they were happy when he called. He could tell.

He had never felt false about including the family pictures in the fall catalog, except during the one rotten period in his marriage, "the lost years," as he thought of them. These began a good while after the fling with Wendy, so he doubted there was a connection. Susan woke up one day suddenly resenting that she was a housewife. She yelled at him for three years. Later, when it was all over, she often said he changed and that was what saved the marriage. He would say, if he could (but he couldn't; who the hell could he tell?), that he hadn't changed at all. Something entirely outside them had saved them—a chance mention by a friend that a publisher was holding a special contest for a teen book, which inspired Susan to write one, which in turn got published, but not by that publisher (she missed the deadline but, happily lost in her writing, hardly noticed). Now she had this other thing she did, and they were fine again. How she could see it any other way amazed him—but not enough for him to bring it up for discussion.

It would always be easy to calculate when the lost years were. All he had to do was look at the kids' ages. Four years separated Andrea from Pam, and four years separated Pam from Karen. But Molly didn't come along for another eight years. There was no point in having a baby if you were about to break up. The big gap would always be there as a reminder, like a scar from a childhood calamity.

George asked some questions about operations. When he asked him what accounting firm he used, Ben grinned. "Don't have one," he said, and he enjoyed the surprise on George's face. He explained that he had taken several accounting courses in college, and that he had a constitutional reluctance to seek the advice of others. He liked to inform himself fully and go it alone. And he enjoyed doing the numbers. He loved it when the end of the month came and it was time to whip up a trial balance, as he had just done on Friday. He was never surprised by the numbers, and he liked it that way.

George worked his way back to scary periods again, and Ben remembered one, not an unusual one in growing catalog businesses. It was a momentary plateau of negative economies of scale, when the business suddenly reached the size that it needed to be, but that at the same time could not quite be sustained by revenues.

"I've heard of that," George said. "It comes at about the two million point in sales, doesn't it? But that was some time ago. So you're well over that number now?"

Ben laughed. "You're forgetting my one ground rule, George. No numbers. Or maybe you're not forgetting, you devil. You're not going to trick me into divulging them. I'm a very private

51

person." Damn, Ben thought. He should have let George have that last thought instead of saying it himself. Then George would have been more likely to write it. He liked the sound of it and wanted to see it in print.

"Okay, okay," said George, feigning good-natured retreat. "I'd like to talk about Crunch in terms of the phases it's been through, from the beginning to today. How would you divide it into periods?"

"Let's get Roberta in here, George," said Ben. He was suddenly tired of talking about the business. Besides, George's slow, heavy manner threatened to eat up Ben's entire morning. George seemed a little unhappy with the plan, but then Ben could see him warm to it. An interesting twist to the story, maybe. Jesus, Ben thought. Nineteen years of looking for twists.

Ben called out to Roberta. When she came in, he asked her to divide the business into phases, just as George had asked.

"Oh my," she said, and her fingertips fluttered at her bosom.

Ben gave her a verbal nudge. "I'd say the store was first." This referred to the retail operation directly across Slattery Road, now closed, thank God. Store retail was a pain in the ass. Roberta stood in place, blank-faced. "She's really very good," Ben said. This made George laugh, but not Roberta. "Then the mail-order Nutpaks." Ben paused long enough to allow Roberta to elaborate. When she didn't, he said to George, "She was a great help. I was only going to offer one option, but Roberta seemed to know there were all kinds of people sitting at home just waiting for the right style to be offered to them, from the ten-dollar box up to the . . . What was our highest-priced offering in the beginning?"

"Nineteen ninety-five," Roberta reported.

"And now?" George said to Ben.

"An even C-note," said Ben.

"Jesus," said George. "For nuts. No offense."

Ben smiled good-naturedly. The markup on the Supreme *was* outrageous. He often wondered if he ought to offer a two-hundred-dollar option, but he thought that might be pushing it.

"The next phase," Ben said, giving up on Roberta-as-narrator, "would be the wholesale operation. Special rates for specialty food stores. They put their name right on the box, or rather, *we* do. We do it in the warehouse. It makes it their product from the beginning. So, to sum up, from a little over-the-counter shop to catalog sales to wholesaling, adding one to the other. We lucked out that it happened in that order. We couldn't have gone from wholesale to catalog retail—"

"—because the stores we sold to would have resented it," Roberta said. She sounded like a child displaying a fragment of catechism.

"Exactly," said Ben.

"Thanks, Roberta," George said. He seemed to want her out of there. When she left, he chuckled. "Helluva talker," he said—too loudly, Ben thought uncomfortably.

"She's really very good," Ben said. It felt like the twentieth time he had said it.

Later, when the leather chair George had sat in was slowly sighing back into shape, Ben found himself staring out the window. On Slattery Road the traffic raced through the ugly suburban stretch of gas stations, fast-food places, and muffler shops. To Ben it was white noise for the eyes.

Five times. The river beach, his office couch (late), the hotel at Union Station, the new minivan, and the same hotel again for their farewell. For Wendy, as for him, it had been a practical affair, begun with passion, continued with curiosity, and concluded with affection, respect, and regret. The damage was contained. No one was hurt, except Susan, moderately, because she lost two friends she liked to do things with. Her failures to schedule get-togethers in the aftermath puzzled her, and she brought it up with him a lot. He participated in the discussion as best he could.

Mainly, he wished it hadn't happened. Sometimes, to cheer himself up, he saw himself as a man who could do everything—raise good kids, run a solid business, and have an affair. He was "larger than life." But the truth was, he was exactly life-size. He could only be a husband and father and hard worker. The guy groping behind the willow bushes with Wendy Marlin was somebody else.

Another regret, much smaller, nagged at him at the moment. He shouldn't have summoned Roberta into his office and called on her like that. He hadn't played to her strength. Roberta was quietly efficient, almost creepily so. Her favorite function was to overhear him looking for something—a stapler, a letter, anything—and then track it down and silently extend it to him. He would take it, thank her, and tell her she was great. He told her that a lot. What was odd about her, among other things, was her utter lack of response to his frequent praise. Most bosses were terrible. Why couldn't she acknowledge how well he treated her?

He stood up and went to her desk in the next room. She was writing checks. A stack of envelopes formed a small wall in front of her. They did it the old-fashioned way, by hand, using the One-Write system they had started with.

"Susan was sorry you couldn't make it to dinner this weekend. How about next?"

"Afraid I can't," she said brightly, her tone and smile at odds with her rejection.

"Well," Ben said, faltering a bit, "we'll count on you for Thanksgiving, at least. As always." He turned to go back to his office.

"Oh, that's a long way off, Ben. We'll have to see. If you'll excuse me now, I have to go to the little girls' room."

It was like Roberta to excuse herself after he had already ended the conversation. But it was unlike her to turn down a Thanksgiving dinner invitation. What was going on? For eighteen years she had made her peculiar contribution to their table. For eighteen years she had been as solid as the desk where she sat. He hoped she wasn't suddenly changing on him.

She disappeared into the bathroom, where she never made any noise whatsoever. His eye went to the fax machine next to her desk. Impatient for Nathan Ravindranathan's price list, he crossed the room to see for himself what had come in, but it was just an advertisement from an office supply company. When he tore off the printout, he heard a high-pitched squeal. For an instant he thought it had come from the machine, protesting some blunder on his part. Then he realized it had come from the bathroom. Unless he was mistaken, Roberta was crying in there.

He stood still a moment, dumbfounded. He thought of her cousin in Indianapolis, her frequent traveling companion. She had had surgery a few weeks ago—a tumor somewhere, Ben couldn't quite remember where. The outlook was good, as he recalled. But maybe Roberta was having a delayed reaction to the stress. That would explain not only the tears but her strange response to his Thanksgiving invitation. Her future was uncertain. After all, she might be traveling to see her cousin. What the hell was her name? Helen—that was it. Roberta was trying to say, in her clumsy way, that her future was uncertain because of Helen.

He went to the door of the bathroom. "Roberta?" he said. Immediately, the crying stopped. He heard the noisy rush of water in the sink. "Roberta?"

"Yes?" she said shakily over the sound of the water.

"Are you all right?"

To his surprise, she flung open the door. "What?" she said. Behind her, the water was still running.

"Is it Helen? Are you worried about Helen?"

Roberta looked blank-faced.

"Is there anything I can do? Do you want to take some time off?"

"Alone?" She threw her shoulders back oddly.

"Or with Helen. But can she travel? Or you could just be with her." Ben was puzzled by her question. Alone? Of course alone. Alone was the way she lived.

But Roberta didn't clarify the question. Instead, she just shook her head and closed the door on him.

# 6

*≈*

The man-essence is control. Therefore, control in bodily congress engenders a man-child. The congress-of-control is accomplished thusly—The man anoints his lingam with powders
of the long pepper, the black pepper, burnt bone of camel, and
honey. He then lies atop th woman without the touch of
flesh save within the folds of ecstasy. He supports himself on
his palms and feet. This is called "the tent." The woman lies
widely accepting with her hands and arms outspread. This is
called "the fallen monkey." The lingam enters no more than
a betel nut's length into the yoni. After entry, the lingam may
not stir. The man, by means of inner agitation—

"Dad? Earth to Dad."

From deep within the moist tangles of the Indian subcontinent, Ben returned to temperate Aberdeen, nearly knocking his
home fax machine off its stand as he spun around. Karen stood at
the door of his study.

"Molly wants to go to the playground. I'm gonna take her, okay?" Karen looked fresh-faced and carried about her the faint smell of soap. Ben slid to one side to block the fax from her view. He had been mortified to discover it there. The kids used the fax machine as a copier, and one of them could have easily seen it. He must have given Nathan Ravindranathan his home fax number in the confusion of that late-night pursuit of Pam.

"That's fine, honey," he said. "Be back in time for dinner. Uncle Ted's coming, and a few other people."

As Karen left, Ben heard a car door slam. Pam and two friends, Dawn and Fawn, were getting out of Dawn's mother's Volvo. As they walked down the driveway toward the basement, Fawn unwrapped a piece of gum and threw the wrapper into the ivy. Ben knocked on the window, but they didn't hear him.

He went back to his fax machine, tore the bizarre text out, and threw it away. A half hour earlier, he had done the same with another transmittal from Nathan Ravindranathan—"The Tale of the Fate Brothers." Ben understood, barely, why Nathan had sent him the sexual instructions, but why the other thing?

Attached to the tale were the cashew numbers Ben had asked for. The numbers were good, but not good enough. It would take a more imaginative stroke than a phone call to India to bring in cashews at the price he had hoped for. He would need to go higher up the chain and acquire a processing plant of his own, maybe even a farm. He could see exotic travel in his family's future, too late for most of the kids, but certainly in time for Molly. *And what did you do this summer, Molly?* "I went to my dad's cashew farm in Tanzania. We saw a pride of lions." *Very good. And you, Artie?* And Art Talbot's son would go home from school and say, "Dad, how come you're a banker? Why can't you own a cashew farm in Africa like Mr. Hudnut?"

It was Friday afternoon, a little after four. Ben liked to come home early on Fridays. A lot of the guys in the neighborhood did it. They would go into the house, come back out in their golf clothes, and throw their clubs into the trunk with a big clatter. It was their way of announcing they were good enough to set their own hours. They were making it, doing just fine. But Ben didn't play golf. In fact, he smuggled work home and usually labored right up to dinnertime. But, like the other guys, he did have that little moment every Friday, around three, when he stepped proudly from the driveway to the front door.

Susan came into the study and sat in the extra swivel chair.

"I'm worried," she said. "Have you talked to Andrea lately?"

"No. Why?"

"Something's bothering her."

"You think so?" Ben had had the same thought, but whenever he shared one of Susan's concerns, he underplayed it slightly. If he confirmed it, she would sink even deeper.

"She's not talking. She just disappears from the scene. We'll be in the kitchen and I'll turn around to say something, and she'll be gone. When she comes home she doesn't stick around to chat. She goes right to her room."

"Well, it's a busy time for her. College applications, the play, her A.P. classes . . ."

Susan was shaking her head. "She feels everything. Maybe she should have gone through what Pam's going through. Maybe it's all bottled up."

Ben listened. He didn't want to pursue this, but he didn't want to be caught not pursuing it.

"Molly's leaking," Susan announced.

"What?"

"She's starting to hold it and let it trickle, like Karen did, exactly at the same age. I've had to change her pants three times today."

"Bummer."

"And Andrea told me Sally Samuelson's mom said to Sally that Jiffy's mother told her Pam's friends are sluts."

"What the hell does that mean?" Now Ben was engaged.

"It means that Pam's friends have a bad reputation."

"So what are you saying? Do you think there's any truth to it?"

"I don't know," said Susan. "I just don't know."

"Jiffy's not popular. Her mother knows that and lashes out at the world by calling the popular girls sluts."

"Actually, *she's* a slut."

"Jiffy?"

"Her mom. I saw her at the Garden Market with a real sleaze-ball."

Ben laughed. For all her maternal wisdom, Susan could get down in the adolescent gutter in a flash.

"Why isn't Roberta coming to dinner tonight?" Susan's tone was lighter now. Her burdens had been eased.

"I can't get her over here. I don't know why."

"She's got a guy, I'll bet."

Ben shook his head. "No way."

"She's got a guy and she's having incredible sex and she's wishing it was you the whole time."

"Stop."

"You'll never believe me, will you? She has this thing for you. She always has. Ooh." Susan suddenly stood up. "The potatoes. I have to cool them off. I never think about making potato salad in time. It's such a drag."

"Who's coming to dinner exactly?"

"Ted and two colleagues of his. They're new in town."

"Three professors? Jesus."

"Don't be nervous. Ted's totally unthreatening, and if they're at all like him—"

"But what if they're not? I'm not the brightest guy in the world, you know."

Susan's face flooded with warmth. She stepped over to him. "You're plenty bright. You're the brightest thing in my life." She hugged his head hard to her body. "I've got to tend to my potatoes."

"Remember our three Roman rules of the road?" Cook said as he turned onto Clayton Road.

Paula grunted an affirmative designed to kill the subject. He looked at her face. It had become flat, almost pan-shaped, which it tended to do when she was unhappy. He figured she was in a funk about work. Her students simply weren't good enough for her. Her daily reports suggested she was at war with them.

He reviewed the Roman rules on his own, but he could remember just two: if any space exists between your car and the car in front, occupy it immediately before someone else does; if lost, follow someone—you will thereby avoid cul-de-sacs and eventually stumble upon a classical pile to orient you. He had discovered the rules the previous fall while driving Paula's father's Fiat after their wedding at the American Embassy. Her father, the deputy chief of mission there, had orchestrated the affair. As far as Cook could tell, this had been his main achievement in office.

"Did you get my message?" Cook said. "I left it on your voice mail."

Paula roused herself. "I forgot to check my messages after class."

"Your father called. Around two." He looked at her. "You should give him your office number."

"Why? Don't you like talking to him?"

"I like it fine. But he wants to talk to you."

Paula mumbled something about students parading through her office all the time. She turned and looked out her window.

The truth was that Cook had always thought that scientists working on interspecies communication, like that between chimpanzees and humans, should instead study Paula's father, Bert, and himself in action. Shortly before Bert was posted to Rome, Cook and Paula drove from Wisconsin to Washington, D.C., where her parents then lived, for their first meeting. Cook quickly established that he had nothing in common with Bert or his cronies, all in foreign service in one way or another, all afflicted with the trick of the trade of referring to places by city (Port Louis, Ouagadougou) rather than country (Mauritius, Burkina Faso), while the hapless listener (Cook) desperately tried to figure out what hemisphere they (the cronies) were talking about so that he (Cook) wouldn't embarrass himself (Cook).

Bert had other discourse tricks as well. "And you're from Monterey," he had said when they first arrived and were settled around drinks in the backyard. Bert gave the town's name a Spanish pronunciation that made Cook feel that Father Serra was still active along the coast. Cook said a few words about Monterey. "And you went to the University of California at Berkeley," Bert said. Cook said a few more words. "And you presently live in Wisconsin." Thus, conjunctivally, Cook was encouraged to give a tour of his life. At each stop Bert did most of the talking, claiming the territory by pinning a topic to the place like a little labeled flag. He knew someone who had known John Steinbeck. He knew the parents of someone filming a documentary about the Free Speech movement. He had a good friend who was an executive high up in Oscar Mayer, headquartered in Madison. Bert's intention was no doubt noble: to suggest that he and Cook already had a great deal in common. Meanwhile, Cook was racing to the opposite view. He could never be like Bert, not even with a lifetime of training.

For the duration of the visit, Cook noted their differences like an anthropologist. Bert chatted, both professionally and after hours; Cook chatted only with himself. Bert loved being at the center of a social whirlwind, with life's endless party spinning around him; whenever Cook dined out, he did so at five P.M. to ensure that the restaurant would be empty. Bert's attire was social—it was meticulous even for tennis and dilettantish home repair; Cook often had to check, upon leaving the apartment, to see that he was in fact fully clothed.

As Cook searched for the street sign that would guide him into new territory, he wondered if there was an alternative world somewhere in which only those people who belonged together actually came together.

# 7

After just a few minutes with their guests, Ben was more uneasy than ever about the evening ahead. The awkwardness had begun almost immediately, while they were still bunched in the narrow entryway, when Susan introduced the couple to Ben as "Paula and Jeremy Cook." Ben knew from the sour look on the woman's face that a correction was coming. "Paula *Nouvelles*," she said firmly. Susan flustered a little and said apologetically that just because she changed her name when she got married, she shouldn't assume everyone else did, and that was twenty years ago anyway. Ben thought the last part was a little obscure, and apparently so did Jeremy, because he leaned toward Susan and said, "Are you saying you would keep your name if you got married today?" Poor Susan flustered all over again. Ben tried to smooth things over by saying he hoped the weekend was off to a good start for them, because they were no doubt busy with their new jobs, and Jeremy said, "My wife has the job, not me." The guy snapped the words at Ben as if he'd been taking speech lessons from Pam. Then Jeremy glanced around the house and said, "This is quite a place. Who says there's a housing problem in this country?" All Ben could do was give him his best "What the hell?" face. Paula said, "Let's move on" and gestured to the living room, and Susan made a funny noise of surprise, because of course the suggestion should have come from her or Ben. They went into the living room and scattered.

Ben took drink orders and helped Susan get them—a white wine spritzer for Paula and a root beer, of all things, for Jeremy. Susan gave Ben a wide-eyed, funny look in the kitchen, in reference to the unevenness of things. "Where's Ted?" he mouthed, and she just gave him a helpless look that said she had no idea.

But Paula answered the question when they returned to the living room. Ted had had to make an emergency trip to Minneapolis to coax a famous but shy linguist into giving the keynote address at an upcoming Buford U. conference. Ted and Paula and a few others had been working hard on the planning. Susan said Ted must have called to tell her too and gotten one of the kids. "They're always forgetting messages," she said. Paula gave her a tiny smile.

"So," Ben said, determined to get the ball rolling, "where do you folks live?"

"On Demun," Paula said as she crossed her long legs. Ben was sure she caught him looking at them. "Above an antiques store."

"Ooh," said Susan. "Which one? There are two antiques stores there. We know the owners of one—the Carters. Their son goes to school with our Pam."

Paula looked at Susan blankly. "Delong's Antiques," she said. "He's our landlord."

"Delong's," Susan said thoughtfully. "We've been to that store, haven't we, honey? I think we went there when we were looking for a brass lamp for the piano." Ben shrugged.

"Who plays?" Paula asked with a glance at the baby grand.

65

"None of us, I'm afraid," said Susan. "The older girls took lessons for a while. Ben, I can't remember now where we bought that lamp. Can you?"

"No." Ben squirmed slightly. Unless he was mistaken, Susan was sounding somewhat limited. She normally didn't sound this way, and he was puzzled. "Where are you folks from originally?" he said, noting that this was the second time he had called them "folks."

"I'm from Washington, D.C.," Paula said—a little haughtily, Ben thought. She looked at her husband. "Jeremy's from California."

Susan said, "Ben and I are pure St. Louis, born and bred. Have you been to the Vietnam Memorial in Washington? I hear it's supposed to be very moving."

Paula soberly affirmed that this was the case. Again, unless Ben was being unfair, it seemed to him that Susan's contribution was really not of the highest caliber.

Susan jumped to her feet. "I forgot the nuts. Excuse me." On her way into the kitchen, she called back, "Jeremy, Ted told me you've written a book. What's it about?" It took her a while to track down the nuts, so Jeremy kind of fidgeted, apparently unsure whether to holler or wait. She finally reappeared with a big smile.

"It's about linguistics," he said. "It's an introduction to linguistics." When he said this, he looked hard at Ben. Why did he do that?

"What's it called?" Ben said.

"*The Woof of Words*," Jeremy said. Ben made a point of keeping a straight face. He thought it was the stupidest title he had ever heard.

"'Woof,'" said Susan. "I love that word. Always have." She looked at Ben. "It's one of Andrea's vocab. words this week."

Ben nodded. Again, he didn't want to be unfair, but wasn't Susan being a bit, well, provincial? These folks didn't know who

Andrea was. They didn't know what a "vocab. word" was. He would have to bring them up to speed.

"Andrea's our oldest daughter," he said. "Her English teacher gives the class ten new words a week, and when they find them in their outside reading, they write down the sentences and hand them in for extra credit." He laughed as if something just occurred to him, even though he had known what he was going to say from the outset. "Last week she was mad because she found two good examples in her reading that she couldn't use—'wizened' and 'surreptitiously.' She was reading some novel or other, and there was a reference to someone's 'wizened penis.' Later someone 'surreptitiously stroked his penis.' She couldn't bring herself to hand the sentences in."

There was some good laughter at this, followed by friendly speculation about whether the wizened penis was the one that got surreptitiously stroked. Ben congratulated himself for getting them all over that initial awkward hump.

Susan said to Ben, "I think it was especially hard for her to take those sentences in because it was Mr. Melon's class." She looked at Paula. "He's always flirting with her."

Paula seemed to jerk in her chair. "Flirting?"

"Not really flirting," Susan said. "Teasing. Little comments."

"And he's her teacher?"

"Oh, it's not that bad," Susan said. "He'll ask her about her boyfriends and say she can do better. That sort of thing. He's just kidding around."

"I think 'that sort of thing' is outrageous," Paula said.

Susan's face lost all expression. "Oh?"

"I have a real problem with that kind of behavior."

Susan, her voice a little thin, said, "I'm sure he means nothing by it. Andrea doesn't seem to mind."

Paula sat still, in judgmental silence. Ben suddenly didn't want these people in his house. They were outsiders in every sense.

They were intruders. He said to Paula, "Don't you think our daughter's opinion matters?"

"Of course it does. But are you sure that's her opinion? Have you explored it with her? Women are so conditioned to accept this stuff that half the time they don't know what they think." She looked at Susan, then back at Ben. "Look, would it be okay if a female teacher talked to a male student that way? If she talked about certain girls not being good enough for him?"

"That's different," Susan said. "That would be coming on to the student."

"Exactly. Because it's not done, whereas it *is* done by male teachers. Historically, they have the right to do it, and females are supposed to play along. But every time a male teacher injects sexuality like that, he's telling a girl that her body is part of the educational process. Boys don't have to deal with that."

"I don't know if it's injecting sexuality, actually," Susan said with a brave smile.

"You called it flirting. I'm just going by your words. In fact you said this teacher's behavior may have contributed to your daughter's self-consciousness about those sentences. Doesn't that show that it gets in the way?"

She was a tough one, Ben thought. What annoyed him more than anything was that she made a convincing case. "That trick of reversing things," he said, "of asking how we would feel if a woman did to a male student what the man did to the female student—does that always work? I mean, is that the best test?"

"It never fails," Jeremy said stonily. Ben almost burst out laughing, man to man, because Jeremy seemed to be saying he spoke from experience since he had to listen to this ballbuster every day. But Ben caught himself just in time. Jeremy probably shared her views right down the line.

Susan was looking more sad than upset. She said, "I know what you're saying, and I can't really disagree. I'm not going to say you're making a big deal out of nothing. I wouldn't say that. But there's actually a positive side to it—to Mr. Melon's flirtation. You see, Andrea isn't traditionally beautiful. I think she's striking, but the boys her age . . . Maybe they're afraid of her. I don't know. Anyway, when a man compliments her like that, he's affirming this sense of her beauty, which I think is very fragile. Now, he's not the one to be doing this, as you say. But we're concerned about her happiness, and it's been a thrill to see this for her. I just want you to know there's this aspect to it."

Paula took this in quietly. Ben felt a swell of pride in Susan. He hadn't seen her think on her feet like this in years.

"She's at a play rehearsal right now," Ben said. "She's directing a student production of *Our Town*."

"'Weaned from the living,'" Jeremy intoned. Then he plunged his hand into the nut bowl. His words just sat there. What the hell did they mean? Even Paula seemed baffled.

"Andrea takes after her mother," Ben said. "Susan's had a novel published."

"It was just a Y.A. novel," Susan said quickly. "For young adults. Twelve and up." She seemed suddenly unsure about how much to say.

"What's it about?" said Paula.

"A girl whose brother gets drafted and goes to Vietnam. It's about the war as experienced by her, at home, and it's about growing up in the late sixties and early seventies."

"Neat," said Paula.

"It was a sheer joy to write," Susan said. She went on to talk about that. It was old material to Ben, and he tuned out. Susan continued to direct her comments to Paula, so Ben was able to look at Paula's legs and still give the appearance that he was quietly participating in the conversation. He felt himself getting

69

agitated and looked away at Jeremy, the silent one. Ben had little sense of him. He wasn't a teacher, but he was a linguist, so he probably had a Ph.D. What did it mean to have a Ph.D., exactly? Did it mean that he had solid views on everything, even religion and politics—views that made more sense than Ben's views? Did he have a complete philosophy of life? What was it like not having kids? Ben no longer knew. Did Jeremy and Paula sleep till noon, get drunk when they felt like it, chase each other naked around the apartment, and finish newspaper articles they started? What was life with Paula like? Clearly she saved all her warmth for the bedroom. When she let it out, was it an explosion or just a little poof?

One thing Ben did know about Jeremy: he liked nuts. He was going to town on that bowl. He was working on the Brazil nuts now, having already polished off the cashews. Ben had watched him throw the cashews to the back of his mouth, one after another, and crunch them with his molars. Early on, he thought he heard a groan of pleasure.

"It sounds like fun," Paula said to Susan. "When I was a teenager, I would have enjoyed a book like that."

"But teenagers don't read them, Paula," Susan said. "Y.A. authors write for an age group that doesn't read the books. We've seen it with our own kids. When they hit twelve they leap right from Judy Blume to adult stuff. Some of them stop reading altogether. They just go to the mall." She threw Ben a look. Pam.

"Maybe the audience doesn't matter," Paula said. "Maybe you're just writing about your own adolescence."

Susan smiled. "That's exactly what I'm doing."

Together, the two women turned and looked at the men. Apparently they were done with the subject. A silence fell.

Jeremy said, "You ever notice how miserable rich people look when they're driving?"

Ben stared at him.

"I noticed coming over here," Jeremy continued in the absence of feedback. "The people driving expensive cars. There are quite a few at this end of Aberdeen. They look really unhappy."

"Actually," said Ben, "if you think about it, everybody looks unhappy when they drive. You notice it with rich people because you look at them. You're going to look at a nice-looking blond in a Jag. Sure, she looks unhappy, but so does the frump in the Fiesta."

Another silence fell. "Have some nuts, you two," said Susan. "Try the Brazils. They're—" She interrupted herself with a laugh because the bowl next to Jeremy was empty. "Relax, Jeremy. That's what they're there for. I'll get some more." The guy did look a little sheepish. Susan took the bowl into the kitchen.

"Where do you get your Brazil nuts?" Paula asked.

Ben relaxed, as he always did when he had a chance to talk about the business. "From my warehouse. Bin number twelve. I'm in the nut business."

"I know," she said. "Ted told me. I meant, where do you import them from?"

"Oh. I get them from a broker in New Jersey. He gets them from Brazil."

Paula nodded—knowingly. What the hell did she know? "Why?" said Ben.

Paula recrossed her legs. "I read an article about the working conditions of the laborers in Brazil who do the shelling. The nuts come out of the furnace and burn their hands. The rooms are horribly hot. The people are underpaid. The conditions are better in Peru, where they also grow Brazil nuts."

Thoughtfully, Ben said, "I wasn't aware of that. I could look into getting Brazils from Peru." But would he? Christ, he had four kids and a wife to take care of. He couldn't take on the entire

Brazilian workforce. He wished Susan would come back from the kitchen.

"I read that article too," Jeremy said to his wife. "It concluded we ought to buy Brazil nuts from Brazil anyway, because it helps keep the rain forest intact. Loggers aren't going to cut down trees that bear money-making nuts."

"I don't recall that as the *conclusion*," Paula said.

Jeremy shrugged and turned to Ben. "Where's Molly?"

Hearing his beloved daughter's name from this eccentric stranger felt like a violation to Ben. "How do you know about Molly?"

"From Ted."

Ben said, "She's off with her sister Karen."

Jeremy seemed a little puzzled. "I'm here to see Molly and talk to you about possibly studying her language. That's one of the things I do." He paused. "That's why we're here. That's the whole point."

"Jesus," said Ben. He leaned back in his chair. He wished to hell he had known this from the beginning. Susan came into the room with more slave-grown nuts, and he told her about Jeremy's wishes.

"Neat," she said as she sat down. "Molly says all sorts of funny things." Then, suddenly self-conscious, she said to Jeremy, "But you're probably interested in . . . in . . ."

"Funny things," Jeremy said, and this made Susan smile. The guy had finally said something to put someone at ease—to raise the comfort level in the room instead of making it plummet. Ben wouldn't have thought he had it in him.

# 8

Cook wasn't entirely happy with his performance thus far. He had been in a dreamlike, shut-down state from the beginning, something akin to what he suspected small animals experienced when they entered a predator's mouth. It had begun when they pulled up to the place, a grand, three-story Tudor house fit for, well, a nut king. Cook had to launch a quick mental counterattack. Why, given life's variety, would a human being devote his life to one thing like nuts? Cook's field, language, ranged over everything. But nuts? Why?

To have a house like this, obviously. As Cook worked his way up the elegant curve of the front walk, he remembered what Veblen wrote about curves—that they existed in an environment like this because they were conspicuously wasteful. He wanted to share the thought with Paula, but before he knew it, there was the couple, opening the door. A handsome couple. Too handsome, really. Too close to a parody, too much the PaineWebber couple confident about their financial future while everyone else was in the toilet.

The guy, Ben, had a wide-open face that Cook immediately distrusted. How could he be the nut king unless he was a cock-sucker in the workplace, a tyrant over his employees, and a liar at tax time? Once inside, standing close to the wife, Cook gently removed her from his circle of contempt. She was milky white, creamy, a pale and wretched captive in this dungeon of commerce. She had flowing auburn hair with an ache in it, an autumnal pain. Still, she smiled. She obviously had no idea how unhappy she was.

He wanted to make an impression. He wanted her to take notice. Unfortunately, the way he jumped in during the screwup over Paula's name was a tad clumsy. He just asked her a simple question about whether she would change her name if she got married now, but it seemed to spook her. The nut king, whose name was aggression, made him confess that he was unemployed, but Cook, inspired by the wife's Christian purity, turned the other cheek and complimented him on the house.

In the living room, Susan (lovely name!) did her best to make them feel welcome, pointing to connections between her life and theirs (she had shopped in his building!). When she asked him about his book, he had an inspiration and directed his answer to the nut king instead of her. Why? To make him say, "What's linguistics?" The word "linguistics" always evoked this question from philistines. He wanted Susan to see what an oaf her husband was. And he could see it coming. He saw the darkening brow, the brutish deliberation.

But, damn it all, he just asked about the title—a title Cook had regretted from the moment he thought of it, a title that he had blamed for the book's poor sales. He was plunging into despair when Susan pulled him out: she loved the title! This told Cook two things: (a) the book's wretched sales were due not to the title but to poor marketing by the publisher, which he would tell them in a letter as soon as he got home, and (b) Susan was fond of him, perhaps more than she realized.

The nut king, all this while, was silent. Cook hated that. Silence was self-protective. People should jump in and make asses of themselves like everyone else. That was Cook's philosophy. But maybe the guy just didn't know how to talk, owing to the lack of words in his life. There wasn't one real book in the living room. Just prints and flowers, doilies and tchotchkes, statues and statuettes, knickknacks and gimcracks. The large bookcase next to the fireplace was a display case for big plates and family photos. There was one quasi-book in the room, on the coffee table, a memento-cum-conversation-piece pertaining to a Matisse exhibit in New York, where the nut king had no doubt gone to broaden himself, but Cook would see him in hell before he asked him about it. There were lots of other things he wanted to ask him first. How much did he make a year? Or rather, since it had to be a lot, at what cost did he make it? If, as Balzac says, behind every great fortune there is a crime, what was his? Child neglect? How did those kids in the family pictures feel about him? What were the family secrets? Where was the dirt?

The king finally deigned to speak. He told a tedious story involving the word "penis"—a calculated shock, Cook guessed, to impress everyone with his unpredictability. It failed. Then Paula stirred things up a bit when she went after Susan on a feminist tack. It was painful for Susan. Cook could tell. He wanted to fold her in his arms and say, "There, there." Paula's view was the right one, of course, but Susan wasn't completely benighted. She just needed nurturing, developing. She had been living in a cave for—what did she say? Twenty years? It was a miracle she could still talk. What really made Cook hate the guy was how he failed to rise to his wife's defense. Prick! Was he hoping to impress Paula? (Good luck, pal.) Or did he just want to distance himself from Susan because she was losing the argument? Bastard! A man shouldn't distance himself from such a woman. He should get close to her, as close as possible. Doofus!

He fell in love with her all over again when she talked about her book for teenagers. He would have to be sure to ask for a copy before he left. Not signed, though. He had always thought that was dumb, based on the one experience he had had with a request for his autograph, and he figured Susan felt the same way. He grew more and more familiar with her while she talked about her writing. In fact, he put his face between her legs. He pretty much set up shop there, canceling meetings, sending out for lunch, filing a change-of-address form. He wanted to be there forever, with the red roar of the fire in his face.

Then at last, thank God, they got to the agenda: Molly. If Cook had known they were ignorant of it he would  have mentioned it sooner, because he now sensed a merciful existential shift. They all seemed to realize they had been brought together in this room not for absurd reasons, not so that the gods could slap their huge knees in laughter, but for a good purpose, to advance the science of linguistics.

Susan stood up (Cook retrieved his face in the nick of time) and walked past his chair. He watched her go to the front window and look for her daughters. There was a lull.

"Linguistics," Ben suddenly said.

Cook went on alert. Was the nut king going to ask the question after all? Was Susan listening? But wait, he thought. Susan's brother, Ted, was a linguist, so Ben would be somewhat familiar with the field. Cook had been on the wrong track.

"Linguistics deals with meaning. Correct?"

"Among other things," said Cook.

"I have a question about meaning."

Cook tried to look eager for a meeting of the minds. Where was the nut king going with this?

"Earlier, you said, 'Who says there's a housing problem in this country?' What was the meaning of that?"

Cook laughed. "Did I say that? It doesn't make much sense, does it?" He threw a glance at Paula to see if she might bail him out. She was staring at him with frigid, Swiss-like neutrality.

"Were you saying it's excessive for people to live in big houses because so many people are homeless?"

Jesus, thought Cook, who unleashed the host? "It's a ridiculous position," he said. He was pleased at the ease with which he distanced himself from it.

"If you were making that claim, I'm not sure where you would draw the line."

"That pesky line. One never knows where to draw it."

"Yet you draw it, Ben," Susan said from the front window. "You have a line like that." Cook's heart soared. *Susan* was bailing him out! "Ben draws the line at fur," she said to him. "I was going to have an old fur of my mother's resewn—"

"That's different," said Ben. "That's —"

"—and he said to me, 'You're married to a man who won't be seen with a woman in fur.' Not because of the animals. It's the showiness of it. Right, honey?"

Ben was scrunching up his face. "Fur coats are smug. A house, though. Well, you live in a house."

In a different tone, Susan said, "I have an idea. Since it's so nice out and there's no sign of Molly and Karen, we could all walk down to the park and meet the kids there."

"Why don't we pack the dinner and have a picnic?" Ben said. He looked from Susan to Cook. "It's a cold dinner anyway. Chicken and potato salad."

77

"A farewell to summer," Susan added.

"Sounds good," Cook said. They all looked at Paula.

"I'm easy," she said.

—

Cook was alone in the living room. Paula was helping Susan in the kitchen, and Ben was somewhere fetching something. Cook stood at the window and tried to imagine what it would be like to own this view: the spacious flagstone patio, the protective low wall of yews at its edge, the broad lawn sloping to the curb, where huge oaks stood sentinel.

Three teenage girls flashed into the scene on Rollerblades. They swerved to a stop in front of a house not far down the road. One of the girls stepped onto the grass and took two black things out of a bush. She slipped them on her wrists.

"That's odd," Cook said, mainly to himself, but Ben heard him as he came into the room.

"What?" Ben joined him at the window.

Cook described what he had seen. Ben listened but said nothing. The three girls Rollerbladed to the curb right in front and clomped up the walk. Ben went to the front door.

"Hi," one of the girls said. "Can you get us some gum?"

"Take your skates off," Ben said.

"I'm not coming in," she said. "We just want some gum."

"You know the rule. You're supposed to wear your wristguards."

"What do you call *these?*" The girl displayed her wrists.

"They're not going to do you any good in the bushes. No more blading today or tomorrow. Take them off."

"Oh, God, don't you have anything better to do?" She whirled away and rejoined her two friends down the walk.

"Pam," Ben said. "Off."

78

"Yeah, yeah." She dropped to the concrete and angrily yanked at her laces. The two other girls stood there like watchful squirrels.

"Oh, and Fawn," Ben said, "please don't throw gum wrappers in the ivy. I'm the one who has to pick them up, and I'll think of you every time I do." One of the girls went stony with embarrassment. Her friend giggled.

Ben rejoined Cook in the living room. "It's not fashionable to wear wristguards," he explained. "You'll notice that Pam's friends, who are on the cutting edge, have bare wrists. They must be eager to break their bones on the asphalt."

"So she wears them as she leaves, then takes them off and hides them—but within full view of the house?"

Ben nodded. "The old cliché: they want to get caught. But then you'd think she'd be more cheerful at the moment of capture." He gave Cook a little smile. It was a small sentence, but Cook liked it. He liked its world-weary tone.

In front, the three girls were talking fast and hard as they removed their Rollerblades. They made Cook uneasy. Their faces were pretty but wildly changeable. The girls were too young to be properly considered sexy, but sexy they were. Cook couldn't imagine how such people were to be dealt with.

"Have you studied children's language before?" Ben said.

Cook decided this was a friendly question and not a demand for credentials. "I did it for six years at a place in Indiana called the Wabash Institute. It was attached to a day-care center, and a small staff of linguists observed the kids. It's where I met Paula."

"Have you ever taught, like Paula?"

Cook shook his head sternly. "You have to say the same things over and over."

Ben seemed to chew on this a while. He asked Cook how he had become interested in linguistics, but just then Susan came into the room, and Cook let the subject die. Susan carried a picnic basket of worn white wicker. Beside her, Paula held a large red thermos. The women had been laughing about something. Ben took the basket. Paula relinquished the thermos to Cook with a hint of reluctance, thereby making a brief political statement.

Susan said, "It's just a short walk. About ten houses down and through the gate." She headed for the door. "Go ahead and answer Ben's question, Jeremy. I'm interested too. How *did* you get interested in linguistics?"

Cook, maneuvering into a position right behind Susan, had a rare feeling. He could be, for a moment, the life of the party. "It happened on the day I learned why so many unrelated languages have words sounding like 'mama' and 'papa' for 'mother' and 'father.'"

"Tell, tell," said Susan, leading the way. They stepped outside.

"Earthly language," said Cook, "is based on sounds made by organs originally evolved for other purposes—for eating and breathing."

The three adolescents, sitting on the curving walk directly ahead, jerked their heads up like deer. Their faces said to Cook, *Do we give a shit?*

"The various sounds," Cook continued as he worked his way by the girls, "are made by altering the flow of air from the lungs."

"Pam, you kids are kind of in the way here," Susan said.

"*Sorry.*"

"There are two kinds of sounds: consonants and vowels."

A shout came from next door. "Goin' on a picnic, Ben?"

"You bet, Mike," Ben said.

The neighbor stood on his front lawn next to a lamppost, grinning and shaking a can of spray paint. The little ball in the can went *gonketa gonketa.* "Tell you what, you picked a good day for it. What you got there? Chicken?"

Susan yelled, "Just enough for us, Mike."

Mike laughed and continued masturbating his paint can as they moved on.

"With consonants—"

"Let's cross here," Ben said. "Sorry, Jeremy. Go ahead."

Cook would have given up, but when they had crossed and settled into formation—Susan and Paula in front, Ben and Cook behind—Susan said, "Consonants. Go on."

"With consonants, the airflow is affected a lot. It can be stopped, it can be narrowed for hissing noises, and so on. With vowels, it's affected much less. Now, here's where it gets interesting."

"Hey, Ben, we gonna beat St. Andrew's tomorrow?" This came from a long-legged man standing next to a black car in a driveway across the street. He had just taken his suit coat and briefcase out of the rear seat. His shirt was the whitest thing Cook had ever seen.

"Hope so, Mort," Ben yelled.

"Tell you what, are we due or what?" the man yelled as he slammed his car door.

"You got that right," Ben called. He turned to Cook. "Soccer. Karen's team."

Cook nodded. Paula and Susan were talking about children's books. The group was approaching a man raking leaves with a little boy of three or four.

"See my helper?" the man said to them. "See my little helper here?" He pointed proudly to the boy, who with his junior rake was dragging leaves out of a large pile into a spotlessly clean area of the lawn.

"You've got a good little helper there, Chuck," Ben said.

"Yeah," the man said proudly. "He's a good helper all right."

"Are you helping your dad, Tommy?" asked Susan.

"He helps me a lot," said Chuck.

Cook wondered if he too should say something structured on the root "help." He was debating between "helpmate" and "help-meet" when the boy suddenly swung his rake in a low, wide arc, smacking his father sharply on the shin and ending the discussion. The group moved on.

"You didn't finish, Jeremy," Susan said. "We didn't get the whole explanation, did we?"

"Not quite," said Cook. "The best consonant is the one that is least like a vowel, for maximum contrast—one that stops the air *completely*, which is 'b' or 'p,' and 'p' is better than 'b' because the vocal cords don't vibrate."

"Neat," said Susan, but her voice had the mild waver of incomplete comprehension. Ben pointed to a gate in a wrought-iron fence and stepped forward to open it. Cook heard the rhythmic squeak of a swing and saw the playground on the other side of a small stand of pine trees.

"There they are," said Ben.

"By the same token, the best possible vowel is the one that contrasts with consonants the most—"

"Molly's not holding on to that swing very well," said Ben. "Excuse me." He hurried ahead. Paula wandered off toward a drinking fountain.

"Go on," Susan said to Cook.

"Well, I'm sort of done," Cook said with a joyless laugh. "If you had just two sounds in your inventory, 'p' and 'ah' would be the best pair, because they contrast the most. Put them together and repeat them, which kids love to do, and you've got 'papa.'"

"Neato," said Susan. She gave him a big smile and hurried to join the others, waving and calling, "Hi, hi."

Cook looked after her, itching with dissatisfaction. He saw himself as a clown, bellowing through this elegant suburb, while the others feigned interest, secretly thinking, Will he never finish, will we never get to the park?

Cook watched Ben. He was pushing Molly on the swing and grinning. Susan got into the swing next to her, and Ben pushed both of them. Molly's mouth opened wide in pleasure at the novelty of the situation. To Cook, Ben suddenly seemed heroic, larger than life. He *was* a king. He had a queen and a palace and heirs. He had a domain. Cook ruled over nothing but words.

Though deep in private despair, Cook sensed something new happening at the swing set—a shift of mood, as if a cloud were passing over. Karen had pointed up the hill, and her parents were looking. There, in a distant set of swings, were a man and a young woman with long black hair. They sat with their backs to Ben's family. They weren't swinging, though the young woman—or girl, perhaps—swayed slightly from side to side in her swing, bringing her close to the man. The girl gestured emotionally once and raised a hand to her face. Cook felt an intensity that made him want to look away.

Susan had stopped swinging and was staring at the couple, her mouth slightly open. Ben stared too. He was no longer pushing the swings, and Molly roared in protest at the abrupt end to something she had been enjoying so much.

# 9

"Do you want to talk to her or should I?" said Susan.

Ben peeled off his shirt and reached for his pajama top. "Either one. How do we approach it?"

"Head on." Susan was sitting up against two pillows, her arms folded across her nightgown. "We know something's going on, and we need to be direct about it."

"We don't *know* something's going on."

"You don't think that was an intimate conversation?"

"Oh, it was intimate," Ben said. "But we don't know what they were being intimate *about*. They could have been talking about some friend of hers."

"You don't really believe that, do you? Don't you think the worst?"

"I never think the worst." Ben climbed into bed. "We don't know what they were saying. Try to remember that. Actually, that's a way to approach it. 'What were you and Mr. Melon talking about on the swings?' That's what we'll say."

"Suppose she says, 'Oh, nothing,' or 'Oh, the play.' Was he the Drama Club adviser last year too?"

"Was she in it last year?" Ben said.

"Toward the end of the year, yeah. Was he the adviser?"

"I don't know. How would I know?"

Susan sighed. "The weirdest thing was the way they left once they saw us."

"After an appropriate interval. That made it even worse."

"Yeah. God. The interval. Did he wave?"

"No," said Ben. "But that doesn't mean anything. We haven't actually met him, so he wouldn't necessarily wave. I mean, he *could* have waved, and it would have been nice, but he didn't have to." Ben thought about it. The guy should have waved.

There was a knock on the door. Karen came in, wearing her pale blue bathrobe with her name embroidered on it. She looked at the TV, which was off. She looked at them, sitting up, neither of them with a book or magazine.

"What are you guys doing?" she said.

"Hanging out," said Ben. "Your game's at noon tomorrow."

"Okay. You gonna watch anything?" It was her bedtime, but on weekends they often let her sprawl with them and watch a late movie.

"I'm kind of tired, honey," Susan said. "Was Andrea at Meredith's house when she called?"

"I think so."

"Did she say where she was going after that?"

"No. What's wrong?"

"Nothing," said Susan.

"Nothing's wrong," said Ben.

Karen took a soapstone turtle from the dresser. "I love this. Can I have it in my room for a while?"

"If it's okay with Dad." Ben felt Susan looking at him and went blank. "You gave it to me," she said.

85

"Oh, yeah," Ben said, rousing himself. "Just be careful with it."

"It'll do until I get my bunny. G'night." Karen threw her father a parting look over her shoulder.

When the door was closed, Susan said, "The world should consist of adults and fourth-graders. Nobody else. You should have seen her with Paula, when you were all down at the pond. Paula asked her what she liked to read, and she really opened up. Paula knew all the books she named—all the classics, anyway. She's read more than me, and I'm the one who writes for kids."

"Did that upset you?"

"Why would it upset me? I was delighted to see Karen so comfortable with a stranger."

"Did she get intense with Karen?"

"Intense?"

"The way she did with you. Didn't it piss you off when she went after you about Melon flirting in class?"

"Not at all. She was right. I felt like an idiot."

"That's what I mean. If she made you feel like an idiot—"

"But I *was* an idiot. So were you. Andrea's been telling us about this guy's misbehavior for weeks, and we just went about our business. God knows what it's developed into now."

Molly cried out from her room—a single yelp. They waited. She had wet the bed a half hour earlier, and they had gone in and changed her and replaced the crib sheet.

"Just a dream," said Susan.

Ben didn't like the way Susan had let Paula off so easy. "There's no *give* to that woman. No lightness."

"She can laugh," Susan said. "We were being very silly after lunch. I like them. They're different. They made me see how lazy I've become. What do we talk about with our friends? Schools, real estate, and grout. Everyone we know says the same things over and over. I'd really like to see them again."

86

"I suppose that's possible," Ben said vaguely.

"How was Jeremy with Molly?"

Ben shrugged. "He let her take the lead. He knows not to push."

"He's cute as a button."

Ben laughed. "You make him sound like a little boy."

"He's awkward as a boy, I'll say that much." Susan shifted under the covers. "So, should I invite them over again or wait for them to return the invitation?"

"I'd wait. Besides, he's going to be here to study Molly. Let's wait." Ben was a firm believer in delay as an avoidance strategy. He didn't want that woman in his house again. Apart from her negative qualities, which were plentiful, there were her positive ones. Tall, broad-shouldered, long-legged, she had one of several kinds of body he was attracted to. Lust, even though he would never be its victim again, stirred him up. Its essence was agitation. It made him irritable and mean to Susan in ways she didn't even know about. Jeremy he could handle, though he found him impossible to read. What could you do with a guy who said one oddball thing after another?

After a long silence, Susan said, "Maybe they were talking about somebody else. Some other mother's problem."

"That's what I'm hoping. That's what I think." Ben stroked her arm. "Enough talking."

Susan looked at the clock. "We can't really do anything. Pam'll be home any minute." Their bedroom was adjacent to hers, with a door connecting them. It was always closed and even blocked by Pam's dresser. But noises easily leaked from one room into the other. "I'm too stirred up anyway."

She gave him a pat on the arm and took a *Vanity Fair* from her nightstand. Ben reached for the book on the Civil War that had been on his nightstand since his birthday four months earlier. He was almost up to the firing of the first shot. As he searched for his place, he heard the front door open. Some kitchen thuds were followed by footsteps up the stairs. Pam's heavy pocket door slid open and slammed shut.

Susan said, "One of us should check the door."

Ben got up and went downstairs. Pam not only had managed to close the front door completely but had also remembered to take her key out of it first. Ben turned off all but one of the downstairs lights, leaving it and the front patio light on for Andrea, whose weekend curfew was two hours later. He stood at the living room window and stared into the darkness over the long slope of grass. He pictured Andrea, seven or eight years old and long of limb, endlessly doing cartwheels on the lawn. Her goal was to do them continuously from the top of the hill to the bottom, from the patio to the curb. It took something like seven rotations. When she finally perfected it, her body stayed as rigid as a wagon wheel all the way down.

He went back upstairs. His legs felt heavy. Susan's light was already off, and she was curled up under the blankets. He took his Civil War book from the bed, set it on the nightstand, and turned off his own light. He lay down on his back and put his hands behind his head.

"Relax," Susan commanded. Her back had been to him, but now she turned and felt for his face. They kissed. It was just a good-night kiss, but she held him for a long while.

*Your ears are like conch shells.*
   *No one's ever said that to me before.*
   *Your hair is like a burning maple tree in autumn—*

*I like it when you bunch it up in your fists. It surprises me, but it doesn't scare me.*

*Your skin is winter milk from an albino cow.*

*You're so . . . different.*

"Jeremy, I just had a horrible thought. Jeremy?"

Cook, floating in a leafy elfin boat of lust, was slow to reengage with reality, at this moment represented by Paula, sitting upright against the headboard with a *Scientific American.* "Mmm?" he said.

"They probably expect us to return the invitation. The circle they move in probably operates that way. You have to have *two* shitty evenings before the relationship is over."

"Don't most social circles operate that way?" Cook would defend the auburn beauty. "I'm sure that's the rule in your parents' world."

Paula huffed. "How can you even mention them in the same breath? In the world I grew up in, if you had a piano in the living room, by God you *played* the piano. We all played it."

She was failing to make the obvious distinction between Susan and her husband. He would have to help her with that. "I'll admit, I could have done without the flapping almond box," he said.

Paula laughed and slapped her magazine against her legs. "What did he call it?"

"A Nutpak."

"God. They're a pack of nuts, all right."

Cook shifted the pillow behind him a bit. "I thought you liked her."

"I'm glad I fooled you. We were guests in their home. I didn't want to be rude."

"But she *is* an author. He's just a merchant, but she—"

"She writes for children."

"So did E. B. White."

Paula laughed. "She's no E. B. White. The book she's writing is about this little doll family that comes to life. She said it's based on a game their little girl plays—"

"Molly."

"Whatever. Apparently Molly puts in hours and hours playing 'Family'—that's what Susan calls it. She gave the girl an old silverware holder, like you put in a drawer—she took pains to show it to me when we got back to the house—and if you stand it on its side it looks like a house in cross section. Molly has this little family of hard plastic dolls—Jesus, I'm going on about it because *she* did. Anyway, she's writing their story. It sounds like half the children's books ever written—the dolls coming to life in the store after hours, blah blah blah."

Cook congratulated himself on not asking to read the work-in-progress, which he had briefly considered doing to get closer to Susan. He wouldn't have known what to say about it.

Paula grabbed the phone on the nightstand and punched a phone number—Ted's, presumably. She had tried it several times already that night. She hung up with a scowl. "He must be spending the night in Minneapolis. I wish he'd call me."

"Why?"

"When I was hired, Chairman Sam said they were going to try to establish a Center for Linguistics here—a center devoted to research. The department's decided to use the conference to launch it, to attract attention and funding. So we all want it to be a bang-up conference. With a center like that, I can get released time from teaching, thank God." She smiled at the prospect, but then she made a face. "Damn. I just remembered Ted is supposed to be my partner for a doubles match tomorrow."

"Who are the other two?"

"A couple I met at Chairman Sam's. They've got a country place next to his."

"I can be your fourth, if you're stuck."

"No, no," she said with a laugh. "I wouldn't ask that of you."

Cook hadn't expected laughter. "I've been known to play tennis. In fact, every time we've played, I've beaten you."

"Beating isn't everything. You beat me by brute force."

"Tennis is running to the ball and hitting it. I run to the ball and hit it."

Paula shook her head. "I've got nothing against good hard hitting. I'm talking about form. You slap your feet on the court like a clown with big shoes."

Cook frowned. Apparently it was his duty to play more beautifully and lose.

Paula said, "In tennis there's a crucial concept of 'level of play.' When you mix levels it's . . ." She sighed. "Still, I suppose four *would* be better than three." She sighed again—heavily. "Okay."

Cook grunted. He would humiliate them all, even if he looked ugly doing it. "What do they do?"

"He's a stockbroker. She's in bonds."

"Jesus. From nuts to Wall Street." But it did not escape him that these two might prove to be dandy reactionary informants. Ben had let him down in that regard. He hadn't uttered one political word the entire evening.

Paula had picked up her magazine, but now she set it back down. "I meant to ask, did something happen when we got to the park? They seemed terribly preoccupied or something."

"I think they saw their daughter there with someone. It might have been the teacher they talked about earlier."

"When did this happen?" Paula seemed irritated to have missed out on the one thing that might have interested her.

"You were at the drinking fountain. This girl and an older guy were up the hill a ways. They saw us and left. Ben and Susan seemed shaken up."

"Well, it's the chickens coming home to roost, if you ask me. If they're involved with each other, the poor girl's life is screwed up forever. The worst people have kids. God, did you see the pictures in the living room? It looked like a shrine. For a moment I thought they'd all been wiped out in some terrible common accident or something. Why have pictures of the kids all over the house if they're right underfoot? I don't get it." Paula set her magazine on the nightstand. "I'm going to sleep." She gave him a kiss, turned off her light, and disappeared under the covers.

"Guess I'll stay up and read some more," Cook said. He turned off his own light. He went into the living room and flopped on the couch. On the coffee table was the Nutpak that Ben had sent him home with, officially dubbed "The Family Sampler." Cook had all but emptied it. He grabbed a handful of broken remnants and munched on them as he lay back. He threw his arm across his forehead.

*I will tell you about "mama" now.*

*Yes. Yes.*

*The baby wants to say the ideal consonant and vowel, "p" and "ah," but he can't because something is in his mouth.*

*What do you mean? Oh I see. Oh!*

*With the surprisingly large breast in his mouth, he can only make a nasal consonant, mmm, a bilabial nasal with mammary coarticulation, mmmmmmm—*

He closed his eyes. He had never felt anything like this for anybody.

# 10

*⌒*

"Service!"

Cook crouched in readiness. To his left, Paula, his partner in all things, bounced on the balls of her feet at the net. He took one quick peek at her ass, then readied himself for Trent's serve in order to avoid being injured by it. The ball bounced and zinged past Cook's right scapula. He didn't budge.

"Pretty!" Paula called out.

From this Cook surmised that the serve, which he hadn't seen in totality, had been good. He moved forward to the net for the next point while Paula stepped back to receive the serve. His present goal, as the foursome neared the end of its first and no doubt last set, was to maintain his dignity. This was the most recent of several coping strategies he had adopted in the past twenty minutes. Brute force had failed. Finesse had failed. Insouciance had failed. Self-deprecating irony had failed. Now he strove for dignity—a composite, derivative pose drawn from the manner of

Gregory Peck, who was not on the court at present, and the words of Trent Houston, who was.

"Fifteen-love. Service!"

Cook heard the serve streak by to his left, a whistling bullet on the battlefield with someone else's name on it. It went deep to Paula's backhand. She lunged and managed to get under it.

"Nice dig!" Trent said, smiling broadly as he loped in on Paula's lob and smashed it past the alert but useless Cook. The ball whispered to him as it passed over his left clavicle.

Cook walked back to the baseline. He said to Paula, as they passed each other, "Nice dig."

"It wouldn't hurt if you backpedaled once in a while," she snapped.

"Right," said Cook. It was his turn to receive the serve again. This would necessarily involve him in the point, if only briefly.

"Thirty-love. Service!"

Cook wondered if he too should say "Service!" every time he served. This thought came to an end as the ball bounced and spun past his zygomatic arch. On his way forward once again, he said to Paula, "Let's bear down now." She made a strange noise in response. He had thought it a good phrase when he had heard it from Trent, early in the set, in self-address: "Bear down, Houston. Bear down."

"Forty-love. Service!"

Trent bore down. Cook watched his long body arc like a Norman bow as he reached up to hit his toss. The ball became invisible again, but Cook did hear a tip as it passed, and he called out, "Net!"

Trent pulled another ball from his deeply pocketed shorts. "First service!" he called. He served, Paula backhanded, Trent's female partner angled, Cook observed, and the set ended.

"Nicely done," Cook said jovially. It made him feel British to say that. In all the movies he had seen where Brits played tennis, they always looked like hell but chatted like gangbusters. That would be his next strategy. Be a Brit on the court.

"The word is *let*, Jeremy," Paula said, her voice biting and metallic. She smacked her racket flatly on the top of the net. "You've been saying *net* all morning. It's a *let* ball when it tips the net. From the Old English *lettan*, meaning 'hinder.' Okay?"

"I knew that," said Cook.

Paula turned away and said, "Sherry, let's you and me hit a few."

"Good idea," said Sherry, hitherto unnamed for punitive reasons, for she had ignored Cook from the moment she had seen the quality of his play.

"I guess that leaves us out, Jeremy," said Trent. "Come on. I want to see what's in that picnic basket."

Trent was Cook's only ally on the court. Tall, graceful, superior but nonjudgmental, he had treated Cook like a gentleman. Cook wanted to address him in those terms: "Sir, you have ever dealt with me fairly." But he just said, "Good idea. I'm hungry."

Trent grabbed his warmups from a bench at mid-court, draped a white towel around his neck, and led Cook out the gate to the shade of a black oak tree. At its base sat a picnic basket so large that it might have been delivered by forklift. Trent dropped to his knees, undid the complicated leather thongs, and paused prayerfully before opening the lid. He began a careful survey of its contents. He pulled out a bottle of white wine from a small ice bucket within and spun it around so he could see the label. Cook watched water drip down the bottle onto Trent's tanned thighs. Trent studied the label the way Cook read monographs in *Neuphilologische Mitteilungen*.

"Looks lovely," Trent said. "One of my many vices is wine with lunch. How about you?"

Cook took an inventory of his own vices. They were all imaginary. Then he saw what Trent meant and said, "I'll just have water." He held up the old plastic Diet 7-UP bottle he had filled from the kitchen tap.

Trent unwrapped a sandwich. "Looks like they did a nice job. Help yourself."

"Didn't you pack this?"

Trent laughed boomingly. "We don't have time for that sort of thing. Arno's packed it. The gourmet shop. We call them up and tell them what we've got planned and they go crazy. It's a real treat."

"Like opening your lunch box and seeing what Mom packed for you?" Cook said.

Trent seemed less taken with this comparison than Cook had wished. He just gestured for Cook to help himself. Cook browsed the basket innards. He rejected an avocado sandwich in favor of one with a meat product in it, some sort of hard spicy sausage. He settled down on the grass with his water bottle wedged between his legs, huddling a bit against the cold. Trent still hadn't put his warmups back on, whereas Cook had never taken his off. They were at the top of a rise. Below them lay expansive Aberdeen Park, a shaded oval green full of picnic tables and playground equipment.

Behind them, Sherry and Paula romped like two hosts finally rid of an unwelcome house guest. Paula moved with long-legged grace on the court. Cook, succumbing conveniently to myth, told himself that his inferior play was a result of those very legs being wrapped around him earlier—and for quite some time. His A.M. sluggishness always translated into granitic endurance, which perhaps explained Paula's preference for that time of day.

Trent tipped the wine bottle toward an iron climber built in the shape of a stagecoach. Several children dangled from it. "St. Louis is a great place to raise kids," he said.

"You have a child?" Cook didn't hide his surprise.

"Three sons. Three, two, and one." Cook braced himself for the inevitable. "The way I see it, everything else pales in significance next to the importance of raising kids."

Cook fought off the sleepiness that overwhelmed him whenever speech matched his prediction. "Do you and Sherry coparent?" He had always wanted to say this word in a human conversation.

"You bet. She has them from six to seven after work, and I get 'em from seven to seven-thirty."

"Where are they now?" It was just shy of high noon on a Saturday.

"With my mom. She's crazy about them."

"She can handle that? A grandmother with three boys that young?"

"She has help. Actually, she was on her way to the mall when we dropped them off. The kids are with her housekeeper." Trent sipped his wine. "Sherry and I need our playtime too. We work hard, and we play hard."

Cook suddenly understood Trent. He was a well-built machine. He produced things: rocket serves with his right arm, children with his sperm, and clichés with his mouth. He pretended to have ideas, but he didn't really. Machines didn't have ideas.

In the distance, Cook saw another father working his way across the park, one who was with his child at the moment. He looked again: it was Ben. It made Cook feel good to recognize him. It made him feel like someone with a home—a St. Louisan. Ben and the girl, Karen, were walking slowly, with Karen pausing at the playground sites to sample the equipment. Ben carried a soccer ball and tossed it up as he walked. Occasionally he bounced it off his head, but erratically.

"'The Nut King of St. Louis,'" Trent said.

"You know him?"

"Ben Hudnut. He's built himself a nice little business. I'd like to handle what he's got." Trent finally slipped into his warmups. Cook watched Ben and Karen climb a distant rise to the plateau of an athletic field. "How about you, Jeremy? Do you have money that's not working as hard as it should for you?" Trent flashed two rows of straight teeth at him. "I like to be direct when I talk about my favorite subject."

Cook deliberated. In his frugal bachelor days at Wabash, he had saved twenty-nine thousand dollars. Of that, just six thousand was left. Two years without a job had drained it. If Trent was a machine—money in, money out—why not crank it up? Why not?

# 11

Karen swung her foot at the rolling soccer ball, but she merely stirred the air. Ben watched her trot after it, well behind a nimbler opponent, who took it on down the field for a goal. The Aberdeen parents on the sideline groaned, but without conviction. The game was already a lost cause.

Karen skipped into position for the kickoff. She didn't have a competitive bone in her body. In late-night talks, Ben and Susan always told each other that it was just fine that she didn't care about being number one. But now it struck Ben that people who didn't want to be number one didn't necessarily end up as number two or three. Those steps on the victory stand were taken by aspirants to the top step. Where did people end up who didn't particularly care?

Ben stamped his feet against the cold. He stood a little apart from the other parents on the sideline, not feeling up to their level of boisterousness. In fact, he felt strangely pessimistic about life in general this morning. He hoped it was just the chill in his bones. Susan had been right to call yesterday's picnic "a farewell to summer."

He heard a faint two-tone whistle—a family signal—and saw Susan waving as she came up from the lower parking lot. She wore a black sweater and head scarf. They combined with the sky of gray clouds behind her to make the whole world look for a moment like a black and white movie. Molly, in bright red pants and green sweater, burst ahead of her mother. Molly ran whenever she had the chance—a born competitor. One of Karen's teammates on the sideline spotted her and dropped to her knees in welcome. The fourth-graders enfolded her in their circle.

"Score?" Susan asked when she reached him.

"Five-zero. Them."

"Six," someone yelled. It was another dad, Art Talbot. Talbot had handled the refinancing of Ben's home mortgage in the early nineties, and therefore he knew more about Ben's life than Ben knew about his. Less for that reason than because of Talbot's streak of aggressive humor, Ben avoided him whenever possible.

"Loss builds character," Ben called to him.

"You'd make a poor banker, Ben," said Talbot.

Ben showed him a smile and turned to Susan. "I may slip away early. My desk is overflowing."

Susan had her eye on the group surrounding Molly. "Andrea was just getting in the shower when I left. I didn't talk to her." This answered the question Ben was about to ask. "Jeremy called," she said. "He's coming by this afternoon."

"Already?"

"He said he was anxious to get started. I don't want to get into any big thing with Andrea when he's around. Let's wait until tonight."

"Fine." Ben was looking at her, so fair in her black sweater. A gust of wind blew some ends of her hair across her mouth. They reached to move it away at the same time. Her eyes met his.

*"Fuck. I say fuck. Fuck."*

"Oh God." Susan ran to Molly, whose outburst had had a phys-ical effect on the fourth-graders, backing them up in embarrass-ment and fascination. "Molly, come with me." Susan said it extra loudly for the sake of those interested, and there were many. Ben joined her as she took Molly aside.

"I say fuck."

"I know you did," said Susan. "Don't."

"I say fuck."

"We've told you. Don't."

"Fuck."

Susan looked at Ben.

"I haven't said it in weeks," he said.

"I'm not accusing you. I'm asking you how we're going to deal with it."

"She enjoys the attention. Ignore it."

"How do you ignore it in public? People expect you to do some-thing."

"You did. You took her aside. Everyone's happy. See?" He looked up. To his chagrin, several parents and kids were still watching them. They looked away now, though.

All but Art Talbot, who grinned and yelled, "Too much cable, Ben?"

Ben smiled. He hated the guy.

"I see Karen," Molly said.

"She's on the field," Susan said. "You can't see her now."

"I see friend."

"You can see her friends, but don't say that word anymore."

Molly looked at her mother, sizing up the opposition. Silently, she eased away and ran back to the group.

"We're completely at her mercy," Susan said.

Ben nodded, feeling this was true of all his children. His and Susan's happiness hung on who they were, what they became. His

101

office beckoned even more strongly, not just as a world where he fully controlled things, but as a place to lay in stores against the future. If any of the kids failed as an adult, he wanted to be able to help.

"You can go," Susan said.

"I don't want to run out on you."

"If she says it again, I'll scoop her up and go home. It won't take two of us to do that. Karen can get a ride."

Ben looked to the field. A knot of players scrambled for control of the ball. Not far away, Karen was chatting with a teammate as if a timeout had been called. He sighed. "Tell her she drove the ball well down the field."

"'Drove the ball well down the field,'" Susan said. "Got it."

Ben kissed her on the lips and headed for his car. He had parked on the upper lot near the high school, under the mistaken impression that the game would be on the upper field. When he and Karen had failed to find her team there, they had walked to the lower field through Aberdeen Park, where Karen had put in many hours at Aberdeen Adventure, her day camp for several summers. On the way, Karen had renewed her acquaintance with the playground equipment, fooling around on the ropes and rings. Most of the equipment was destined for replacement with modern, safer structures next spring, as provided for in a recent bond vote. Ben was always impressed with the way bond issues passed in Aberdeen. Its residents had the money to spend on good things, and they knew how to elect people who presented ballot issues with merit. In a basic sense, its citizens had mastered the art of living.

The high school parking lot was filling with cars belonging to students busy with weekend projects. Andrea would be here later for a play rehearsal. Ben noted the shiny new Jeeps, Jeep Cherokees, and Land Cruisers, and he bristled. When he was in high school, he counted himself lucky on the days he got to drive his father's ten-year-old Rambler Classic with the Flash-O-Matic transmission. Trying to strike a balance between these extremes, Ben and Susan had arranged for Andrea to own a six-year-old Accord. It had been Susan's car before her new van, and Andrea was buying it over time with money earned from waitressing at Renault's, a French restaurant in the Central West End.

To provide without spoiling—that was the goal. Every time Ben reached into his wallet he asked himself on which side of the line the expenditure fell. If his own watch cost eighty dollars, why should his daughter's cost two hundred? Fortunately, Andrea had passed quickly through the phase where life was a catalog store. If anything, she now went overboard the other way, shopping for two-dollar jeans at resale stores like Veteran's Village—"thrifting," she called it. But Pam was fast becoming fashion's slave, and Karen was right behind her. Years of conflict and negotiation lay ahead of him. Molly lurked in the far distance, a weapon still in research and development.

When Ben was about halfway down the long row of cars, a beige sedan of indeterminate brand pulled into the spot next to his. A teacher's car, he guessed, and he was right: it was Melon. Ben watched him take a cardboard box out of the backseat and head quickly for the school building.

When Ben called out his name, Melon turned but kept walking backward, briskly—clearly a man in a hurry. But then he stopped. He seemed undecided, as if too many courses of action were open to him. Ben walked up to him.

"I'm Ben Hudnut," he said.

"I recognized you. Paul Melon." The box precluded handshakes. "I'm a bit late for something." He had a face that was young without being bland. It was rich in expression, almost too rich.

"I need to talk to you," Ben said.

Melon avoided Ben's gaze, looking to the cardboard box instead. "I have to take this inside. Some students are waiting for me. I need to say a few words to get them started. Then I can come back."

"It's about Andrea."

"I know. I'll be back soon."

The minutes passed. Ben tried to keep his mind clear. He refused to spin his wheels. In this, he and Susan were different. Ben made a point of never thinking without full knowledge of the facts. Susan took incomplete information and added other bits to it, completing the picture—or rather, completing several pictures and worrying about all of them.

So now, standing there in the parking lot, Ben willed himself to think about anything but Andrea and this man. His thoughts went to his other children for solace. Sweet Karen. But if she was passive, couldn't she end up as someone's doormat? And what if Pam wasn't just experimenting? What if she had reached her final identity? What if Molly's smouldering "fuck" summed up his whole family—an unsuspected failure at the core?

What if Andrea loved this guy? What would that say about who she was? If she had a thing for older men, it had to be Ben's fault. What if she had slept with Melon? *What if she was pregnant?* They could have been discussing that when they were on the swings, when she drifted sideways, almost touching him. "I'll pay for it," the guy probably said. The hell you will, Ben thought angrily. I can pay for my own children's abortions, thank you. But what if she wanted to have the baby? He calculated—pregnant now, in October, no, certain about it now, so probably pregnant in September, so the baby would come along in June. Molly would be three. As they grew up, they could be playmates. Aunt Molly.

He decided he could handle it as long as she wasn't pregnant. He would let that be the bad thing. Let him just hear the news that she wasn't pregnant, and everything would be fine. As for Melon, he would be departing the prestigious Aberdeen School District sooner than he expected, if Ben knew the school board—and he did, six out of the seven of them. "Can't you keep your hands to yourself, Melon?" Ben imagined yelling across the boardroom at him. "Can't you?"

Melon walked with his head cocked slightly to the side. It made him look sheepish and even younger than he was. As he neared Ben, he pointed to a stone bench under a pear tree. The gesture had an everyday quality that infuriated Ben. When they sat down, Ben took charge.

"I assume you have something to tell me," he said.

Melon frowned and wriggled, as if for an angle.

"Just do me a favor," Ben added. "Tell the truth. From beginning to end."

Melon looked him in the eye. "Fair enough," he said. But then he looked away. "Andrea has presented me with a gift. You saw us talking, so you know that. It's an incredible gift, really, and I'm always grateful for it. It happens a lot, I don't know why. Maybe I encourage it, maybe I don't. I am who I am, and students come to me. It's a glorious gift. It's almost tangible—"

Ben clutched the cold stone of the bench. His mouth was dry with fury.

"—tactile. It happens most often with girls, but the boys can surprise me too. They'll seek me out after hours. I'm talking about trust, Ben. The gift of trust. Let me share with you what your daughter shared with me. Andrea is upset. She learned something that shook her down to the roots of her being. It shook her in a way that suggests a fragility I wouldn't have suspected in her. I don't have the whole story, but I've pieced together enough so that you'll know if there's truth in it. She learned of an instance in your family, on your part, of what I would have called, at a

105

younger age, when, believe it or not, I actually considered the ministry as a vocation, adultery."

"What?"

Melon was looking not at Ben, but straight ahead, like a confessor. "Someone she knows—I don't know who, but it was someone reliable enough to upset her—told her that you had an affair a number of years ago."

"That's impossible," Ben said.

"It involved a camping trip, apparently a trip where she was present. She has the feeling it occurred right under her nose, and that sharpens the pain, I think. She told me she will never trust anyone again. I told her that wasn't true, that she was trusting me—that's what I was trying to tell her yesterday, when you saw us. She's been turned upside down by this. What's more, she knows her reaction is extreme, and that scares her. She told me she thought she might be crazy. She's been reading about schizophrenia, and she's obsessed with the idea that because it can have such a late onset, with no previous signs, she must be a schizophrenic. Well, I wouldn't have any of that. I went right after her and told her she was crazy if she thought that. It made her laugh, and I must say I felt good about that. She's talked about suicide, of course, but I've heard enough of that sort of talk to know when there's real danger. She's safe—for the moment." Melon paused.

Ben was deep in the throes of a struggle to minimize the disaster. In some sense it couldn't be as bad as it felt. There had to be a way of seeing it that made it less bad. This was the only way he knew how to deal with terrible news. As he sensed his usual strategy failing, a cold hand closed around his heart.

"Her mother doesn't even know," Ben said softly.

"Yes, Andrea's under that impression," Melon said matter-of-factly. "She wants to keep it that way. And she doesn't want you to know that she knows. I've betrayed the gift she gave me by

telling you. It's a judgment call. I think I've done the right thing."
Melon looked at Ben. "It was long ago, I take it. Don't blame
yourself for Andrea's feelings. She's the victim of a somewhat ex-
alted view of you."

"I think I'm to blame a *little*," Ben said bitterly.

Melon made a small gesture with his hand. If you say so, it
seemed to say.

"How did she find out?"

Melon frowned. "I'm a little unclear on that. She said the person who told her didn't seem to know completely what he was
telling her. He knew something, or said something, that allowed
her to put certain things together."

Scott Marlin, Ben thought. Wendy's son. Andrea had gone out
with him the night Ben had chased Pam and her gang across Aberdeen. She had seemed a little down after her date. Not that
down, though. Maybe it started as a suspicion, then grew. But how
could Scott *partly* know?

"I have to get back," Melon said. "You're a good father, Ben.
You have to be to have raised someone like Andrea. You'll both
get through this. There are worse things, let me tell you."

"I suppose so," Ben mumbled. In a way, this *was* a relief compared to what he had feared. As Melon stood up, Ben looked at
his face. Though he was grateful for Melon's openness and fair-
ness—and, yes, for his forgiveness—Ben sensed the man had a
need for this kind of intimate crisis on a regular basis. He could almost feel Melon drawing nourishment from his pain.

Melon said good-bye and left Ben there, sitting in the shade of
the pear tree. His pessimism gave way to an equally unfamiliar
state: panic. He needed a plan. He would talk to Andrea. It would
be awful, but he would talk to her and try to explain what happened. But how? He hadn't loved Wendy, so what could he say?
"It was hot, her breasts looked wet and big under her swimming

suit, and I just wanted to do it." He would have to tell her he loved Wendy, or thought he loved her. He would tell her he had been young and confused. He would stress his strong feelings for Susan, his own pain and regret. Pain and regret, that would be his theme. Hell, that *was* his theme.

He sat for some time under the pear tree, happy to have a plan. Still, he fluttered with panic.

He drove to his office. This was what he did best. He put in the hours, he sold nuts, he provided. One mistake, he thought bitterly. One little mistake. Well, five mistakes. No—one mistake five times. It was unfair that it should dog him now, eleven years later. It was damned unfair.

He pulled into the industrial park entrance and saw with surprise that Roberta's Datsun was parked on the gravel lot near the front door. She never came in on weekends. He saw her arm reach out the window and stay stiff for a moment—a morning stretch, even though it was well into the afternoon. Her pale wrist and fingers reached lazily into the air.

He parked next to her, facing the building. She turned a laughing face to her left, toward his car. How could she be laughing when she was staring at a blank wall? Then he glimpsed someone in the seat next to her. A male companion. This was the language that occurred to him, because it was Roberta's kind of language. Ben waved and got out of his car.

Roberta's companion was a little man with a big cigarette. He transferred this to his left hand and, smiling broadly, reached across the seat to shake hands, presenting himself as "Orson." Ben reached in at Roberta's window, and she leaned back with an intake of breath to avoid contact with his arm. Ben looked down and noticed that Roberta was not wearing a bra under her sweater—a partly unbuttoned peach cardigan number that allowed Ben to see more of her than he had ever seen before. He stared at her breasts, and in his mind they merged with Wendy's, wet with river water. Roberta quickly pulled the top of the sweater together, and Ben tried to grin away his disorientation.

"What's up?" he said.

Roberta giggled. Orson seemed to be fighting laughter too. "We were out driving around," Roberta said, "and I thought I would come by and show Orson the home office."

This language—"home office"—was unusually playful for Roberta. Or rather, it was playful without being tedious. "Do you want to come in?" Ben said to Orson. "There isn't much to see, but—"

"No, no," Roberta said. "I just wanted to show him where I've been working all this time. Eighteen years."

"I've seen your products in the stores, Ben," Orson said. He enunciated slowly, like one who had conquered a speech impediment. "You've got a very nice business. I know how hard it is to make a go of a business."

Ben said he'd just been lucky. He wondered if Orson was confessing to a string of failures. Ben couldn't get over the man's size. He looked like a jockey. Still, he had a good smile. Ben hoped he was successful at something.

"We met at church," Orson said.

"He dropped his hymnal right on my foot," Roberta said with a loud laugh. "Right on my foot."

Ben nodded. He had trouble getting from the church to this moment, in the morning, with the whiff of the bedroom about them.

"We're on our way to a picnic now," Roberta said.

"A church picnic," Orson chimed in, and he reached out for Ben's hand again. As he took it, Ben had an impulse to tell them they should relax, they could get it on as much as they wanted, he was happy to see Roberta having fun. It was no wonder she was turning down his invitations to family dinner. Braless!

Roberta started her car and backed out, kicking up some gravel when she accelerated too rapidly. Orson laughed and leaned out his window. "Women drivers!" he yelled. Ben waved as they drove off.

When he entered the office, he could still smell Orson's tobacco about him. He sniffed his right hand. It smelled not just of tobacco, but of lime cologne as well. He went to the bathroom and washed up. At his desk, the first thing he did was wholly spontaneous, yet fitting. He made a note to himself to call his New Jersey nut broker, Zender Nut Co., on Monday, to explore the possibility of getting his Brazil nuts from Peru. This change in his farm source might mean employment for one or two Peruvians under good conditions instead of one or two Brazilians under bad ones. And if every nut dealer in the world took this step, Brazil would be forced to improve. It wasn't just that Paula woman who had brought this about. Nathan Ravindranathan had too, with his grim tale of the Indian cashew shellers. Two such reports within such a short time—it was almost like a sign. Ben had done some bad things in his life. He felt he owed the world a good thing now.

He called up his inventory on the computer and checked it against orders. The balance was about right. He had never gotten around to programming this part of the business with built-in warnings when inventory dropped too low. Why should he, when he could do it in a jiffy with a glance? He couldn't understand why companies went high-tech when they didn't have to.

Next, he searched through his recent correspondence for a package from an international trade company that he thought might grease the wheels for his cashew venture. He put his feet up on the corner of his desk and settled down with its literature.

The leather couch across the office sighed at him. He looked at it. An indentation ran its length. He couldn't see it rising, but it must have been. He could see something else though, with little effort: Roberta on her back and her little jockey riding her to the finish line.

He was happy she was having fun, sure, but in his office? Had they been overcome with passion? But maybe they had just settled there to talk. He got up and went to the couch to examine it closely. He felt like a crime scene investigator. There was no real evidence—for which, now that he thought about it, he was thankful—but the cushions were definitely rising, all three of them, swelling back into shape.

His mind full of male interlopers and general dread, he quickly gathered up his materials. He would do his work at home.

# 12

*"Six thousand dollars?"*

"That's right," Cook said.

"How much does that leave in the account?"

"Not a lot."

"How much?"

"Zero."

Paula slowly set down her blue pen. She had been grading exercises at the kitchen table. She used blue ink instead of red in order to seem less judgmental to the students. "So you cleaned us out?"

"Well, I cleaned myself out. It's my money."

"Your money, my money, what's the difference? Couldn't you have at least talked to me first?"

"You were busy playing tennis with Sherry."

Paula stared at him. "Do you know what a cushion is? A financial cushion?"

Rather than answer a clearly rhetorical question, Cook grabbed his car keys from the kitchen counter. It was going to feel good to leave the apartment instead of being left in it.

"We no longer have a financial cushion," Paula said. She shook her head. "You and money. You just don't have clue."

"Are you afraid it's lost?"

"I have no idea about that. I'm talking about how screwed up you are in the way you feel about it. You pretend money means nothing to you."

"It's not a pretense. It does mean nothing to me." He headed for the door.

"It means *everything* to you. You're crazy on the subject. You met Trent and got all stirred up and you wanted to impress him so you threw money at him."

As he reached for the doorknob, Cook saw his list before his eyes as clearly as if it were posted on the door like Luther's Theses: "thug," "throw money at," "happen to." Was Paula, despite her feminism, a closet conservative?

⌒

"I'm excited," said Susan. "Are you excited?"

"I'm very excited," Cook said to her. Be professional, he said to himself.

"I'll get Molly. She's in the kitchen. She's been painting, but she's just squishing it in her fingers now." As Susan turned to go, Cook noted the striking way her jeans, viewed from the rear, separated her legs. This completed one phase of his data collection, for on arrival he had scanned this part of her body from the front. She whirled around quickly. "You could be in the kitchen while I clean her up—you know, to hang around and listen to her. Is that what you want to do?"

"Hanging around is exactly what I want to do. Short of being a nuisance."

Susan laughed lightly. "I'll let you know when that happens."

Cook sagged with disappointment. She had passed up the opportunity to say, "You could never be a nuisance, Jeremy." He followed her into the kitchen, where Molly sat at the table, talking quietly to her paint-covered fingers.

"Molly, do you remember Jeremy?"

Molly looked him in the eye. "Fuck you, buster."

"Oh God," said Susan. She threw her hands up. "I'm sorry. She hears these things and just parrots them."

"Where did she hear that one?"

"I have no idea. I don't know what to do. She's way too young to punish. If we took away something, she wouldn't get the connection no matter how much we explained it."

Molly's eyes went from Cook to her mother and back again. She knew they were talking about her. But did she know *what* they were talking about?"

"Does she say any other taboo words?"

"Oh! You name it. Sometimes she hears one and shouts out a different one." Susan leaned over the table and began putting caps on the tiny paint jars.

"You mean she'll hear F-U-C-K and say S-H-I-T?"

"Yes."

"I say fuck."

"That's enough, Molly."

"I say fuck."

"Please don't, honey. Help me clean up now." Susan shook her head. "She does that too. Brags."

Cook looked at Molly—at her blond hair, her broad forehead, her wide-open face. "She must know the words belong to a class, since she's saying one in response to another." He said this half to himself. To Susan he said, "Have you tried a direct approach—

talking to her about words that people shouldn't say? There's tremendous power in language acquisition. She feels powerful saying the words. Try cultivating her power *not* to say them."

"Right now? You mean I should talk to her now?"

"Unless you're worried that it might increase production."

Susan gave a little laugh of despair as she went to the sink. "Production is already at record levels." She moistened a paper towel and went back to the table. Molly squirmed under her mother's wiping. Susan finished with the towel and sat down. "Molly," she said, "I've got something very important to say to you. Listen to me."

Cook wandered into the living room, tactfully leaving Susan alone. This didn't preclude eavesdropping, of course, at which he was very skilled. From what he could hear, she handled it well. She spoke without reproach, but with an urgency that commanded attention. He listened closely to her list of forbidden words. Mommy's little glossary. He hoped his advice didn't backfire. Molly was saying the words back as she heard them, so the plan clearly involved a short-term setback. But a moment later, when they came into the living room, Susan gave him a bright, hopeful smile.

"We'll see what happens," she said. She looked around the room. "I'll tell you what. If you play Grocery Store with Molly, she'll be your friend forever."

With an eerie robotic quality, Molly silently swung into action. She wheeled a miniature shopping cart to where Cook had sat down on the couch, banging it lightly into his foot. Then she installed herself behind a yellow plastic cash register at the end of the coffee table in front of him, so that she stood close to him at a right angle. Cook looked at Susan.

"You take the stuff out of the cart, let her identify it, then tell her how much it costs. Then put it into the shopping bag there next to your feet. Sometimes she works Raggedy Anne and Andy into it. It changes all the time. I'll be downstairs. Laundry." With that, she exited.

Cook inspected the props. He took a large plastic green pepper out of the cart and held it up.

"Green peppuh," said Molly.

"Five cents," said Cook.

"Five cent," said Molly. She pressed a yellow key on the cash register. Then she looked at him. He put the pepper into the shopping bag and took a plastic cucumber from the cart.

"Cucumbuh," said Molly.

"Ten cents," said Cook.

"Ten cent," said Molly. She punched the same key and looked at him. He put the cucumber into the bag and took an orange out of the cart.

"Orange," said Molly.

"Five cents," said Cook.

"Five cent." Molly punched the key and looked at him. He felt a wave of pure sleepiness, as if someone had drawn a magic blanket over him in a fairy tale. He sorted through the cart, stirring the contents. Like boulders in the earth, the large items had risen to the top. There were more below, many more than he had realized—miniature fruits, vegetables, frozen foods, cans, boxes, steaks, chops. Most were the size of a small grape. The items numbered well over a hundred.

"Jesus," Cook said under his breath.

"I no say shit, I no say fuck, I no say Jeezah Chrise."

"Whoa," Cook said. "Listen—"

"I no say shit, I no say fuck, I no say Jeezah Chrise."

"That's great, Molly, but—"

"I no say shit, I no say fuck, I no say Jeezah Chrise."

Cook grabbed a tomato from the cart and held it up.

"Pomato," Molly said, and the game resumed.

About halfway through the inventory, Cook took out a note-book and wrote down a few observations of Molly's speech. She calmly continued to play by herself, and he realized he could have gotten away with resigning earlier. Linguistically, the game hadn't been too fertile, but he had drawn her out a bit. In pronouns she had full case differentiation, at least in first person ("I," "me," "my/mines"), but no gender distinction in third person, "he" serving for both "he" and "she." She had serial intonation for series of two or more. Her "pomato" for "tomato" interested him, but he wasn't sure how general the governing rule was. The reduplication Ted had told him about—"box-ox" for "boxes"—was apparently dead. She seemed to have no plural marking of any kind.

Susan appeared from the basement, bearing her husband's shirts on hangers. As she carried them on up the stairs, they swayed, ghostly reminders to Cook of the real man of the house. As if to drive the point home, that man in the flesh was suddenly visible on the patio, heading for the front door. Cook's heart sank.

"Hey, hey," Ben said as he strode into the living room, thrusting a hand out. Cook obliged, although in his world eighteen hours of separation didn't require a handshake. "How's it going?" Ben glanced at Molly.

"Fine," said Cook. "She's great."

"Grocery Store, eh? It's a killer." Ben's smile changed to a mild frown. "Look at her. I come home and she doesn't react. She doesn't run to me and say, 'Daddy Daddy Daddy.' What do you make of that?"

Cook had to speak the truth. "It means she takes you for granted—as she should. She's secure."

"So . . . it's good." Ben seemed in need of reassurance.

"Yes. It's good."

Susan came downstairs, and there were some predictable ex-clamations of surprise that the big guy was home and some mouth kissing that didn't involve Cook. The phone rang. Susan stepped into the kitchen and answered it. She exclaimed, apologized, and hung up. Cook and Ben watched with interest as she threw open the closet door and grabbed her pocketbook.

"Molly's hairdresser," she said, hustling into the living room. "I forgot her appointment."

Cook rose. "I'll be off then."

"Stick around," said Ben. "They'll be right back."

Susan had turned her attention to Molly, but she said, "Twenty minutes at the most. Stay here, Jeremy." She scooped Molly up and hurried out the door.

Ben chuckled as he watched them pass by the front window on their way to the driveway. "Two and a half years old and she gets a professional haircut. We cut Andrea's hair ourselves until she was five or six. I remember doing it on the front porch of our old house and watching the wind blow it away." He headed for the kitchen. "I'm gonna have a beer. Can I get you anything?"

Cook declined.

"I could make a list of things I used to do that I have other people do now," Ben said when he returned. "Mowing the lawn. Cleaning the gutters. Changing the oil in the car. Even *washing* the car." He laughed. "I have a guy do everything but sleep with my wife."

Cook gave a public chuckle while he put out several spot-fires that flared in his imagination. Ben suggested they go outside, since it had warmed up. On their way out, Karen came down the stairs with two other girls. She said hi to Cook in the front hall and gave her father a playful punch on the arm. "Mom said I drove the ball well down the field. How about that?"

"Good job," Ben said. The girls went out and headed up the street while the two men sat down on the wrought-iron patio chairs.

"Did they beat St. Andrew's?" Cook said.

"Nope. Good for you for remembering, though." Ben took a swig of his beer. "The only exception is finances," he said, continuing, though certainly not at Cook's request, the earlier topic. "No one messes with my finances." He pointed into the air with the neck of his beer bottle as if it were an index finger. "I know enough accounting to handle my business stuff, and I don't use anyone for financial advice. I tried it for a while, tried using a guy, and I found that to understand what he was doing took as much work as doing it myself. And you've *got* to understand it—either that or you're a total vegetable, just rolling over and letting them stick it to you. I could never do that. *Action.* That's what I like. Knowing stuff and then acting on it. There was an English king named Edmund the Deed-Doer. I don't know what the hell he did. For all I know, he did everything wrong. But I like him just because of his name."

Cook nodded. He felt weak, as he always felt when in thrall to a speechmaker. But Ben hadn't been this way yesterday. He seemed different—on edge, out to prove something.

"People around here like to hire professionals all the time, but professionals can get it wrong. Take the average tax strategy. Everybody tells you to put money in the children's name, right?"

"Right," said Cook, who had little money, no children, nary a clue.

"It's good advice as far as taxes go. But it's terrible advice when it comes to any hope of getting financial aid for college. My two middle kids, Pam and Karen, have trust funds for college. I set them up when I was being guided by a money man—a cousin of Susan's. I've since learned that those trust funds, which I'm completely powerless to change, will kill their chances of getting financial aid."

Cook was now deeply confused. How could this man, with this

house looming behind them, its sheer bulk giving Cook the sensation it was nudging him off the property, honestly talk about needing financial aid for college?

"So I'm not going to set up a trust fund for Molly. I'll handle her differently. As for Andrea—she starts college next year—fortunately I was too broke to set one up when she was young, so there's hope of getting some help for her. I figure the aid is out there, and if you can qualify, you should go after it aggressively. But trying to get the aid, putting myself in a position to get it, has been a real juggling act." Ben took a swig of his beer. "Am I boring you?"

"Not at all," said Cook. In truth, he was stimulated in the extreme.

"Shall I tell you what I've done?" Ben said. "It's kind of nifty. It's not in your line or anything—"

"Go ahead. I like to learn about people."

Ben gave him a quizzical look. "Okay. Here's the story. The financial aid formula kills you if your child has any money in her name, like I said. The formula goes after thirty-five percent of the kid's assets each year. Let's say, hypothetically, the kid has a hundred thousand in a trust fund. The formula says congratulations, you've planned your future well, you can now pay thirty-five thou of that toward college in the kid's first year, then thirty-five percent of the balance in the second year, and so on. Eats it right up. But let's say that hundred thou is in the parents' name. The formula assesses parental assets at a much lower rate—six percent. If it's in their name, they've only got to come up with six thou from savings in the kid's first year."

"I see," said Cook, who wished he had a hundred "thou" he could talk about like this. "That's quite a difference."

"But let's say the parents have more than a hundred thou in savings. I mean accessible savings, not including retirement accounts. Let's say they have"—Ben waved a hand helplessly, then plucked a figure from the air—"two hundred and twenty thou." The unroundedness of the figure, combined with the transparent display of improvisation, told all: Ben had two hundred twenty thousand dollars in ready savings. He was naming numbers.

"Now, there's a formula that protects a certain amount of the assets before this six-percent assessment. In this case, the six per-cent works out to be about eleven thousand dollars. The college expects the parents to kick that in before they can get any aid. But that's just their expected contribution based on their cash as-sets. What about income? We need to talk about income. Let's say the family makes a hundred ninety thousand a year, okay?"

"Okay." In Cook's experience, once people started naming numbers, they couldn't stop.

"Salary is assessed by the formula at about fifty percent, but only after all sorts of reductions based on an income protection allowance. In this case, the parents get socked for about fifty thousand. Combine that with the eleven thou, and you've got an expected family contribution of sixty-one thousand in the first year." Ben laughed. "That's quite a bit more than even the high-est tuition in the land. So this family, wherever it might be, gets no aid."

As is only right, Cook wanted to say.

"So how can they possibly get aid? I'll tell you how. The trick is to own your own business. If they own their own business, they can do four things: they can reduce the salary the business pays them; they can make up the deficit by living off their savings, thereby reducing their household assets; a fluctuating salary from a closely held business can trigger an audit lickety-split, and to avoid that they can make sure the salary reduction is gradual and that the difference is recorded as retained salary, which of course infuses a lot of cash into the business; and, also for audit reasons, they can make sure they have an argument ready for all that cash in the business, like a new expansion requiring an outlay." Ben took another pull on his beer. "You with me?"

Cook's head was spinning. The only words he could think of were "pomato" and "Fuck you, buster."

"I worked out a four-year plan. I'm in the fourth year of it now, Andrea's 'base year' for determining her eligibility for aid. The effect of the plan, year by year, is to reduce how good I look on paper and shift money to the business. Of course, you're probably thinking that since I own the business, it's a personal asset too, and you're right, that's part of the picture. But the aid formula assesses a business you own at a lower rate than other assets. It's a progressive assessment, kind of complicated, but trust me, I'm ahead of the game doing this."

"I trust you."

"So where am I? The business is flush. Me, I'm broke!" Ben laughed again—a quick blast that seemed to echo off the faces of the brick houses across the street. "I don't turn in the aid application until January 1, so I can't be sure what we'll get. I'd like something real small, a thousand or less, just for the satisfaction of it. I'm not doing anything underhanded, you know. If Susan and I tried to hide our assets by, say, giving twenty thousand a year to her brother Ted with the understanding that he'd give it back after Andrea finished college, *that* would be underhanded. In fact, the new money in the business has affected the profit picture there and actually raised my corporate taxes, and since the bulk of college aid is federal money, I'm paying into the same pot that I'm trying to draw from."

"So why do it?" Cook had understood enough to know that this question was in order.

Ben shrugged. "It's there. I want to go for it. It's just something I need to do. Like I said: *action*." He took a big breath and expelled it, blew it across his huge front lawn. "Anyway, I'm glad all that's in place. It was fun figuring it out, kind of a weekend lark. But you're probably wondering what new venture I have in mind to justify the infusion of capital into the business. I've noticed you like cashews. Hell, who doesn't? You'll be happy to know that my goal is to bring a cheap, quality cashew to America. Let me tell you about it."

⌐⌐

"Trent Houston," Cook said into the phone. "And pronto. . . . If you *must* know, it's Jeremy Cook. I'm a client." Cook made a face into the phone, and when he was sure he was on hold, shrilly imitated the secretary: "'May I say who's calling? May I say who's calling?'"

He looked from the kitchen into the den, where Molly was watching some noisy nonsense on television. Cook had been put in charge of her. This was the last in a breathtaking series of annoying events:

After Ben had unzipped his pants, shown Cook his financial penis, and then beat him over the head with it, Susan had returned from the hairdresser's with Molly and told Ben that she had just discovered that an end table she had had her eye on had just gone on sale, and this would be a great opportunity for him to look at it. She also wanted to get his opinion on some trundle-bed affair for Molly and a couple of lamps. But Molly was always difficult in furniture stores, and there was no one to watch her. Susan was almost whining by this point, and Cook found himself loving her a little less than he had before. He halfheartedly offered his own services, fully expecting rejection, but there wasn't the faintest demurral, not a single we-couldn't-possibly. Ben and Susan zoomed off in their Saab like two horny kids on a date.

He couldn't figure Ben. Even by the standards of his class, he had gone too far, not only naming numbers but bragging about his brash dance along the cliff edge of ethics. By God, he *was* a liar at tax time. And it wasn't enough that he smashed Cook over the head with his family financial portrait. He had to pull down the battle-plan chart for his saturation bombing of the country with cashews. In the future, Cook would make a point of observing Molly only on weekdays, when Ben was at the office, juggling his nuts and his funds.

One good thing had happened on the patio. Ben had inadvertently given Cook useful investment information. He now had a rare opportunity, probably the only one he would ever have in his life, to get in on the ground floor, to have a leg up, to outfox the competition, to be ahead of the curve—in sum, to fulfill all the clichés of capitalistic greed.

Trent ("Bear Down") Houston came on the phone. "Houston," he said.

"Trent? Jeremy Cook." He paused. "Tennis? Paula Nouvelles's husband?"

"Ah. Jeremy. Good to hear your voice."

"Listen. My six thousand dollars—the 'small account,' as you called it—I want you to put it all in an outfit called Archway International."

"Archway. I don't know the company, Jeremy."

"Well, now you do."

"Let me check it out. What's the stock symbol?"

"How do I know? Look it up. What am I paying you a commission for?" Cook felt a surge of power. Apparently aggression was contagious. "It's an international trade organization. It cuts through red tape for businesses and ensures compliance with all the laws and just generally does fuck-all. It doesn't matter. My source has a cashew deal with them, and he says he chose them because someone there told him they're about ten minutes away from a merger with an even larger outfit."

"It sounds dangerously close to an insider tip, Jeremy."

"What are you talking about? Of course it's an insider tip. How the hell else do you expect to make any money in this game? Are you gonna play ball or not?"

"Well, it's the kind of thing we'll—"

"Of *course* we'll keep it under our hats. Whaddya think, I'm naive? Now get your head out of your picnic basket and start earning your keep." Cook slammed the phone down.

# 13

Pam had been bad again. She and three of the gang of six had spent Saturday afternoon making prank telephone calls to one of the middle school science teachers, a gentle soul with a high voice vulnerable to mockery. The teacher had recorded the second, third, and fourth calls, and on a hunch he had called Susan and played them back for her. Susan's punishment was swift and terrible. Pam, her weekend nighttime privileges having just been restored, was now sentenced to weekend house arrest day *and* night for the next month.

To enforce the new order, Ben and Susan would have to make sacrifices. It was the last Sunday before Halloween, the time for the traditional family outing to Olfield's Farm in Illinois to pick apples and look at the rustically humorous, faintly repellent pumpkin displays. Should they take Pam? If she had fun, her punishment would have little sting on its first day. If she didn't, she would poison the excursion for everyone else. If she stayed home alone, she could slip out and taste life for several hours. Susan resolved to stay behind and sit on her squirming body. It wasn't the first time in Ben's experience that punishing a child meant punishing one of them as well.

"It's part of the process," Susan said as she helped Ben pick out toys for Molly to play with in the van. As far as Ben could tell, this was what people said when things went to hell. "Families that are rigid about traditions are actually afraid of something," Susan went on. She had picked up a plastic wand filled with blue liquid and sparkles, and she distractedly tapped it against one palm. "They're afraid of flying apart. We don't have that fear, so we can be flexible."

Ben was debating between Gonga and a Barbie. "Right," he said. He threw both into Molly's backpack. It had occurred to him, and no doubt to Susan, that because Andrea would be in college next year, their annual apple-picking trip would never involve the whole family again.

He followed Susan into the kitchen to help with the bag lunches. Andrea was leaning into the refrigerator, sorting through film boxes in the meat drawer. Susan leaned over and kissed her on top of the head.

"Take some normal pictures for me, okay?" she said. Andrea eased out of the kitchen with a vague smile. She did not look at her father.

Ben first picked up a friend of Karen's, a girl named Samantha who lived near Moorlands School. Then he headed for the highway. Andrea sat in the front of the van and quietly fooled with her camera lenses. As he shifted gears and navigated the traffic, he felt stiff and unnatural. He felt exactly the way he felt when he and Susan were fighting and were forced by circumstances to be near each other. Over the years, the way he related to Andrea had taken on the feel of the way he related to his wife.

Two weeks had passed since his talk with Melon. Two cowardly weeks. The only action he had taken was to lie to Susan. Beginning with a tiny piece of truth, he had told her that he had run into Melon outside the high school after leaving Karen's soccer game and had pointedly asked him about the subject he and Andrea had been discussing on the swings. Melon's answer? Casting for the production of *Our Town*. Andrea had promised a major role to a girl who had proved to be unstable—one Brigitte Duvray, said Ben, plucking the name from he knew not where—and Andrea didn't know how to handle it. Melon advised her, and now all was well. However, Andrea was embarrassed by her lapse in judgment and didn't want her parents to know about it. ("She's so demanding of herself!" Susan declared.) The important point, Ben said, afraid Susan might have missed it, was that the problem was solved, and that Susan should not follow up with any kind of questions about it to Andrea. Susan wanted to know if Ben had confronted Melon about his treatment of female students. No, Ben said, for the reason that Melon spontaneously addressed the issue to his satisfaction. Melon, in the course of singing Andrea's praises, had said that her maturity had inspired him to rethink the way he treated girls in his class. Ben met Susan's astonished look with extreme amazement of his own, agreeing that it was indeed a stunning development. When he was all done, he felt as if he had slept with Wendy Marlin for a sixth time.

As hard as it had been to lie to Susan, it would be at least that hard to face the truth with Andrea. In the two weeks that had passed, given their schedules and the activity in the house, he hadn't been alone with Andrea for any significant length of time—a justification for inaction that he was prepared to cite if summoned to some kind of judgment.

In the rear seat, Karen and her friend Samantha had been playing a modified version of Name That Tune with Molly, who was able to hold her own within a narrow range. Karen respected that range, but Samantha kept straying from it, to Ben's annoyance. As they neared the Mississippi, Samantha howled and said to Karen, "She calls the song 'Twinklestar.' She says everything wrong." Ben made an unhappy noise and looked at Andrea. By way of response, she fiddled with her f-stops.

The approach to Olfield's Farm, twenty miles into Illinois, was a long dirt road running through the middle of a pumpkin patch, a road that ordinarily gave Ben the pleasant feeling that he was entering a fairy tale. In the distance he saw a tractor towing a trailer full of apple pickers from the city.

"Apple time, Molly," said Karen.

"Apple time," Molly echoed.

Ben pulled into the damp but not quite muddy parking lot. The lot always seemed to be exactly this damp. They piled out. Karen and Samantha ran ahead with Molly toward a scarecrow slouched on a bale of hay. As Ben waited for Andrea to get her camera bag together, he watched Karen encourage Molly to shake the scarecrow's hand.

"Molly is most desirable," Ben said, "when someone else is taking care of her." Andrea slammed the van door.

Another tractor arrived. Ben called out to the kids. They grabbed some bags and climbed aboard the long trailer with its high bench seat in the middle. It filled quickly. The driver stood up on his tractor and called out that the first stop would be for your Golden Delicious, the second for your Jonathans, the third for your Rome Beauties.

"Beauty," Molly said. She was thinking of Beauty and the Beast. Karen looked at her dad over Molly's head and smiled.

They climbed down at the second stop. Samantha ran off and grabbed an apple knocker—a long pole with a small wire basket on the end, topped off by double prongs that plucked apples into the basket. Molly immediately lost her footing on a windfall Jonathan. She got up and seemed puzzled. Karen took Molly's hand and showed her the apples on the ground. Then she took a pole and set up a rhythm with her. She would reach the pole high and pick an apple, then lower the basket to Molly, who put the apple into the bag. Molly concentrated so hard that she looked angry.

Andrea was busy taking pictures, not of this charming duo, but of three apple knockers leaning against a tree, their baskets all touching. She took one picture after another, shifting her position, holding her elbows tightly against her body, planting her legs as if braced against a gale.

Ben began to pick apples as well. He found himself looking around for Susan, expecting to hear her strong voice. He called a halt when they had filled three bags—no doubt too many. What seemed like a reasonable number in the orchard took over the house when they unpacked them.

They caught a ride back to the weighing station. Then, while Ben and Andrea wordlessly put the apples in the van, the others played on an elaborate wooden fort manned by scarecrows. By the time Ben and Andrea returned, the kids had abandoned the fort and were running across a field toward a distant orange mountain of pumpkins. Ben and Andrea followed.

"That'd be a good picture," Ben said, looking to the mound. "Of course, I don't know about black and white."

"No, you don't," Andrea said.

They walked halfway across the field before Ben said, "Let's sit down here a minute." He pointed to a hay bale.

Andrea stiffened. "Why?"

"We need to talk."

"About what?"

"You know."

She stared at him, then looked away.

"Come on," he said.

She stood still.

"Come on."

Andrea was looking toward her sisters and the mountain of pumpkins. "I don't want to do this."

"We need to talk about it a lot, for a really long time."

She laughed unpleasantly and threw herself onto the hay bale. She stuck her legs out, straight and stiff, and stared at them.

"First, I'm sorry," he said. "I'm sorry I did it, sorry I betrayed Mom's trust—"

"God."

"—sorry that you found out. That's what I'm most sorry about."

"Why do we have to talk about it? It was eleven years ago, right?"

"It's upsetting you. That's why we have to talk."

"I'll get over it."

"You hate me."

"I'll get over that too."

"Can't you see it was a mistake? People make mistakes."

"How long did it go on?" she asked sharply.

Ben considered his response. "It was a mistake that lasted about a month."

"So you can't exactly say you got carried away. You had to set things up, you had to *make plans*."

"I'm the same man I was before you found out."

"No, you aren't. If you were, I wouldn't keep thinking about it. I'll be in the middle of a rehearsal, yelling at someone, and there it is." She held her hands out in front of her as if holding an idea. "My father slept with Wendy Marlin." She let her hands drop. "He slept with her on a camping trip. I was seven years old. He taught me the J-stroke, he baited my sister's hook, he gave my

131

mom a kiss, and he sneaked off and fucked Wendy Marlin." She looked away, at the pumpkin mountain.

They were silent for some time. A few people passed by.

Andrea said, "Did you love her?"

He had known this would come up. He was glad he was prepared. "Yes."

Andrea stared at him. She raised her camera from her lap and took a quick picture of him.

"What was that for?"

"I'm going to take this home and develop it, and I'll show you the face of a liar. You're the worst."

He hesitated. "All right. I didn't love her."

Andrea shook her head. "No woman would do what you did. No woman I know anyway."

"But a woman did," he said, on firm ground here. "*She* did. She felt the same way I did."

Andrea stared directly at him again. He was struck at her ability to do this—at the way she could hold her own. Even though she was going after him, even though *he* was the object of her scorn, he was pleasantly impressed with how well she could take care of herself.

She said, "Well, now you're telling the truth, I guess. Or you're trying to. You're just ignorant. Scott told me his mom was destroyed when you broke it off. She was a wreck."

"I was under the impression he didn't know who the man was—"

"Jesus, is that the important point—what he knows or doesn't know?"

Ben shrank into himself a bit. "No. You're right."

"You didn't know she loved you?"

"Loved me? No. When we were together, she never—" He stopped.

"Don't want to get into the details, huh? Good. Me neither."

They watched a family pass by—parents, two kids, and a grandma. Grandma was smoking, and she threw her cigarette into the pumpkin patch.

"This is unreal," Andrea said softly. "I feel like two people—one talking and one watching me talk. I feel like *ten* people." She looked at her father. "There's nothing beautiful about it, is there? It's not the tale of a love that was not meant to be—of two mature people parting for the sake of their families. That's a tale I can live with. It's not exactly the tale of a one-nighter either. It's just a tale of rotten behavior."

"I was bad."

"Did you ever apologize to her?"

"Wendy? No. I thought it was a mutual deal."

"What happens when you see her?"

"We say hi."

"No meaningful looks? No funny looks?"

"No." This wasn't exactly true. Wendy seemed to look at him half a second longer than anyone else did. He was always the first to look away.

"Well, you should apologize to her."

"I'll think about it."

"Liar." Andrea picked a piece of straw from a buckle in her shoe. "I thought I knew you. I mean, I thought I knew you *a little*, anyway. I guess I was wrong about even that little bit." She rummaged through her camera case. "I brought something you should read. It's the essay for my Swarthmore application. We're supposed to write about some problem we haven't solved. Mom thinks it's too weird. She didn't say that, but it's what she thinks. I was going to show it to you anyway. Now, I don't know, it seems especially appropriate. Or inappropriate. I don't know." She handed him some typed pages. "See what you think. I have time if I need to start all over. Which I probably will."

Ben took the essay. It was a strangely ordinary thing to be

happening right now—him helping her with her homework, as it were. Andrea got up and walked toward the three girls running around the mound of pumpkins. He began to read.

I remember sitting in the car, in front of the Candy Barrel, amazed at how he always knew right where it was. I'd try to follow the route he took, try to figure out how he knew where to turn, but it was so long and complicated that it would make my head spin, and then *boom*, there we were, right in front of it. How did he know where it was?

Or the movies. How did he know when they started? We would buy the tickets and popcorn and soda, grab two good seats, and *boom*, the movie would start. I figured he knew the owner, who was peeking at the crowd from somewhere (I'd try to spot him), and they had agreed that when we sat down it was time to start the movie.

He used to read me an old book, *Mystery Mountain*, that his father read to him. The jacket was falling apart, and my dad's little-boy signature was on the title page. These two kids (boys, of course) lived on adjacent ranches at the base of a mountain, and they had all sorts of adventures up there. I've forgotten the story, except for a cave full of bats. I remember that part all right.

To kids, dads are mountains. We climb them and fall from them. They're mountains with gentle roars, exotic smells, and cushioned slopes. But they're not just mountains. They're mountains of mystery.

My mom and I have long talks. It's almost like talking with a friend. Sometimes she'll ruin it by sneaking in some advice, or I'll ruin it by making a joke only my friends could get. But it's surprising how long we can go on, how long we can talk like friends. If my dad's around, he'll get in on it too. It's great when that happens. But he could never do that alone with me. He needs Mom for it. It's not in his repertoire.

My being female isn't the issue. The guys I know don't connect with their fathers either. If they need to bring up something awkward or important, or if they have to confess to wrongdoing, they'll pick their mom every time, just like when they were children. They're embarrassed to admit it, but it's the truth.

Dads are mysterious. They just come that way, and they'll never change. They've always got other stuff going on that we'll never know about. They're like mobsters keeping secrets from their loved ones. So, as children, we try to learn about them by snooping, by sitting at their desks or poring over their simple apparatus—their keys, their watches, their pens.

They're mysterious, but we must want it that way. We send them out into the world and say, "Don't come back until you have some meat to bring home." And when they're home, we say, "Don't get too involved. You should be thinking about your next hunt." We like our dads focused, so that we can have all the goodies. We do like our goodies. In a way, we've sacrificed our dads for those goodies.

Sometimes I'll look at my dad and try to see the world from his point of view. He agrees to live the way he does, so he must like being mysterious. But how can he? It means, literally, that nobody really knows him, nobody understands him. How satisfying can that be? When someone understands what I'm going through, it's the best feeling in the world. He can never have that feeling.

There must be something about it that he likes, something that makes up for the not being understood. It's a mystery to me. I figured out how he knows where the Candy Barrel is. Maybe one day I'll figure out this mystery too.

Ben was still sitting on the hay bale when the kids came back, each carrying a pumpkin from the mound. Molly had a green one the size of an apple. Andrea trailed after the group. Ben stood up and gave her the essay back. She took it with a surprised look, as if she'd forgotten giving it to him. He said it was well written but he would have to think about it.

"In what connection?" she said.

"Both," he said.

They were quiet on the way home, but not the awful kind of quiet. Andrea seemed calm. She fooled with the radio and settled on an oldies station, purely for his sake, he knew. She sprawled in her seat with her shoeless feet on the dash, twirled her hair, and watched the Illinois farmland roll by.

Ben was quiet because he was thinking about her essay. He didn't quite get the point of it. What was the big mystery? He was who he was. What did she want to know about him? If it was something specific, why didn't she just ask him? If she was saying she didn't know him as well as she knew her mother, well, hell, what was so strange about that? What did she expect? She seemed to want to blame it on his job—his "hunting." What the hell? Should he have hung around the house all day? What house? They wouldn't have had one.

It wasn't exactly that he didn't get the point of the essay. It was that he got it and it pissed him off. How did she expect him to take it? It occurred to him that the essay was a punishment for his affair—not the writing of it, since he thought she wrote it before she found out, but showing it to him. She didn't have to do that. He hadn't seen her other essays. Susan was the one helping her with them. Andrea had gone out of her way to lay this one on him.

136

He looked at her Birkenstocks on the van floor. She liked her goodies, no doubt about it. The whole damn family liked them. And the whole damn family expected him to provide them. And the whole damn family got them because he pushed, and pushed harder, and stayed at the office until ten and eleven at night, and thought about money every hour of every day, and still did, right in the middle of dinner, or while riding bikes with one of them, or opening Christmas presents, or brushing his teeth, or watching a field hockey game. What the hell else was he supposed to do?

These thoughts kept him quiet all the way home.

# 14

Molly was a grump. In the past hour, all she had said was "no," "no way," and "go 'way." This was Cook's fifth session with her, and her mood caught him by surprise. He tried plastic finger puppets he found in the wicker toy bin, giving them his very best high voice with uvular trill. She just stared. He set up for Grocery Store, but this drove her into a possessive frenzy, and she clutched her tiny wares to her bosom. He even offered to read her *Pat the Bunny*—a household copy so worn that it lacked most of the interior props. She wrenched it from him with a "Mines!" At the moment, she was picking at globs of dried glue on the pages.

Cook could faintly hear Susan talking on the phone upstairs, enlisting volunteers for some school function. One of Molly's sisters—Pam, the reckless Rollerblader—had come home from school with what seemed like a dozen friends and one very little boy, presumably a younger brother of one of the girls. They had stormed the kitchen, then stomped up the stairs. They had set up directly over Cook's head, where they were presently shrieking.

Cook spied another sister coming up the front walk, Karen, the one who always looked excessively content. "Who's that?" he said to Molly. She dropped the book and stood up on the couch next to him. Her eyes went to the window.

"Karen," she said softly—and perfectly, although she was years away from a consistent *r*. Her eyes were on a level with Cook's, and she had laid a hand lightly on his shoulder. He gazed deeply into her face and lost himself there.

She sat with a bounce on the couch and slid to the floor. She ran to the door, where Karen scooped her up and wished her a happy Halloween.

Cook called out a hello.

"Hi," she said. "Molly say anything interesting?"

"No. She's been a grump. How do you get her out of it?"

Karen set Molly down. Or tried to. Molly's legs went rubbery when her feet touched the floor.

"None of that," said Karen, laying her on the carpet. "Do you know what it's time for? It's time"—Karen paused dramatically— "for *the running game!*" Karen dashed into the kitchen. Molly jumped up and hustled after her. A moment later they appeared again, with Karen several steps ahead. The downstairs had an open, looping layout, allowing laps, and Cook, seated on the couch, watched them run along one edge of the living room, disappear into the kitchen, and reemerge later via the den and entryway. Karen would slow tantalizingly, then speed up. It did not occur to Molly to reverse direction.

Susan appeared at the bottom of the stairs. Cook expected her to put an end to the rumpus. Instead, she picked up a helicopter pull-toy that one of them could have tripped over. "Don't you have soccer practice?" she asked Karen during one pass.

"Forgot my shoes."

"Well, you'd better get them and get going."

"Gotta go, Molly," Karen said on her next pass, and she darted up the stairs. Molly stopped in her tracks, on the verge of howling, when the front door opened with a new arrival. It was the girl from the swings, Andrea, the only daughter Cook hadn't met. She didn't see him. She tossed her backpack aside and, in a cadence exactly like Karen's, said, "Is someone . . . playing . . . *the running game?*"

Molly's screams made her mother wince. She took off on the circuit again, and when she reached Andrea, she screamed and ran the other way. Andrea took off after her.

Susan called up the stairs, "I'll give you a ride, honey. You'll be late otherwise." Hearing no response, she muttered and went up.

Andrea rounded the corner, all legs and arms and long, black hair, and she saw Cook for the first time. She laughed at herself and slowed to a stop.

"I'm Jeremy," he said.

"Your reputation precedes you. I'm Andrea."

Molly plowed into Andrea and grabbed her legs, her little white arms circling the black jeans. Then she let go and took off on her own.

"How's it going?" she asked Cook. "With Molly, I mean."

"Good," said Cook. He stood up and approached, trying to think of what else to say. Andrea seemed to have twice the self-possession he had.

Susan reappeared on the stairs. "Don't you have a rehearsal?"

"There was a debate scheduled in the auditorium. It's nice to have a break, actually. I wish there were some way to be involved in the theater without being involved with theater *people*. God."

Susan turned to Cook. "Andrea won the directing competition last spring. Every year students present plans for directing a play. They say what play they want to do and how they'd stage it. Andrea picked *Our Town*."

"That's enough, Mom."

"'Weaned from the living,'" said Cook.

Andrea nodded. "The play shouldn't be any good, really. It's too obvious. Plain old everyday life, a wedding, a funeral, then the curtain. That's it. But it works. Plus it breaks a basic rule of writing that you can't write directly about a theme."

Susan was watching Andrea with undisguised pride. From above there came more foot stompings and shrieks, and Susan hollered up the stairs that they needed to settle down.

Andrea said to her, "I have to go look at some dresses for the play in the Central West End. I'll be back for dinner." Andrea looked at Cook. "I'm being nibbled to death by ducks." He laughed.

Susan asked her if she could hand out Halloween candy at home for an hour after dinner so that she and Ben could take Molly trick-or-treating. Andrea said she could.

"Molly's costume is a field hockey goalie," Susan said. "Just like her big sister." She gave Andrea a pat on the back.

"I'm humbled," Andrea said. "Humbled."

Karen appeared, cleated shoes in hand. Molly was still running laps. Susan corralled her and explained she was going to Karen's school and would be right back.

"I come wit' you," Molly said.

Cook said, "I'll take off."

"We'll be right back," said Susan. "Things'll quiet down. Honest." Cook shrugged and returned to the couch. Susan grabbed Molly's coat from the closet and wrestled her into it. Karen had disappeared, and Susan was about to yell in exasperation, but she emerged from the kitchen with a large apple, and they left.

"The theme," Andrea said with an emphasis signaling delayed return to topic, "is the enjoyment of daily life." She was standing and he was sitting, and he felt like her pupil. "I keep asking myself, why is the play so sad? The only answer I can come up with is activity."

"Activity?" said Cook.

"People are active. They deliver papers, they deliver babies, they string green beans. They're busy living. It's sad because it'll all come to an end. It's the saddest thing in the world." She made a face. "I'm having trouble getting my people to see that."

"The actors?"

"Yeah. They don't feel the pain."

"How do you feel it?"

"How can you *not* feel it? It's in every word."

What Cook had meant—but was uncomfortable explaining—was how could Andrea, whose life was just beginning, feel it?

She went into the kitchen. Overhead, Pam and her friends stomped and shrieked, making the floor lamp next to Cook jingle faintly. Andrea reappeared, carrying a water bottle and chomping on a large pretzel. As she headed for the front door, she said, "I am realizing this pretzel while I eat it—every, every minute." She didn't look at Cook for his reaction. She just called out "Bye" and was gone.

Fresh screams from above issued into the rumble of a hundred hooves on the stairs. The herd pounded into the living room, but their movement became confused at the sight of the solitary linguist on the couch.

"Where's Mom?" Pam said. She was bent over, clutching her brown hair.

Cook explained that she had taken Karen to her school. "Is something wrong?"

Pam moaned in despair. Another girl said, "Pam got a brush stuck in her hair, and Willy's locked in the bathroom."

"Willy?" said Cook.

"Terri's brother," said Pam. "He's all freaked out."

Cook stood up. "How old is he?"

"Three and a half," Pam said. She was standing straight up now, but her face was red.

"Let's go," said Cook.

Pam led the way, rapidly explaining that Willy had turned a key in the door and was now unable to turn it the other way. Cook asked if any other keys in the house matched it. Pam said no. His mind raced. If the hinge pins were outside the door, he could remove them and slip the door off the hinges.

However, when they arrived he saw that the door didn't even have hinges. It was a sliding door—a thick one that closed flush with the doorjamb and threshold. He couldn't imagine how the lock worked. He asked Pam if she thought Willy could get the key out of the lock. She said yes, if he positioned it the right way. But the door hugged the hall rug so tightly that Willy wouldn't have been able to slide the key under it. And he was certainly too young to open a window to throw it out.

Cook grew uncomfortable as the potential solutions toppled. He could hear the boy crying. "It's okay, Willy," a girl said—Terri, he assumed. "Turn the key. Turn it."

Cook heard some futile rattling in the lock. He decided to explore access from the outside and asked Pam to show him. She led him down the stairs and out to the back lawn. The window was high and perilously close to the electrical line entering the house. When Pam showed him the available ladders in the garage, it was clear that none could reach it in any case.

The garage connected directly with the basement, and Pam led him back into the house by this route. Cook's eye fell on two large plastic pipes descending from the basement ceiling. They merged into one larger pipe, which disappeared into the concrete floor. The waste stack.

"Go tell Willy to flush the toilet. He can do that, can't he? Then come back."

Pam frowned, but she ran up. Cook positioned himself at the stack. He put a palm on each branch of the pipe. In a moment, he heard and felt a whoosh of water down the pipe on his right. Pam came back.

"Tools. Wrenches. Where are they?"

Pam led him to a well-organized tool room, set apart from the rest of the basement. He grabbed the biggest wrenches there. With one of them he was able to get a grip on the square head of a cleanout cap in the side of the pipe. He unscrewed it. His hand just fit inside.

"Tell Willy to take the key out of the door and flush it down the toilet."

Pam stared, and comprehension dawned. "Cool!" She took off.

Cook readied himself. After what seemed like a very long time, the water rushed down. It cascaded over his hands and plunged through his fingers. He came up empty. Had he missed it? His heart sank. Then another gush came, and when the key hit his palm, it surprised him so much that he jerked and almost fumbled it. He pulled the key out just as Pam came back, and he gave it to her. She gasped and took off again, her stuck hairbrush flopping against her head.

Cook replaced the stack cap and washed up in the first-floor bathroom. He smiled at the shouts of celebration upstairs. Pam and the others came down with Willy, who was about Molly's height, but chubbier. He had a haunted look about him, but Terri was comforting him.

"I hate to bother you again, but can you do my brush?" Pam said. "It feels like it's been in there forever."

"This shouldn't be too bad," said Cook. He approached and gingerly touched her hair where the brush was stuck. He began to separate the strands. The girls gathered around. At these close quarters, with a quieter crisis, Cook felt uncomfortably aware of the girls' strangeness.

But he soon lost himself completely in the task. He had never seen anything like it. The brush had no proper top or bottom but had bristles all around it. Apparently Pam had twisted it enough to entangle it, then worsened things by fussing with it. The futile efforts by her friends had sensitized her, and she yowled at the slightest tug on her scalp. After five minutes of delicate work, Cook felt like a surgeon up to his wrists in the young girl's life.

"Scissors," he said.

"Don't cut it!" Pam yelled.

"I'm going to cut the brush bristles."

"Cool," one of the girls said.

"In the big kitchen drawer," Pam said.

Scissors were produced, and Cook went for the base of the bristles, snipping them one by one. By the time Susan and Molly returned, Pam and Cook were down on the floor. Pam was seated with her legs crossed, and Cook knelt behind her. Susan said, "Not again! I'm throwing them out. All of them." She stormed up the stairs. Molly pulled up next to Cook and watched the operation with fascination.

When he finally eased the brush out, Cook felt the same measure of satisfaction he had felt upon attaining his doctoral degree. Pam broke free with a hurried thank-you and ran up the stairs. The gang followed her, babbling.

Cook sat back on the floor and stretched. He seemed to see Pam's tangled hair still before his eyes. Molly, alone with him, stared at his face.

"So," he said to her, "what's this running game I've been hearing so much about?"

—

Cook stopped at a used bookstore on his way home and found what he wanted without any difficulty. When he arrived home, he heard Paula singing, after a fashion.

"*Wrong!*" she sang out from her study. She was grading student exercises. He took off his coat and called out a hello, but it was drowned out by another *"Wrong!"* He heard a third one as he stepped into her study.

"The Great Vowel Shift," she said, throwing down her pen. "They're crashing and burning."

"It's a tough change for beginners."

Paula slowly turned her head to him. "What are you saying? That I'm pushing them? Of course I'm pushing them. They've never been pushed in their lives. These people can't think, and they sure can't write. Look at this." She rummaged through a pile and pulled out a sheet. "This guy, Bob. Instead of 'all of a sudden,' he writes 'all of *the* sudden.' What the hell's that about?"

Cook stepped forward and looked at it. Bob had written, "All of the sudden, the vowels moved." The penmanship was sad and vulnerable. It seemed to say, "Hurt me." Paula had obliged in the margin: "Not English!"

"It's a developmental relic," said Cook. "When Bob was little and first heard 'all of a sudden,' he interpreted the 'a' as a reduced form of 'the' because it gets so little stress."

"I know that. But his theory should have been contradicted the first time he read the correct form."

"Maybe he doesn't read enough."

"He should read more. I'm punishing him for not reading enough. That's part of my job."

He suspected Paula was punishing the lad for a different reason: for being average, like Buford U. itself.

"Excellence in all things," said Paula. "That's my new motto."

"Oh?" To Cook it sounded like a General Electric motto.

"For example"—she reached across the desk for a thick manila file—"the conference. I'm running it now. My goal is to blow everyone away with the excellence of it."

"What happened to Ted?"

"He stepped aside. We're close to getting long-term funding for the new center from this one branch of the Buford family, a pair of twins with a ton of money. They're very straitlaced, a brother-sister pair who live together." She laughed softly. "They look like the couple in 'American Gothic.' Anyway, I'm running the show now because of them."

Cook was having trouble following this. "Why you instead of Ted?"

"Because he's gay."

Many thoughts besieged him. He felt out of the loop—that was one. Another was about Susan: she had a gay brother. In his complicated mind, this enriched her. But the main thought he had was still confusion. "Why does Ted's being gay disqualify him from running the conference?"

"It doesn't disqualify him. It's just politic under the circumstances to have a heterosexual at the helm."

Cook imagined the phrase in an ad for a cruise line for fundamentalists: "A Heterosexual at the Helm." The language was as odd as her "Excellence in all things." He said, "This doesn't sound like you."

"It's not. It's Chairman Sam's idea."

"How does Ted feel about it?"

"He's pissed off." She rose and picked up her coffee cup. "To tell the truth, he's kind of not talking to me. He's mad that I've accepted the helm. I guess he'd rather there be *no* conference."

Cook followed her to the kitchen. He was silent because the only words he could think of supported Ted's case.

"I have a favor to ask," she said as she poured herself some coffee. "Tilley won't give the keynote address." This was the shy Minnesotan whom Ted had been wooing. "I've upgraded one of the regular presenters, Sid Meltzer, to give the keynote, and he's almost as distinguished. But now I need a new presenter to fill in. Do you have anything you could do?"

"Sure."

"That's great. What?"

It was too early to tell her. "Thug," "throw money at," and "happen to" were good for just five minutes, not forty-five. "I'll have something. Don't worry."

"I'm not worried. I'll just need a title by November 10, okay?" As she headed for her study, she spotted his newly purchased book on the counter.

"*Our Town*? Why are you reading that?"

He shrugged.

"Isn't it kind of sappy?"

"It doesn't hurt to look at the big questions. People like us, we're clever with certain questions—the ones at the top of the pyramid, like the Great Vowel Shift. But there are underlying ones. Like this one: Do you love life?"

"*What?*"

"I mean it. Do you love life?"

Paula hesitated, then looked across the room. "I love my field. I love language. I love the life of the mind. I love tennis. I love the outdoors. I love travel. If that adds up to a love of life, then yes."

"I love life," he said.

His wife laughed hard at him.

"I do. I love life. I decided today."

"Jeremy, you're the most negative person I know. You are a total nay-sayer. A cynic. A misanthrope."

"I love life."

She shook her head as she returned to her study. He took the play to the couch, kicked off his shoes, and propped his feet on the coffee table. Pretty soon, she was singing again.

# 15

"Knock knock."

"Who's there?"

"William."

"William who?"

"William miss me when I'm gone?"

After a token laugh, Ben found his place in his reading. This was easy to do because he hadn't taken his eyes from the page. Roberta remained standing on the other side of his desk, right in front of him.

"Knock knock."

"Who's there?"

"Sir."

"Sir who."

"*Sir View Right!*" The sharp tone made him look up. Roberta grinned at the way she had gotten his attention. "My, aren't we vain this morning," she said as she walked to the file cabinet against the wall behind him. She was referring to the story about

Crunch in the *St. Louis Business Journal*, which he was eager to finish reading.

"Yeah," said Ben. "Finally. I'd almost forgotten about it."

"No, you hadn't."

"Fair enough." Ben looked at her as she fluttered her fingers through the folders in the bottom drawer—hard copies of their orders from years gone by, years when "hard copy" didn't exist as a term because there was no other kind. He wondered what she was doing in these ancient files, but not enough to ask. Her explanation would be tedious. He took in her profile as she squatted at the drawer. Her skirt had ridden up her thigh so far that he could see the edge of her white panties. With his glimpse down her chest in the parking lot a few weeks earlier, a map of Roberta was coming together.

He scooted his chair forward a bit and resumed reading. Roberta, still squatting, shifted her position and cleared her throat unnaturally. This made him look at her again. He almost gasped. She was exposing her entire flank to him—all of one buttock, or at least all that could be seen in profile. She continued to search the files, but with her near arm she pressed her bunched-up skirt against her hip, revealing below it an expanse of white skin, stark white, fishbelly white. Still, it was an ass. Where were her panties? All he could figure was that they had ridden up around her cheek all the way into her crack. But how? Wouldn't that require a deliberate tug?

His eyes hurried back to the article. He said, "I think George did a nice job. Did you read it?"

Roberta stood up and kicked the cabinet drawer closed. "I read it."

"Did you like it?"

"He patronized me."

Ben looked up. "You think so?"

"He patronized you too."

Ben frowned. "By 'patronize' you mean . . ."

"'To treat in a superior manner disguised as a friendly one.' I've become very adept at spotting it." She clutched a green file folder to her chest.

"I missed that. What—"

"He makes fun of the Supreme."

"Well, he does express a little astonishment at the price. Hell, I'm astonished too."

"He ridicules *all* the Nutpaks. He's laughing behind his hand."

"You think so?"

"Ben, you are so *blind*. He calls the Nutpaks 'mysteriously successful.' Don't you see what he's saying? He's saying our success is undeserved. My question is, why would he do something like that? Does he have something against you?"

"I can't imagine what."

"It's a cruel story, Ben. It's just terribly cruel." She spun on her heel and left his office.

In the course of the next half hour, Ben puzzled over Roberta's words. He reread the article and tried to reach Susan at home to read it to her, but she was out somewhere with Molly, and he left a message. It was possible that between the interview and the writing, George had discovered the affair (Andrea's discovery around that time underscored the possibility); still, it was hard for Ben to find anything really objectionable in the story. He finally decided that Roberta was wrong—that it was a damned fine article. He had just one regret: that he hadn't let George in on his cashew venture. He wanted the readers to know that he was trying to leap to a new level, that he was a striver. Benjamin the Deed-Doer.

At one point he stepped into the bathroom, not just to relieve himself but also to determine experimentally if it was possible to slide his own jockey underwear entirely across his buttock cheek *inadvertently*. The question was decided in the negative.

He made a few phone calls—goodwill calls to retailers and one get-well call to an employee at the warehouse across the street who had severely strained his back, on his own time, thank God. Then he spent an hour analyzing whether to switch from his regular California almond supplier to one who had been wooing him. It was a debate between loyalty and savings, mere pennies per tons, but pennies had a way of turning into dollars. He finally decided to stick with his old supplier and hoped something good would happen to him as a reward.

He heard the buzz of the fax machine next to Roberta's desk. A few minutes later, he heard her zany musical laughter. She didn't explain, and he didn't ask. Later, she came into his office and returned the early-years file to the bottom drawer. He kept his eyes locked on the papers in front of him. She rose.

"Interesting fax reading this morning, Ben."

"Oh?"

"From India. Hot and spicy. Very stimulating."

Ben frowned. He had given Nathan Ravindranathan his office fax number and asked him to use it if he had more information, but he certainly hadn't asked for any more erotic literature.

Roberta was still standing by the cabinet. Instead of going straight to the door, she took a roundabout route behind his chair, squeezing between its back and the bookcase behind it. She paused directly behind him, *as he knew she would*. Leaning over him, she reached out and touched the top of his right hand. Her white fingers lightly resting there made his own hand look hairy and brawny, almost apelike. She ran a single finger up the length of his arm, across his shoulders, and down his left arm to his other hand. He sat still, weighing his options. Her maneuvers came to an end, and she walked across his office, not to the door but to the window, where she stood for what must have been a full minute, facing the distant traffic.

Ben sat. He felt like a dumb cluck. He knew he should say something, but what? He finally hit on something that he thought would embarrass neither of them. Just as he was about to speak, she made a noise, a kind of sigh or moan of exasperation, and turned and walked to the door. He said his sentence.

"Roberta, is something on your mind?"

She laughed hollowly and paused. "Depends, Ben. Is something on yours?"

"No."

"Then nothing's on mine." She went back to her own desk and immediately resumed work.

The way Ben saw it, life at the office as he had known it was over. Roberta, for eighteen years a silent and predictable servant, had changed. She had discovered sex, thanks to the little man with the big cigarette. When Ben put this discovery together with her evident feelings for him (Susan must have been right about that after all), the sum was a disaster: having discovered sex, she wanted to have it *with him*. The best he could hope was that this was her one shot at it. She had made her overture or whatever, he had passed, and things would return to what they had been—but not completely. He would always be on edge, wondering when she might put the moves on him again, when she might flash more white at him. The suspense would kill him.

And what if there were no suspense? What if, after her mid-morning break, fortified by a doughnut, she came right back at him? Well, what if she did? He was the boss, wasn't he? He could fire her, couldn't he?

*William miss me when I'm gone?* Not really.

~

153

Ben squirmed in his chair with a sense of unease. A second awkward thing had just happened, this one involving not Roberta but the Zender Nut Co. in New Jersey. He had finally gotten around to calling to explore Peru as a source of Brazil nuts—more than two weeks had passed since his initial resolve—and he had reached old Bill Zender himself, the gruff, impatient patriarch of the firm. Ben usually dealt with his son, but he went ahead and put the idea to the old guy that since most of their nuts came from poor, tropical countries, they should perhaps try to give their business to those with the best working conditions. Zender had all but blown Ben's ear off. "How dare you!" he said, over and over, and Ben knew he was in trouble. Zender hung up on him, and after pacing the office for a few minutes, Ben called back and reached the son, who said that he hadn't learned what had happened, but that he could see his father approaching across the warehouse as they were speaking. Ben apologized to the son for any offense he had given and received assurance that the old man would settle down. "Hell, he's probably forgotten about it already, Ben," he said, to which Ben replied, "If he has, then I have." So it was over. Still, it had been awkward.

The phone rang in Roberta's office, but she had left. Ten minutes earlier, while Ben was stewing between his two calls to New Jersey, Roberta had leaned her head in the door, acting as if nothing unusual had happened, and complained of "a tummy ache." Ben, having tensed as soon as he heard her chair wheels squeak, relaxed and told her to go home for the rest of the day. She left immediately. On top of his worries about old man Zender, Ben now wondered if Roberta was going to launch a rebellion of malingering.

After the fourth ring, the call jumped to his desk. He had never bothered to figure out his own phone system. Now, unable to modify it, he was doomed to answer the phone this way until five o'clock.

"Ben? This is Tina Fairweather from Countywide."

"Who?"

"Tina Fairweather. Your personal banker from Countywide Bank. How are you today?"

"Fine. What's up?"

"Well, that's a good question, Ben. You've been with us going on twenty-five years. You should be getting your twenty-five-year paperweight any day now."

Jesus, Ben thought. Was this why she called?

"I'm speaking of your personal accounts. Twenty-five years. As for your business accounts, they've been part of the Countywide family for almost twenty years, and we're very happy with the relationship." She paused. "Our records show that there are two Crunch accounts."

"That's right."

"An investment savings account and a commercial checking account."

"Is there some problem?" Ben asked—not sharply, but not dully either.

"A small one, Ben. That's why I'm calling. That's why you have a personal banker. There 's a three-check limit, per month, on the investment savings account."

"I know. That's why we don't use it to pay bills."

"Well, let me just tell you what our records show. We show four checks written against this account in a one-month period. That's a violation of federal guidelines. This is just a warning call, but—"

"Look, can you talk to my secretary about this? She handles all this stuff."

"I just did. Roberta said I should speak with you about it."

Ben was simultaneously bored and confused. "When did she say this?"

"About five minutes ago. She noticed the oversight before we

155

did, and she called to alert me to it. I think that's a first—the customer reporting the limit violation. She's very efficient, isn't she? Anyway, she asked me to call you about it."

Ben couldn't figure this. By his calculations, Roberta should still be on her way home. Why would she call this woman and have her call him? And how could she have screwed up with the account like this? She wasn't supposed to write checks from it. The only draws they made from it were internal transfers to the other account. Ben said, "Let's make sure we're talking about the right accounts. What balance do you show?"

"Well, that's another point. As you know, the interest rate on an investment savings account drops when the balance goes under a thousand dollars."

"Whoa. You're looking at the wrong account. First of all, the checking account has four or five thousand. And the other one has a ton of money in it. I just moved some money out of some mutual funds, and I parked it in the investment savings account. Almost two hundred and fifty thousand. Right?"

"Yes. I see what you mean. Two hundred forty-eight thousand, rounded off. That's the figure that was the balance on October sixteenth."

"Okay. And it should be close to the same today."

"I show a balance of eighteen dollars and eighteen cents."

Ben laughed. But he was sitting up now. "Roberta must have moved it all to the other account. I can't imagine why she would, but will you check that balance?"

"Glad to." The woman tapped on her keyboard. Then she discovered something that made her laugh lightly. "This is very funny," she said.

"What?"

"It's exactly the same figure. Eighteen dollars and eighteen cents."

Ben wanted one thing: to get this settled, with an innocent explanation, fast. "Someone has blundered," he said.

"Well, that's what we're trying to establish, Ben."

"Can you check all my personal accounts? Mine, my wife's, the kids'—everything having to do with my family. It's all in my name."

"Glad to." She hit the keys.

"I'm thinking Roberta must have gotten hold of one of my personal deposit slips."

"That can happen, yes."

"I leave stuff lying around—"

"Yes."

A call-waiting signal beeped in his ear. Susan, he guessed. He ignored it. Tina read out the names heading the family accounts, seven in all, along with the balances. The numbers were exactly what he had expected, no more, no less. Fear began to crowd in on him.

"You said four checks were written on the Crunch account. What do your records show about them?" His voice was tight in his own ears.

"Let me get that back on my screen . . . Here we are. Three checks were in the amount of eighty-two thousand, five hundred dollars each. The fourth was for three hundred six dollars and nine cents. That brought the balance down to eighteen dollars, eighteen cents, as I said before."

Ben cleared his throat. "Who were the checks made out to? Do you know?"

"Let me call up the copies. Here we are. Let's see. The checks are all payable to the same party. 'O. McSweeney Asset Management.'"

Ben stared across the room. It seemed ridiculous that a name so completely foreign to him, so utterly without meaning, would offer itself as the apparent solution. It was no solution at all. Had Roberta shifted the money back into a mutual fund? It was his plan, ultimately. She was good at anticipating his moves, but that would have been too bold. But maybe boldness like that went with the boldness of a flashing flank. Maybe she was trying to impress him on several fronts.

"Ben? Are you there?"

"I'm thinking. Let me check something." He grabbed the white pages but found no listing for O. McSweeney Asset Management. "Tina?"

"Yes?"

"Check the endorsement. Do you have that?"

"Yes. I'll call up the copies."

While he waited, the call-waiting signal came back.

"What I'm thinking," Ben said, fighting a creeping feebleness in his throat, "is that the endorsement might show an address."

"They often do, yes," said Tina. "Sorry to take so long. The endorsement is in a separate file, if you can believe it. I'll have it in just a moment." In her voice was something Ben wasn't used to: pity. It made him see things as she saw them. She was unpacking a disaster right before his eyes.

Another call-waiting beep. He was finding it hard to think. "I have to get rid of that call," Ben said. "I'll be right back." As he clicked the switchhook, he thought, If it's Susan, she'll have the answer.

"Knock knock." Roberta said it before he had even said hello.

"Roberta? Thank God. Listen—"

"Knock knock."

"Listen to me. The investment savings account—where in the hell is the money?"

"Knock knock."

"Jesus! *Who's there?*"

"Orson."

"Orson *who?*" Ben snarled.

"Just Orson around with your money." Roberta laughed her zany laugh. "Thanks for the memories, Ben." In the background, before Roberta hung up, Ben heard a male voice begin to sing those words with exaggerated feeling.

Ben had kept Fear at bay. He was good at that. Even when Roberta had given him the punch line, he had said to himself, "She's saying she's just horsing around. It's a practical joke. It's not a *good* joke, but it's still a joke." But then she said, "Thanks for the memories, Ben." Between the punch line and those words, Ben inhabited a tiny island of hope around which Fear could only circle.

But now Fear was upon him.

# 16

"Now, Ben, let's go back. Let's take it nice and slow. When did you get this phone call?"

"About ten forty-five."

Sergeant Klaus, of the Bigelow Hills Police Department, looked at his watch. It rode high on his wrist. "It's gone three o'clock."

"So?"

"Is there some strange reason you waited so long to call?"

Ben glared at him. "No reason." The sergeant did not return his look because he was writing something in a tiny spiral notebook in his lap. How ironic, Ben thought, that he was being interviewed again. The mature business indeed.

Sergeant Klaus shifted in the chair, which he overoccupied. "When did your secretary leave the office?"

"About twenty minutes before that."

"Any idea where she called you from?"

"No. I wondered if she—"

"Just wait now. Could she have called from home?"

"I was going to *say*," Ben said, "that I wondered if she was home. As soon as she hung up, I tried that number. I got a recording."

"Well, all by itself that don't mean nothin'. She could have still been home."

Ben stared at the master of deduction. How could someone who said "don't mean nothin'" ever find his money? The man was a moron. Ben had a story to tell, a simple story that held all the facts, but Sergeant Klaus kept trying to put together his own version based on tiny questions.

Ben suddenly realized the error he had made in calling this man's department. Bigelow Hills, the municipality where Crunch was located, had a population of under two thousand. Roberta had embezzled a quarter of a million dollars. This was a big jump from the typical local property crime, like last summer's ransacking of the coin laundry down the street. He had known the moment he had called that Bigelow Hills was all wrong. He had known it from the accent, which wasn't educated enough for the magnitude of the crime. But he went ahead anyway. Why did he do that?

"You're right," he said to Klaus, reining in his impatience. "The recording itself means nothing. It's what the recording says that's important." Ben grabbed his phone and punched Roberta's number. He held the receiver out for Klaus, who had anticipated this and had begun shifting forward in his chair. Ben watched him listen to the duet he himself had obsessively listened to several times already. It was Orson and Roberta singing a lyric Ben always found annoying under the best of circumstances: "Nah nah nah nah, nah nah nah nah, hey hey, good-bye."

Klaus blinked stupidly as he listened. Then he broke into a grin.

Ben jumped to his feet. "Get out."

Klaus's face emptied of expression. "What?"

"Get out. You're fired. I called the wrong office. Go away."

"You gone off your nut?"

"The money was taken from an account in the Countywide Bank in University City. The suspect lives in Glendale. I live in Aberdeen. It's a county matter. I'm calling the County Police Department."

Ben didn't know what he was talking about, but something in his manner convinced Klaus. He closed his tiny notebook with a mini-slam. "I was gonna call 'em anyway," he said, "but if you ain't gonna cooperate, *you* call 'em." When he reached the door, he turned. "One thing for sure—if I had that kind of money, I wouldn't be callin' a podunk police department to report it missin'. I'd take care it wasn't missin' in the first place."

Ben found he had nothing to say against this. He watched the sergeant go. Then he sat at his desk. The phone rang in Roberta's office, then it rang on his desk, and then it stopped. This happened several times. It was background noise to the rushing sounds in his head. Among those sounds were the words from Klaus: "strange reason," "podunk," "take care."

Yes, there was a reason why he hadn't called immediately, but it wasn't strange at all. To make that phone call meant admitting that it had really happened. He could not let go of the hope that it was a joke. As morning gave way to afternoon and the afternoon wore on, he saw that the only argument for that hope was the enormity of the alternative. He hoped because he couldn't stand the idea of being without hope. Hour by hour the balance between hope and no-hope tilted, until he found himself with the phone in his hand, giving the undeniable facts to Sergeant Klaus.

Now he had to do it all over again—had to take his sorry tale to the outside world. He had had two samples of the responses waiting for him—pity from personal banker Tina and sadistic pleasure from Klaus.

But this time, at the St. Louis County Police Department, he found a response he could live with: respectful curiosity. Detective Phillips was fascinated by the case. He was also a man of action. Ben sensed him holding calls and shutting out the world of his office to focus on Ben's words. As Phillips learned things, he called out orders to people. As soon as Ben gave him Roberta's name, he obtained the license number of her Datsun and immediately learned that her car had been towed an hour earlier from a handicapped parking spot at the airport. Ben imagined Roberta and Orson giggling as she parked it there, emboldened to mischief by their higher crime.

"I've sent some people out to comb the terminal, Ben," said Phillips, whose speech was crisp without being cold, "but my guess is they're airborne or already on the ground somewhere else. I've got another man checking the names against passenger lists."

"Wouldn't they use aliases?"

"Look, I don't want to make you feel worse, but if you'd called earlier, we might have nailed them. I understand, though. It happens with embezzlement. The boss sits there openmouthed. Or he spends the day checking and rechecking the books. I've seen weeks go by before the boss calls. Some never do. We learn about them from the other side, when a suspect suddenly gives us the whole history, and we go to the victim and he says yeah, it happened."

Ben made some vague noises. He didn't like being called a victim.

"You haven't mentioned insurance, Ben. The carrier's going to want to be involved from the beginning. Do you have an employee dishonesty rider on your policy?"

Ben felt the weight on his chest of yet another regret. "My employees pack nuts. They're not going to ruin me by sneaking nuts home. Only one handled the money, and I trusted her. She'd been with me eighteen years."

"I understand," said Phillips, who seemed to understand all.

Ben had a thought. Eighteen years and how many days? He did a quick calculation. Roberta had begun work a month before Andrea was born. He remembered it well. Susan had been slowing down at the office, and, between naps and trips to the toilet, she had trained Roberta. Working from Andrea's upcoming birthday, he calculated precisely how long Roberta had been with him: eighteen years and eighteen days. Eighteen dollars and eighteen cents.

"How about we take a look at where they might have flown to." Phillips said this in the free-and-easy manner of a man with time on his hands. "What do you know about Orson McSweeney?"

"He smokes big cigarettes."

"Oh? Hundred-millimeter jobs, huh? Okay, that's something. That's a start."

"That's the end, I'm afraid. I told you he was short. Thin mustache. Big cigarettes. That's it. That's all I know. I don't even know if the name 'Orson McSweeney' is real."

"Probably about as real as 'Asset Management.' That's going to be a dummy corp. If those big checks on your account had been written to individuals, your bank might have called you to check up on it. But with 'Asset Management,' they'd figure you were just making an investment. Does Orson have an accent of any kind? Foreign? Southern?"

"Not that I noticed. He didn't say much."

"Let's try Roberta. Does she have connections elsewhere?"

"Indianapolis. A cousin. Helen Bonner. B-O-N-N-E-R."

"Got an address?"

"No. I'm sorry."

"We'll find her. What else about Roberta?"

Ben thought. Efficient. Bad dresser. Boring. Awkward. And, he now knew, a thief. "She travels a lot. It's the one thing she does. Europe, Asia. All over."

"Any place in particular she's talked about wanting to return to, maybe settle down in?"

Ben thought about this. "No. Nothing comes to mind."

Phillips was silent a moment. "I've noticed something. Correct me if I'm wrong. You don't sound mad at her."

Ben sat up in his chair. "The woman stole a quarter of a million dollars. That's my money."

"Okay. Sorry. Now, can you guess how long the theft might have been in the planning?"

"How could I know that?" Ben said. "I suppose from the time this Orson came on the scene. The first I heard of him was when I met him, two or three weeks ago."

Phillips asked for an exact date. Ben recalled the events of that day. A Saturday, because Roberta was off work and had brought Orson by to see the place—and to be screwed on the couch. Ben had driven to the office after watching Karen play soccer. He rose and checked the copy of the soccer schedule taped to the side of the file cabinet. As he reported the date to Phillips, he felt tricked by time. Why couldn't he be back on that field with his future ahead of him instead of behind him?

"So, Ben, no hint of it in the works? No sign it was coming?"

"Well, Roberta was acting weird a few weeks before then. She kept turning down dinner invitations to our house. She'd always accepted them before. It started about a month before I met him."

"So he could have come into the picture then. Mid-September."

"I guess."

"Let me tell you the reason I dwell on this. We're going to look at the passenger lists for all the flights out of Lambert today after ten forty-five, which is the earliest they could have left. I've got someone on it right now. We're going to want to flush out the aliases. You do that by finding a name without a history—no Social Security number, nothing. Your Roberta sounds like a completely straight arrow who got swept up in something. If she just met this guy, her alias is going to be about ten minutes old. The Orson dick is gonna be a different story. He could have half a dozen names with histories. Roberta is the key."

"What if she booked a ticket as Mary Smith? Or M. Smith?"

"It gets tricky, sure."

Ben sagged. Phillips, because he had a plan, had begun to give Ben hope. But now the hope was gone again.

"The wheels are in motion, Ben. I'll get a warrant to search her house. We'll dust the Datsun for Orson's prints. I want to come out to your office for a look-see. You going to be there for a while?"

"I'll stay as long as you want."

"It'll be about an hour."

"One thing," Ben said nervously.

"Yeah?"

"Can you keep this quiet?"

Phillips said nothing for a moment. "The papers call the office every day. We choose whether or not we tell them of ongoing investigations."

"Can you choose not to?"

"For now, yes."

As he hung up the phone, Ben thought maybe it wasn't hopeless. There were lots of scenarios in which everything worked out okay. Phillips could catch them at the airport as they boarded. Or catch them when they landed in New York or Dallas or L.A. (Foreign cities made the scenario less okay.) Or Roberta could cave in, her essential blandness carrying the day and sending her to the police with a confession—and an account number.

Or, best of all, it could be a joke. This notion struck him with something very like the freshness of a bold new idea. There could easily be some signal lying around somewhere that it was all harmless—some sort of "Gotcha!" It could be lying on her desk, which he hadn't even checked. He imagined the wording of the note: "Ben, I'm sorry if I gave you a scare. I just wanted to get your attention. I opened a new Crunch account at Glendale Bank. It's all there. Good-bye forever, Roberta."

He had so worked himself up with positive thinking that he was mildly distressed to find the top of Roberta's desk exactly as she left it at the end of every workday—bare, as bare as the half-ass she had flashed at him that morning. He opened the top drawer. Essence of Roberta wafted from it. It was neatly packed with the boring tools of the secretarial trade. He tried the drawers on the right side. They contained blank paper in aqua and pink hues, the colors she wore. The top and bottom drawers on the left contained travel magazines and brochures. This was her lunch-time reading, which she often told him about as he passed through the office, making him slow in his walk but never making him stop.

The large middle drawer on the left contained files. Ben scanned the labels, looking among the business names for something more personal. He found it, right between "Imperial Almond Co." and "North Valley Tree Nuts," but it wasn't what he expected. It was a file labeled "Marlin, Wendy." In it Ben found a single small envelope, addressed to him. Roberta had opened it, as she opened all correspondence sent to the office. After all, what did he have to hide?

The stamp looked ancient, insufficient. The postmark was eleven years old. With a sinking feeling, Ben took out the letter.

167

In it Wendy said she loved him; their parting broke her heart; he had cut her off without giving their love a chance. She played back their times together, each one, each place, every memory. Couldn't they still be together in some way? Couldn't they? She would wait for his response. To Ben, it was like reading a new chapter to a familiar book, a wild, tacked-on ending that didn't belong. He was mortified at the pain of the letter—pain he hadn't felt, ever, during their brief relationship.

Of more immediate concern, the letter meant that Roberta knew of the affair. Ben saw it all in a flash, everything, the whole picture of Roberta's warped psyche set against the scorched landscape of his fate. He knew this with certainty: Roberta could have lived with her feelings for him, could have reconciled herself to a life of denial, if he had been faithful to Susan. But Wendy came along, and Roberta knew about it. That the affair happened eleven years ago without consequence didn't shake Ben's belief in it as a root cause. The formula for action probably required two ingredients together: an Orson to suggest it, and an active jealousy for the suggestion to appeal to her. Eleven years ago, she lacked an Orson.

As for active jealousy, Ben remembered Roberta as unusually flustered the day George was in the office, useless when he called on her to help him narrate the history of the business. "Does he have something against you, Ben?" she had asked after reading the article. Then had come the overture—Jesus, the overture—and the standing at the window. She had been waiting for him to make his move. If he had—if he had taken her to the couch as Orson had taken her and as he had taken Wendy—she would have called the embezzlement off. He was sure of it.

What Ben wanted to know above all was this: When would this really quite human indiscretion of eleven years ago stop dogging him? What ridiculously unforgiving gods were running this show?

Up till now, Ben had been troubled by Roberta's motive—troubled happily, because greed alone didn't seem to suit her, and if the crime was senseless, it could all still be a joke. Now he let go of his last grip on hope. It was like watching a loved one slip from his grasp forever.

He was forced to do something he had been able to avoid earlier: take stock. His overly clever fund juggling now put him in double jeopardy. Roberta had taken virtually all his business cash, but most of that cash, two hundred and twenty thousand of it, was really household money he had shifted to the business over the past four years. Which ruin should he survey first?

At home, he had about twenty-two thousand dollars in his joint savings account and another four thousand in his checking account. Looking at the other side of the ledger, which he was reluctant to do, he saw monthly mortgage payments of $4,025—steep because he had opted to finance the house almost to the max in the early nineties, when low interest rates had everyone scrambling. That figure didn't include homeowner's insurance and taxes, both of which would fall due at the end of next month—another six thousand there. Susan needed two thousand a month, at least, and he needed a thousand. Some time in January, a little over two months from now, he would be broke from household expenses alone.

This schedule for disaster assumed he drew no salary—unfortunately a safe assumption. The business generated steady money, but it also sucked it back up, and he wasn't used to opening envelopes and putting the contents right into his wallet. He was used to a plentiful bucket whose level could rise and fall without causing any worry. Now the bucket was empty. There wasn't even a bucket. He needed a loan—for the business, not for him personally. The way his house was in hock, no one would give him a personal loan. But he thought he could get a business loan. He *had* to get one. Art Talbot. Art was an ass, but he could bail Ben out. He looked at his watch. What the hell *were* bankers' hours, anyway? He grabbed the phone book and tracked down the number.

He was in luck. "You just got me, Ben. I was almost a gone banker. What's up? You calling to brag about soccer scouts recruiting Karen? Why do I doubt that?"

"I want to see if you guys live up to your advertising."

"Hell, Ben, you know those campaigns are a pack of lies. Which particular crock are you talking about?"

"Business QuikCash."

"What—you expanding? Going into sunflower seeds?"

"We're starting the New Year with an expanded mailing list," he said. "I can use thirty thousand."

Talbot laughed. "You sending each catalog special delivery?"

"Well," Ben said, flustered, "it's for other expenses too. Is thirty thousand the limit?"

"For QuikCash, yeah. But, you know, Ben, that kind of money is just for our preferred customers." After a long pause, Talbot burst out laughing. What Ben went through in that pause told him how much his life had changed in just a few hours. "Tell you what, with your track record and all, I don't need to see your financials. I'll fax you an application, and you dash off some answers—hell, just fill in your business name and address and sign it. Forget the other questions, six through fifteen. I'll fax you the terms too. It's a three-year payback with a balloon. Nothing fancy. You sign it and fax that baby back to me, right now. I'll stick around for a few minutes, and I'll pop the check in the mail on my way home. Fair enough?"

"You're a prince, Art."

"Just make it snappy. I want to get home and kick back with a brew and some beer nuts. Oops, sorry, pal."

When Ben hung up, the receiver stuck to his palm.

Thirty thousand. It was a start. He called up the twelve-month cash-flow budget on Roberta's screen. A December blip under payroll reminded him of Christmas bonuses. He wouldn't stint on those. January held two nasty surges—an insurance premium and a payment due to the printer. But that was a ways off. And if he had to, he could stretch his payables. It was no way to operate, but he had done it before, and he could do it again.

Next to Roberta's desk, the fax whined into action with Talbot's transmittal. As Ben surveyed the cash-flow figures on the screen, it occurred to him that Roberta could have sabotaged the business and utterly ruined him. There was no evidence she had done that. Up to the moment of her departure, she had placed and filled orders and paid bills as if she would be here forever. That was something, anyway.

Ben read over the loan application and filled it out. He was faxing it back to Talbot's office when Detective Phillips arrived. Phillips was lean, good-looking, and quick with a smile. He seemed Western to Ben, as if he might have parked a horse instead of a police car out on the lot. He had brought another cop with him, to Ben's dismay. Ben would have preferred that the problem remain a private thing between the two of them.

The new guy, an eager beaver, dived right into Roberta's files. He wouldn't find the Wendy Marlin letter there. Ben had pocketed it, along with the identifying plastic file tab. Meanwhile, Phillips asked Ben a few more questions. Then, with the dinner hour upon them, Phillips urged Ben to go on home. He would call him there if he had questions about anything they found. There was nothing more Ben could do for now. He left the two policemen with instructions to pull the door closed to lock it.

The loan had buoyed him, briefly. But on the road, confidence

drained from his body, and he flinched and overreacted like a beginning driver. When he entered the neighborhood where he had
lived for nearly twelve years, the houses seemed hostile. They
seemed to say, "It's hard to live in a house like this, Ben. Are you
up to it?"

A car zoomed up close behind him, its lights, though low,
bright in his mirror. It followed him into the driveway. It was their
van, with Susan behind the wheel. She beeped a hello as he hit
the remote for the garage door and pulled in right after him.

"Groceries," she said as she got out. "Can you help? Two hundred dollars' worth." She had popped the hatch and lifted it. Ben
stood between the cars. She said, "I've got some bad news. Andrea went to Dolgin today. She has to have her wisdom teeth out
or they'll mess up all the work she had done. All four of them.
Can you believe it? I'll try to schedule it for the Christmas break.
And speaking of teeth, we got the insurance statement for my
bridge. It only covered fifty percent, not eighty." She passed by
him with a bag of groceries and gave him a pat on the arm with
her free hand. "I've got to check on Molly. Karen's got her.
Thanks." At the entrance to the basement she hit the garage door
switch. The opener over Ben's head buzzed futilely. Susan
smacked the switch several times.

"Great," she said. "Can you close it manually? I'll call the guy
tomorrow. He said if it happened again the motor might need re-
placing." She went on into the basement.

The garage became a spinning ride. Ben stood between the
cars, a hand pressed hard against each. Both were leased—Susan's
at $312 per month, his at $385. He braced himself against his lia-
bilities and rode his garage around and around and around.

"Ben! Ben!" He heard these words as distant noises before rec-
ognizing them as his name. He yelled some sort of answer.

"Phone!" Susan called from the basement.

Phone. Possibly Detective Phillips, with possible news. It was possible. Ben took a gulp of air and worked his way forward between the cars, using them like parallel bars for support. He spotted the downstairs phone waiting for him on the laundry room table. He felt a little hazy. Susan, on the stairs, bent down and peered through the railing to be sure he was getting it.

"It's Scott Marlin," she said.

Marlin. Not Phillips. Too bad. Marlin calling to see how he liked the *Business Journal* article. Wait—*Scott* Marlin? The son?

"For me?" Ben said, but the door to the kitchen banged on his words. Ben's step faltered. It had never been clear to him how much Scott knew. He was under the impression that Scott had been fuzzy on some details, and he had hoped the identity of his mother's partner was one. Was he no longer fuzzy? Was he calling to accuse Ben?

"Hello?" Ben said. He was stepping into a dense mist.

"Mr. Hudnut?"

"Yes. Hi, Scott."

"Sorry to bother you at the dinner hour, but I'm on deadline, as Dad likes to say."

Ben stared at the laundry piled at his feet. "Deadline?"

"Maybe Andrea didn't tell you. Dad pulled some strings and got me an internship at the paper. The *Post-Dispatch*. That's where I am right now. I do research for Tommy Toronado."

Ben struggled for clear thought. Too much was coming at him, and none of it matched his expectations. Tommy Toronado was a gossip columnist for the *Post*. He liked to find out whose lives were in ruin and then add public shame to their private pain.

"Tommy's all mad at me because I didn't call you for a comment. Do you have a comment?"

Ben cleared his throat. "A comment?"

"You know. The embezzlement. I was making calls to the police departments—they give the little departments to the interns. Sergeant Klaus from Bigelow Hills was incredibly helpful. He says your secretary stole a quarter of a million dollars. Tommy's going to run it in tomorrow's column. Do you have a comment?"

# 17

Molly awoke the next morning with no knowledge of how poor she was. Likewise Susan, who was already in her study, chugging coffee and writing whatever she wrote. As he piggybacked Molly down the stairs, Ben heard the noise of the shower kicking off and the radio alarm in Karen's room. For all of them, this morning was like any other.

As for the rest of the world, the extent of its knowledge would become clear once Ben saw the morning paper. He had slept poorly, imagining several times that he heard the smack of the *Post-Dispatch* hitting the sidewalk, but each time it was too early. The next thing he knew, it was daylight and Molly was hollering from her crib.

On the phone, he had told Scott Marlin, cub reporter, that he hadn't yet figured out what was going on. This silenced the lad, whose inexperience left him bereft of follow-up questions that might have revealed more. Ben felt good about the tactic for about one minute, until he realized he could have gotten away with a straight denial, claiming that a mere bookkeeping error, discovered only later, had led him to summon Sergeant Klaus needlessly to his office. Still, Ben hadn't exactly confirmed the report, and that would weaken whatever Tommy Toronado had to say.

Or not. As he reached the bottom of the stairs, he imagined the wording: "GUESS WHO: He's the Nut King of St. Louis, his license plate says '4 GIRLZ,' and his secretary just skipped town with 250 K. That ain't peanuts, Ben!"

Susan had asked about Scott Marlin's call as Ben had carted groceries in from the van, but a mumble about a request for a letter of recommendation had satisfied her. Nobody else had phoned him, not even Detective Phillips. The evening had been eerily ordinary. Ben was struck by the fact that he could inhabit the house with the weight of his awful knowledge bearing down on him, and no one noticed a thing. Susan had gone to her study right after she had put Molly down—unusual behavior, suggesting her writing was going well. The kids wouldn't notice anything unless he bled from an open head wound. In their world he had multiple functions—banker, chauffeur, enforcer. Man in dire straights was not one of them.

But the secrecy would have to end this morning. He couldn't let his children trot off to school and get blindsided by some Toronado-reading classmate, or, more likely, by the child of some Toronado-reading Aberdeen gossip. Ben imagined the parent calling out as the kid was about to leave for school, "Hey, Junior, isn't one of the Hudnut kids in your class? Listen to this."

What Ben would tell them depended on what was in the paper. If Toronado didn't give the dollar amount, Ben could downplay the disaster. If he did give it, Ben's job would be tougher, but he could tell them it was just a business loss. It wouldn't affect any of them. He was almost beginning to see it that way himself. Why did it have to change anything? He was just a guy without significant personal savings. There were lots of people like that. Maybe not in this neighborhood, but . . .

"Get the paper," Molly said as she wriggled out of his arms. This was not a command but a statement about their next joint activity, a morning ritual he had introduced for the fun of it a few weeks earlier and was now a slave to. He tightened Molly's terry-cloth bathrobe. As he followed her out the door, he heard one of his other girls clatter down the stairs into the kitchen. He padded along behind Molly, the cold of the sidewalk penetrating his slippers. She grabbed the paper, dropped it, and grabbed it again.

Mort Samuelson's black BMW hove into view. Mort was a hugely successful lawyer specializing in trusts. Their morning schedules had already intersected like this once, and Mort had slowed and called out a greeting to Molly. But this morning he gave a curt wave behind a sealed window. Ben felt one wild spin of his house and yard around his body. He steeled himself and followed Molly, his eyes on the paper, which she dragged by its yellow plastic wrapper all the way up to the house.

As soon as the door banged closed behind him, Ben heard "Funnies!" from the kitchen.

"I called them first," Pam said.

"No, you didn't," said Karen.

"My mouth was full. You just didn't hear me."

"Karen called them," Andrea said calmly.

"Oh, the great judge," Pam said. "The wise one."

Molly, drawn to the acrimony, dropped the newspaper and rushed off to join her sisters. In the entryway, Ben slid the wrapper off the paper.

"Dad," Karen yelled, "you got the funnies?"

"A minute," Ben said. Tommy Toronado's column was in the

177

same section as the funnies. He took a deep breath and read. From beginning to end. It was the best news ever. Kudos, charity galas, celebrity sightings, divorces, and not a word about him. The bullet had whizzed over his head. Then a stab of fear hit him: he might be the subject of a full-length article. He began to search the whole paper, page by page.

"Dad?" Karen said.

"Hang on." He walked slowly, skimming and turning the pages, and when he reached the table he relinquished the paper section by section. When the last one left his hands, going to a frowning Andrea, he smiled. He was safe for the day.

All through breakfast, Ben pondered the meaning of Tommy Toronado's column. Perhaps as the deadline approached, the columnist didn't trust the research of a high-school intern. But if so, why hadn't Toronado called him? Lazy? Column full? Small potatoes? Maybe it *was* small potatoes. His secretary stole some money. So what? Why should that be in the paper? Or maybe the newspaper didn't run the story in any form because they knew something he didn't—something good. He wasn't sure what this might be, exactly, but it was still an inspiration to him. On the other hand, if the news was good, why hadn't Detective Phillips called him? Why hadn't he called him in any case?

"You okay?" Andrea said.

He looked at her. "Sure."

"You're just sitting there."

Ben picked up his bowl of Grape-Nuts and carried it from the table. "Not hungry," he said. His furtiveness made him feel like one of his kids.

But he got away with it. Ten minutes later, they were gone. They would be tucked in at their schools, insulated from the news. He began to clean up the kitchen.

"More toast," Molly yelled, and he grabbed the already-buttered slice from the breadboard. *Storytime* was on Channel 9. Ben put the toast on Molly's high-chair tray and looked at the TV. The story was about a baby locomotive named Tootle. A lady in an engineer's cap was reading from the book. Tootle went to locomotive school to learn important lessons like Whistle Blowing, Puffing Loudly When Starting, and Stopping for a Red Flag Waving. Tootle was a smart little locomotive, but he had trouble with one lesson: Staying on the Rails No Matter What. Tootle jumped off the tracks to chase a horse across a meadow. Tootle strayed after buttercups. Tootle wandered off and made daisy chains. Tootle didn't Stay on the Rails No Matter What. Tootle was a Fucking Loser.

Two hundred fifty thousand dollars.

Two hundred fifty thousand dollars.

Two . . . hundred . . . fifty . . . thousand . . .

Susan's footsteps thudded in the bedroom overhead. He heard the shower come on. What she knew, and didn't, made him think of other secrets, which made him think of Scott Marlin, which made him jump to his feet. "Jesus!" he yelled.

"Jesus!" yelled Molly.

Ben rushed into the kitchen. He could just possibly catch Andrea on her car phone. What he said to her about the embezzlement would be an unplanned mess, but it would still be better than letting her find out from Scott Marlin. How could he have not thought of that?

When he picked up the phone, he heard nothing. It was off the hook somewhere. Molly liked to play phone in his study and then leave the receiver dangling, but when he checked it, it was in place. He ran up the stairs to Pam's room. She kept her phone on the floor, amid her shirts, bras, and empty soda cans. As a result, she often kicked it off the hook, as she had done in this case, either late last night or early this morning. Ben hung it back up and tumbled down the stairs to call from the kitchen, in case Molly needed him.

The phone rang just as he was reaching for it. He took a breath and answered it.

"Ben Hudnut, please," a man's voice said.

"Speaking."

"Barney Schramm of the *Post-Dispatch*. I'm calling about the apparent embezzlement of funds from your business. Is this a good time for you to talk, sir?"

"No." So much for silence meaning good news.

"When is a good time to talk?"

"A week ago, when I could have prevented it."

The reporter seemed momentarily thrown. "What was the exact amount, sir?"

"Listen, this *is* a bad time. I'm watching my baby girl." To make it convincing, he yelled, "Just a minute, Molly. Just a minute, honey." Christ, he thought. He was turning into Pam.

"What?" Molly barked back. "What?"

"Call me at the office in an hour," Ben said.

"I'd like to make good use of that hour," the reporter said quickly. "This looks like it's going to get pretty big play in the paper, and I want to get as much as I can into the first story. I've got your secretary's name and address. I'll call her neighbors. Did she have any friends you can think of?"

"No. No friends. Call me at the office." Ben hung up. He heard the shower being turned off, followed by the *boing* of the shower door opening. The phone rang again.

"Ben. Stan Phillips. Has your phone been off the hook?"

"Yes. I'm sorry. I—"

"No matter. I just want to bring you up to date. We got plenty of prints from the Orson guy—I assume they're his, anyway—but no match with anything on file. We found a train schedule in

Roberta's apartment. It's possible they didn't fly out at all. They could have taken the Metrolink to the Amtrak station and left town that way. No passenger record, if they did. It's an annoyance. We also found some documents that shed light on things. Love letters from Roberta."

"To Orson?"

"To you, Ben. Forty or fifty of them. I take it you've never read them?"

"God, no."

"I should be so lucky. You never slept with her, did you?"

"Me? God, no."

"I didn't think so. The letters seem kind of . . . inaccurate. Ever come close?"

"No. I mean, well, she made a pass at me about ten minutes before she robbed me."

"What did you do?"

"Sat there."

"I see," said Phillips. He seemed to understand.

"The *Post* is calling." It felt good to share something with somebody.

"Us too. I was going to tell you. I won't mention the letters to anyone, though. They're too weird."

"Okay."

After a pause, Phillips said, "Hang in there." Then he said good-bye.

Ben hung up and took two steps toward the den before the phone rang again.

"Hello? Ben Hudnut, please. This is Tracy Aubuchon from the newsroom of—"

"No comment at all whatsoever ever," Ben said. He hit the switchhook, held it down a moment, and threw the receiver into a drawer. He staggered into the den. Molly was watching a story with a lady in it who kept saying "Tee hee hee." It made Ben want to kick the screen in. Molly's toast was on the floor. He scooped her out of her high chair and set her on the den couch.

Susan came into the kitchen, dressed in a soft sweater and jeans, rubbing her hair dry with a white towel.

"You've gotta hear this, honey," she said to him. "I forgot to tell you last night. Listen." She stepped into Molly's line of sight to the TV. "Hey, Molly, can you say 'Jonathan'?"

Distractedly, leaning to one side to see around her mother, Molly said, "Joffanan."

Susan laughed and turned to Ben. "Jeremy found a new rule. He's coming by later to test it some more. 'Joffanan' for 'Jonathan,' 'mesinin' for 'medicine,' and 'elfenen,' or something like that, for 'elephant.' Let me see if I can describe the rule. In a three-syllable word—"

"We're broke."

"What?"

"We're not really broke. We're just a lot worse off than we were yesterday. At this hour yesterday."

She stared at him. "What are you talking about?"

"We'll be able to bounce back, even if we don't get it back, which we probably won't, but we'll bounce back."

Now she was scared. His voice was dry, and he sounded crazy even to himself.

"Come into the living room," he said. "Sit down."

She did. And he told her.

&#10547;

It did not go well. He kept wanting to hurry on to the good parts, the reasons for hope. She could only dwell on the bad.

"Can you tell me," she said, each word sounding sharply tipped at the end, "what your thinking was in putting all that money into the business account? Can you run that by me again?"

"I wanted to help Andrea qualify for financial aid for college."

Susan stared at him blankly. The white towel was still draped around her shoulders. "Well, you've accomplished your goal," she said. She looked pale, a little sick.

He said, "I told you about it four years ago, when I first thought of it as a strategy."

"Four years ago?"

"I've mentioned it now and then since. You know what I wanted. Just to see if we could get a thousand or so for Andrea."

"But . . . why?"

"What do you mean why? The aid is there. I went after it."

"But you took all this other money—Jesus Christ, Ben, enough for two or three college educations—and you put it at risk."

"How the hell did I know it was at risk? It was in my business. Who would suspect Roberta? She was like a piece of furniture. How could I know she was a thief?"

"But for such a small amount of aid, which you didn't even know you could get in the first place, you took all our money, and—"

"What's this you crap? You've got me hanging out there all by myself. It was a joint decision."

"I don't remember. You're always talking about the business and money, and you're always moving things here and there and going on about tax consequences. I don't understand half the stuff you say."

"Oh, but now you do. Now you choose to listen and judge."

At this point, Molly began to agitate. The PBS station had switched from kids' shows to cooking shows, and Molly came running into the living room. Susan took her back into the den and stuck a *Tom and Jerry* tape into the VCR. Although the family fortune was in deep trouble, Molly's had decidedly improved for the moment. She rarely got to watch this much TV at one time.

When Susan returned to the living room, she said, "Go ahead. Let's get off this point. You were talking about the guy she met."

"Orson. I was done." Now it was time to tell her about Roberta's pass at him. The story all but threw Susan out of her chair.

"That bitch," she said. "What did you do?"

"I kind of pulled away. I indicated I wasn't interested."

"Indicated? What did you say?"

"Nothing."

"Nothing?"

Ben shrugged. "Not really."

"Jesus," she said under her breath.

When he told her that the theft would be written up in tomorrow's paper, she plunged to another level of gloom. He had to tell her twice about the loan from Art Talbot's bank.

"How about bankruptcy?" she said.

"Bankruptcy! What are you talking about? The business is a moneymaker. It's our bread and butter. It's our only hope."

"I just thought—"

"It's a ridiculous suggestion. How can you even think it?"

"Well, it's nothing to be ashamed of. People do it."

"You don't even know what bankruptcy is, do you? I'm not in debt. I'm not failing. I'm thriving. Don't you know that?"

"Okay. Fine. Drop it."

"I can't believe you'd suggest that."

"*Fine.* How about selling the business? Have you thought of that?"

"Christ," he said. "You've got fifty ideas and they're all bad. What would I do if I sold the business?"

"How would I know?"

"I'll tell you what I'd do. I'd start a business just like Crunch and grow it into its present size. That's what I would do. And the capital outlay required for a new business would use up every penny I got by selling the old one, plus it would fail, because it would have to compete directly against the successful business I spent twenty years building and stupidly sold. Isn't all of that obvious?"

"Look, I'm just throwing some ideas out, okay?"

"What am I supposed to do with them?"

"I don't know. You figure it out. Act on the good ones. How would I know?"

"It's easy to sit there and throw ideas out. You sit in a safe position and make little suggestions. You don't have to take the ultimate responsibility. You just lob stuff at me."

"What are you talking about?"

"And then," he said, "if it's a good idea and I act on it, you take the credit. If it's a good idea and I don't act—if we learn *later* it was a good idea—I get the blame. If I act and it's a bad idea, I get the blame." Ben laughed. The noise sounded strange to him. "The wife's got it made. She can't lose. The guy eats all the shit."

"You have no right to be mad at me about this. I'm the one who should be mad. Isn't this all your fault, basically?"

"Yes." It was easy to say. It was the truth. But in admitting this, he wasn't taking back a word of what he had said. He felt all of that deep in his bones.

"You should have been able to sense Roberta's feelings," Susan went on. Ben didn't know if she was citing a new blunder or elaborating on the basic one. "You should have done something about it. You should have sat her down and told her, 'Look, get over this or I'll have to let you go.' I'm not surprised. I've been telling you for years how she feels about you."

"You just did it!" he said. He was almost happy. "That's a perfect example. All these years you've sat there and thrown out this stuff about Roberta, and I didn't act on it, so now it's all my fault. If you really believed it, why didn't you *insist* I do something?"

"Fine. Yell at me. Whatever."

"Don't you see? It's all on me, all the time. You just throw stuff—"

"Will you for Christ's sake stop saying that? I'll throw stuff, all right." She looked to the window and closed her eyes against the bright morning light. She became aware of the towel still around her shoulders and slowly stroked her hair with it. She turned back to Ben. "You shouldn't be mad at me. Be mad at Roberta. Why aren't you?"

"Because it's my fault. My mistake."

"But she's the thief. She stole it."

Ben shook his head. "It's my fault. Anybody else's role is insignificant. Including yours." He rubbed his eyes with the heels of his hands.

Susan gave him a long look. "You talked about a loan. When can you get it?"

"It's on its way. Thirty thousand dollars. From my good friend, Art Talbot."

Susan flickered a smile. She scooted forward and reached for his hands. He lifted them for her. They didn't seem to be part of him. Susan said, "I'm thinking of Andrea right now. She's earned the right to go to whatever college she wants to. No matter what it takes, we can still make that possible, one way or another. That's what we'll do. I want your promise on that."

"Promise."

"We've got the business. You're right about that. It'll be okay. You'll work like a dog. You can do it. It's twenty years ago all over again."

Ben thought back to that time. His mind seemed to be working

186

in slow motion. Or was Susan's just working extra fast? "It's not quite that bad."

"You're right. And that's good. It's a solid, established business, and you know it backward and forward. Crunch will save us. I'll take Roberta's place until you hire someone. I can do that again. We'll find a sitter for Molly. We'll bounce back."

Ben rose from the couch and, with his hands holding Susan's, encouraged her to rise so that he could hug her. As he took her in his arms, he was more than a little surprised to see George and Wendy Marlin, stone-faced, coming up the front walk to the house. Neither had set foot on their property in eleven years.

Susan sensed his tension and pulled her head back to look at him. "What is it?" She turned to the window. "My God," she said. "I wonder what they want. They look miserable." She headed for the front door.

"Susan!" Ben blurted out.

"What?" she said, frowning in the entryway. Her hand was on the doorknob.

"I don't want you to learn from them or anyone else, so I'm going to tell you now. Eleven years ago—"

A new figure appeared in the window, coming from Ben's right. He had come up the stairs from the driveway and was beginning to cross the patio toward the front door. It was Jeremy. He was whistling and snapping his fingers.

Susan had already opened the door. The Marlins were still a few steps away. Ben, standing near the window, could see everyone—Susan inside, the others outside. He could see everything with perfect clarity.

"Eleven years ago I slept with Wendy Marlin. Five times. Andrea found out last month. That's what she was so upset about. I don't want you to find out from someone else, like she did." Even in the midst of this emergency, with his wife's mouth working

187

soundlessly, Ben realized he was guilty of another lapse: he hadn't called Andrea after all, and Scott would shock her with the embezzlement news. And another: the Marlins, having learned from their son about the embezzlement, were here not because of the affair, but as old friends, to offer solace. He wanted to grab all his words and stuff them back in his mouth.

"*Oh God!*" The three visitors, now at the door, rocked back on their heels from the force of Susan's cry. She ran up the stairs.

"Ben," George called, trying to see inside. "We got wind of your terrible news. We tried to call. Is there anything we can do?"

Ben went to the front door and looked blankly at the threesome.

"We just wanted to tell you how sorry we are," Wendy said. "We're just very sorry."

Behind the Marlins, Jeremy seemed to be fishing for something to say. He was coming up short.

Ben thanked them one and all for coming and closed the door on them.

# 18

*Oh God!*

What was going on? Cook didn't see Susan's face—only the back of her head as she whirled away from the door. Her outcry, all by itself, suggested a horrible tragedy, but Ben's face was part of the picture too, and it modified Cook's interpretation. Ben's reticence, his eagerness to be rid of the intruders, his embarrassment—all these told Cook the ancient story of marital blood being shed. Ben's face said, "You don't want to be here now." He was right.

His fieldwork momentarily on hold, Cook drove back to his apartment. His rent check was due, but the time was still well before Delong's stingy hours of operation. He went up the stairs and to his desk, where he took a first step aimed at data collection for the other linguistic project in his life: he called Show-Me Cablevision.

A simple sequence of events had led to this act. Earlier, as

Cook was leaving the apartment, Paula's father had phoned for her. Cook impressed upon him that Paula had a phone in her office at Buford U. He did this as diplomatically as possible, though he was certainly no match for the master himself. The two men made some offerings to the God of Chat, but the smoke didn't rise and they said good-bye. The call had come from Rome, but as Cook drove to Ben and Susan's, he thought about Bert's D.C. home. Cook remembered his visit there as one long withdrawal into the guest room, where he watched cable TV, mainly C-SPAN. He remembered seeing conservatives speaking at conferences and in panel discussions, and it occurred to him that this was exactly what he needed: conservatives preaching to the faithful, their language unchecked by fear of giving offense. He had recently sampled conservatives on the broadcast channels, but these spoke to all of North America, not just to their studio audiences. Since C-SPAN had a tiny audience, watching it was just like being there and eavesdropping. C-SPAN was a linguist's heaven.

Now, in pursuit of a hookup, Cook spent the next twenty minutes on the phone with the cable lady, who must have worked from a form as complicated as a grant proposal. She kept throwing obstacles in his way. Had he secured his landlord's permission for the hookup? Did he want any of the countless premium channels? Was his TV cable-ready, or did he need a box? At one point he cried out, "I just want to watch right-wingers say obnoxious things!" Apparently there was no such category of cable user on her order form.

After he hung up, he fished through his domestic file folder in the hall closet and found the receipt for the TV he and Paula had bought a year earlier at Badger Electronics in Stoughton, Wisconsin. At the bottom of the receipt was scribbled "Ralph." This was his "dealer"—the person in his life who, according to the cable lady, could tell him if his TV was cable-ready and possibly save him the three-ninety-five monthly surcharge for "the box."

Ralph was equal to the task. "That puppy is cable-ready, Jeremy, and anybody who says otherwise is lying." So it was back to Show-Me Cablevision, but Cook got a different woman, a tough cookie who brooked no contradiction. She read from the official cable-unready list, which damned Cook's TV. So it was back to Ralph, who whistled with respect at Show-Me's dogged pursuit of Cook's three-ninety-five. "They're playin' hardball," he said, adding that he was looking at a TV just like Cook's, right now, right there in front of him, and he was looking at the mount for the feed.

"Are those the key words?" said Cook. "If I say them to the cable lady, will she say, 'Oh! It's got a mount for the feed!' and will everything be all right?"

"Well, now you're asking me to make a prediction, Jeremy. I can't do that. I can't make a prediction."

Cook, fortified nonetheless, called and got another Show-Me lady, one who was sweet but deadly, with intimidating syntax. She commended Cook for his research, then pointed out that if he had a VCR, as she suspected he did, he should know that most users put the VCR between the cable line and the TV, which meant that the question of his TV's cable-readiness was superseded by this question: Was his VCR cable-ready? Cook, out of ammo, retreated and said he would get back to her. He felt like Rip Van Winkle. When had watching TV become so complicated?

Delong's jazz began to irritate his feet through the floorboards. He wrote a rent check and went downstairs with it. The store's inventory seemed unchanged since his last visit. It reminded him of the playthings in "Little Boy Blue," which stood in faithful readiness long after the kid bought the farm. Stepping lively to some sort of vibes–snare drum duo, Cook made his way past the jewelry cases into a logjam of cabinetry, squeezing past the Victorian

Rococo Rosewood Chest ($1,490), the Federal Armchair with Chamfered Stiles ($810), and an unlabeled, unpriced narrow pine wardrobe. This he nudged in passing, causing one of its doors to creak open. He waited to see if a corpse would topple out, then moved on.

As he neared Delong's office, the jazz piece gave way to the disc jockey naming the performers responsible. The list seemed to feature lots of men named Eddie. Accompanying this was Delong's Brahmin voice, reciting a list of a different sort:

"Seventy-one thirty-nine Dartmouth, nine-thirty. Sixty-one seventy Pershing, nine-fifty. Three oh three three Nordic at ten-fifteen . . ." Cook guessed they were addresses of estate sales, though the times seemed odd. Maybe Delong had private appointments.

Delong broke off with a start when he saw Cook at the office door. "I'll get back to you," he said into the phone, and he hung up.

"Sorry to interrupt," Cook said.

Delong gave an aristocratic cock of an eyebrow.

"Do you have any glass unicorn collectibles?" Cook said.

Delong shut his eyes and gave a quick headshake.

"Too bad. Here's the rent. It's a day late. Sorry."

Delong took Cook's check.

"One other thing. I'd like to have cable service brought into our apartment. I'll need your signature when I get the form."

Delong became engaged. He had been leaning back in his wooden chair, but now he brought his weight forward and planted his feet flat on the floor. "Out of the question."

Cook hadn't expected this. "They just drill a little hole—"

"Those people rape buildings. I won't have them assaulting my property. No Delong property will ever endure that."

"I'll patch up the hole afterward, when we move out."

Delong laughed and gestured to his furniture. "What if I took that approach to my pieces? Drilled holes and patched them up. Wouldn't that detract from their value in your eyes?"

"I'm the wrong person to ask," Cook said. "Look, it's for my work. I just want the C-SPAN channel."

Delong raised his hands. "What you watch in the privacy of your apartment is your own affair."

"I just—"

"The structure itself is *my* affair. I will not have my structure penetrated by the tools of crass popular culture." The phone rang. Before answering it, Delong raised both eyebrows to ask if there was anything else. Cook hated the way he was able to talk with his face.

"*No*," said Cook. "The answer is *no*. There's nothing else."

To cleanse his mind, Cook put his lust for cable on hold, went back to his desk, and took out his several pages of notes on Molly's speech. As he leafed through them, he saw three pronunciations that were clearly related. He wrote them down along with the adult targets:

tomato > pomato
Rebecca > pabecca
balloon > paboon

The words all had an unstressed first syllable. In such an environment, reduction of different sounds to a common one—in this case of the three initial consonants to "p"—was a common occurrence in language. But if that were the only operative rule, the third word should have been "palloon," not "paboon." An additional rule seemed to govern the initial consonant of the *stressed* syllable: it had to be bilabial.

How to test it? He could sit around with Molly and wait for

more examples, or he could elicit. But there were severe vocabulary constraints with a two-year-old. He leaned back in his chair and went on a search through her vocabulary—that is, through her world as he knew it. He came up with two possible examples. She almost certainly knew the word "banana," which his rule predicted as "pamana." And since Susan sometimes put barrettes in her hair, she probably had that word, which would be "pabette."

He couldn't wait any longer. He dialed Susan and Ben's number, realizing as it rang that the battle might still be raging. He was relieved to get their answering machine. He left a simple message asking that they call him at their convenience.

⌇

That night over lentil soup and a sourdough baguette, Cook and Paula talked about their day. At least they started that way. Then, without warning, the topic broadened. Paula's conference, a mere month away, was all set up. Ted still wasn't talking to her, but he didn't need to. His files were well organized, and she was helming like a true heterosexual. She had lunched with the Buford twins at the faculty club and listened to scintillating stories about their pet dogs. The Bufords lived a plain life in the rural house where they had grown up, hoarding their share of the Buford wealth, occasionally donating it to groups but often yanking it back if conditions dictated—"if they don't do right by us." Cook wasn't sure which of the twins had said this. Paula drawled the imitation without attribution. Her disdain for them made Cook wonder just where they ranked on her new scale based on "excellence in all things."

Cook told Paula about catching Ben and Susan at an awkward moment and about his chat with Delong. He was just warming to the subject of Delong when she asked why on earth he wanted cable in the apartment. For the news and educational channels, he said. "For *ideas*—something Delong doesn't care about. There are no ideas in his 'pieces,' as he calls them."

"He's not nearly as unpleasant as you make him out to be," she said. "He offered to give a free appraisal of my grandmother's opal necklace. That was nice. And he's very successful."

"That's another reason to hate him. I prefer the company of failures. Cheerful failures."

Paula laughed. "When you choose a doctor, is that your policy? You'd pick a surgeon with the highest failure rate?"

Cook helped himself to another bowl of soup and struggled to address this nontrivial challenge. "I'm talking about attitude. The guy who has failed doesn't think he's better than other people."

"Successful people are proud of their success," Paula said matter-of-factly. "What's wrong with a little pride?"

"Joe's pride is Bill's shame. No pride, no shame. I want all of life to be neutral. Achievement should mean nothing except for the goodies it brings—comfort, travel, and such like. Failure should mean nothing except you're less comfortable, you've got to take the bus, you read *National Geographic* instead of traveling, and so on. The government, of course, needs to take care of failures. Otherwise they'll be *too* uncomfortable. They need food, clothing, shelter, education, health care, and cable TV, but just one outlet."

"If some people," Paula said, her lips tightening strangely, "by virtue of their talent and hard work, achieve something of value, they deserve praise. Period."

"Not really," Cook said cheerfully. "They're just pursuing their own interests. Do you praise a lion for bringing down a wildebeest? They're just doing what they're programmed to do."

"But praise is an incentive. It helps society push forward."

"First"—Cook had no idea where he was going, but he had the

195

feeling there would be more than one stop on the way—"I don't care if society pushes forward. Everyone ought to slow down. Second, if you take away the praise, enough people will still strive for the goodies I mentioned, so society will progress anyway. Third, even if we agree in principle that praise has a purely encouraging function, we lose sight of that. If we say 'You're terrific' enough times, we end up believing it. But nobody's terrific. Praise the product, not the producer."

"The producer *deserves* praise."

Cook shook his head. "Hotshots become hotshots by virtue of the body and brains they were born with and the personal history that rains down on them."

"You're saying *they* are products."

Cook hesitated. He didn't know if agreeing would hurt or help his argument. "Yes."

"Fine," said Paula. "I praise hotshots—or *achievers*, as I prefer to call them—I praise them for being products who produce good products." She seemed happy with her conclusion.

Cook mulled this over until he heard the crescendoing hoof-beats of a distinction coming to rescue him. "I was wrong to rule out praise. Praise is fine. But not pride. No *product* can be proud. It's a ridiculous notion."

Paula looked thoughtful for a long while, and then she gave a quick headshake and resumed eating. It was the gesture of one who deeply wanted to be asked to say what she had ostentatiously just decided not to say.

Cook bit. "What were you going to say?"

"That it all sounds like rationalization."

"Mmm. Are you calling me a failure?"

She took a long moment to swallow her soup. "I must admit my heart sank when you talked about getting cable. You can't spend the rest of your life in this apartment, Jeremy."

"I'm doing things," he said, his voice letting him down a little. "I'm working with Molly. I'm writing this other thing for the conference."

"Which you won't even tell me about."

"It's too early. You know what that's like."

"I just . . ." She held her hands out as if they supported something weighty. "I have a plan, a life plan, an ambitious one, and it's disturbing to hear you discount ambition. I feel we're on different tracks."

"Is teaching at Buford part of your plan?"

She recoiled. "I must have really hurt your feelings. That was very nasty. I'm supporting you right now, you know."

"And I supported you last year, with my savings from six years of work."

"Fair enough. But what happens after this year? We'll be even. My debt will be paid."

He didn't recoil, but he did frown.

"Actually," she said as she rose and collected her dishes, "I couldn't have hurt your feelings. In your view there's nothing wrong with being a failure. Right? In fact, it's a positive thing. Right?"

# 19

Ralph the Badger burst out laughing. "What the hell?"

"Just bear with me, Ralph." Cook was in Paula's office, joining telephonic battle. "I want you to tell the cable people directly that my VCR is cable-ready. If *I* tell them, they'll say it's on a special list or something like they did with my TV, and I'm caught in the old runaround."

"I'm not giving you any runaround."

"Of course you're not, Ralph. You've been wonderful. It's the cable people. They're driving me nuts."

"Yeah. They get you comin' and goin'."

"Exactly. So can you bear with me?"

"Sure. What the hell. Go for it."

"Back in a flash."

Cook parked Ralph. In the bold new vocabulary of Buford University's Galacto 9 Phone System, one didn't put a caller on hold. One "parked" him. Cook accomplished this by first hitting the button mysteriously labeled "TAP," followed by "*" and "44," and then hanging up. He was confident in his strokes because he had spent a good hour hunched over the Galacto 9 guide spread open before him on Paula's desk. Its complexity was dizzying. When had phones turned into Hydras? Why hadn't Paula warned him the night before, when he had asked if he could use her equipment to make this conference call? To hell with her, he thought. And to hell with Delong. Cook was focused. He would get that cable line into his apartment even if it killed him.

He called Show-Me Cablevision and explained to the woman that he yearned for cable installation but that he wasn't sure if his VCR, a Perfector QC, was cable-ready.

"Let me see, Mr. Cook. Oh, here it is on our list. It's *not* cable-ready. You'll need a box."

Cook suppressed a snort. "My dealer says it's cable-ready."

"It's on our list, sir. Perhaps he was thinking of a different Perfector model."

"How about if I let the two of you talk?"

"Pardon?"

"I've got him on the line. I can connect you."

"Well . . ."

"Look, you answer the phone by saying, 'How may I help you?' I'm telling you how. I'd like to connect you. His name is Ralph."

"Very well," she said curtly.

Cook shot her with "TAP + * + 44 + HANG UP" and allowed himself a quick bark of laughter. He had a physical sense of the situation. Ralph the Badger was in one wing of a house, the cable lady was in another wing, and Cook, dressed in a butler's suit, was bustling to and fro between them.

The phone rang. Cook jumped in his chair. How could it ring now? Was Ralph calling him back? How would he know how to do that? Cook gingerly picked up the phone and said hello.

"Paula?" a woman's voice said.

"She's not here," Cook snapped. "Call back in an hour."

"Who's this?" the woman demanded.

"Phone repair. Stay off the line."

"Oh. Sorry." The woman hung up.

Cook wondered if the interruption had ruined everything. To check, he dialed the three-digit code that would take him back to Badger Electronics. "Ralph? Are you there?"

"This is Ralph," he said a little tiredly.

"Good man," Cook said. "I've got the cable lady. I'm going to bi-link you now."

"I can hardly wait."

Cook parked Ralph all over again. He looked at the Galacto 9 guide and reviewed the steps to bi-link the two calls. First he would have to shift the cable lady from park to link-park. Then he would do the same to Ralph. Then he would bi-link the two link-parked calls. But he couldn't just let them talk to each other. He would have to be there too: he would have to tri-link with the already bi-linked calls. An error at any point would be fatal. He scooted his chair forward and initiated the process, feeling like an astronaut performing a prelaunch sequence. He easily imagined himself, with the push of the last button, being shot through the window into the blue sky.

As soon as he completed step one of the procedure, the phone rang again. Was this the phone's way of saying "Nice job," or was it another intruder? He picked it up.

"Is Dr. Nouvelles there?"

"No," said Cook. "She's in surgery." He laughed at his own joke and hung up. It was a subtle joke, indeed not a very good one: Cook found the doctoral form of address ridiculous for Ph.D.s. For that matter, he found it ridiculous for physicians too.

He attacked the phone buttons and put Ralph in the land of

link-park, where he hoped the cable lady still was. As far as he knew, they weren't together yet, but he couldn't be sure. He no longer felt like a butler on the same floor—more like a basement captive, shouting up at concrete slabs.

The last punch of the bi-linking series was "TAP." An instant before he hit it, the phone rang again, going off like an overstimulated organ. Cook hit "TAP," and the phone stopped ringing. Now it was time to tri-link with Ralph and the cable lady. He began the process, as uncertain of success as if he were about to insert himself into an already established sexual union. He punched two buttons, lifted the receiver, and clicked the switchhook twice.

"Hello?" he said.

". . . ever buy those kind. They pinch. Yeah, I'm still waiting for him to come back." It was the cable lady, but in a relaxed condition. Cook heard other women's voices in the background.

"Hello?" he said.

"Some man who talks real fast. He seemed sorta high-strung. Don't those kind pinch?"

"Hello?"

"They pinch *me*."

"I'll get back to you!" Cook shouted, as if volume were the issue. But there was obviously no connection between his voice and her ears. He hung up, picked up, and clicked twice.

"Hello?" said Cook.

". . . guy's got me on hold while he calls them."

"Hello? Ralph?"

"Thinks he can beat the fuckin' system." There was a chorus of hearty male laughter.

Cook slammed the phone down. He had the sensation he was rolling in a gigantic kaleidoscope, tumbling head over heels on the jagged rocks. He picked up the receiver and clicked twice.

This time there was nothing but air whooshing at him. In a rage, he hit numbers at random, thrilling to the jangle of tones. He ranged far and wide, and he didn't neglect "TAP" either. He settled on three keys in a row, rolling out a descending triplet again and again.

*"You have m-two m-new messages. Press m-one if you wish to hear them."*

"M-what the fuck?" shouted Cook.

*"You have m-two m-new messages. Press m-one if you wish to hear them."*

He had stumbled into a voice mailbox. Paula's? He hit the "1" button.

"Hello? Dr. Nouvelles? This is Mavis Necker? I like your class and everything, but I'm going to have to drop it? I put the drop slip in your mailbox for you to sign? I'll call back? Thank you."

Cook imagined Satan greeting Mavis Necker at the door of perdition, where she had gone at Cook's recommendation: "Welcome to hell, Mavis? You're here because you talk like this?"

A second beep sounded.

"Paula, it's Dad. I think I've finally found a way to pull it off. It's been an ordeal, and I've certainly endured my share of Mediterranean smirks from the people I've broached the subject with, but here's what it boils down to. If you really want to contrive a way to annul your marriage, we can simply claim we bought the wrong stamps for the certificate. Do you remember how I had to dash out to a tobacconist's on the Via Veneto at the last minute? That's where they're sold—at tobacco shops. I bought the stamps in a rush and slathered them onto the certificate, and that made it legal. It's plausible that I could have bought the wrong ones. It's so plausible, in fact, that it helps me live with the white lie we're telling. So here's what I suggest. Write me a letter—we'll want a paper trail, of course—in which you casually mention that you

202

were looking at your marriage certificate and you noticed the stamps didn't seem right. I'll check my records and—shocked! shocked!—I'll write back telling you your marriage is technically invalid. *If* you are sure this is what you want to do. Your mother and I have discussed this into the wee hours over many nights, and we feel we understand the reasons for your approach to the problem. Of course, we've always had reservations about Jeremy himself—enough said on that score. What we've had to struggle with is your desire to annul the marriage rather than simply get a divorce. But we've come to appreciate the desire for a clean slate, a blemish-free record. In all other respects, your life has been perfect—'excellent in all ways,' as I think you put it—and I can see why you would want to keep it that way. In the future, if someone asks if you've ever been married, you won't have to go into a long explanation. So, dear, if you want to go ahead, I'll be happy to cooperate. Just send me that letter. Until then—oh, one more thing. Be prepared for some minor practical ramifications. If you filed a joint tax return this year, you're going to have to file an amended return. I don't know your financial situation intimately, but you weren't teaching last year, and Jeremy's earnings were no doubt negligible, so the tax consequences couldn't be too great. Call if you want to talk about any of this again. I love you, and I look forward, as I know you do, to the time when this gross error in judgment is behind you."

—

"Here's what it sounds like to me, Jeremy. You characterize yourself in your younger days as something of an asshole."

"That's right."

"And Paula as something of a bitch."

"I'm not sure about that, actually."

"Whoa. She's a bitch now, isn't she?"

"Definitely."

"Well, you know what Faulkner says: 'Once a bitch, always a bitch.' *Ergo*, she was a bitch when you met her. So, asshole meets bitch, asshole courts bitch, but bitch is cool to him."

"Yes."

"Then, asshole changes."

"Yes. I did change to win her. I did."

"Bitch now wants ex-asshole."

"Does she know—"

"That he's changed? Doesn't matter. The point is—"

"She's still a bitch."

"Exactly. Ex-asshole marries bitch, ends up in deep confusion because they now inhabit different moral planes. And you know the old saying."

"'You can't save a marriage with a bitch in it.'"

"A *fortiori* in this case, because bitch intends to rewrite history. If the plan succeeds, ex-asshole, *mirabile dictu*, will become an ex-husband."

"One question. Why the Latin?"

"Comes with the territory. Logical rigor."

Cook had this interesting conversation with himself as he drove, erratically, from Buford U. back to the apartment. He had begun the dialogue as an open-ended exercise to see where it might lead. He was stunned by the speed with which he had raced to cold clarity.

He felt like a chump. He was a good enough linguist to determine from language—in this case Paula's father's—whether a topic was old or new. This sucker was positively antediluvian. She must have been trying to erase him for months. But when he tried to go back and find a point from which she must have started, he couldn't. There was seamless continuity from the day they married to the present moment. What cool self-possession she had.

She was Ray Milland in *Dial M for Murder*. She was plotting spousal elimination.

As he pulled to a stop in front of the apartment, another thought struck him, hitting him full in the face like a cold stick of Volpi salami: where did that diplomatic weenie come off calling Cook's earnings from last year "no doubt negligible"?

His legs quaked as he climbed the wooden stairs, and he had to stop on the balcony—shaking with rage or fear, he couldn't say which. He did not know what to do, how to be. Thus armed with ambiguous resolve, he threw open the door.

"Got to go now," he heard from her study. Her door was slightly ajar. "Ciao, Papa." She came out and gave him a flicker of acknowledgment. "Been here long?"

"Nope."

"I was just talking to Dad. He says hi. Did your conference call go okay?"

Cook felt a blur before his eyes. He said nothing.

Paula went into the kitchen and opened the refrigerator door. "Do you want to hear about *my* day?"

"Fuck no," he said. With that, it would begin.

"It went pretty well, all in all."

She must have banged something in the refrigerator at the precise moment he had spoken. Either that, or he had crossed over into a realm of utter insignificance. She lugged a big pot out of the refrigerator and set it on the stove. She fired up the burner.

"Only one bad thing with a student happened, which I think is a record. I was in the middle of a call with Susumo, and this student barges in waving an exercise that I'd given him a 'C' on. You know what I'm beginning to think 'C' stands for? 'Complain.' I tell him I'm on the phone. He tells me I'm in the middle of an office hour—he had me there, the shit—so I ask Susumo to give me a second so we can go over it. I've got Susumo Shumatso at MIT on hold so I can talk with a goddamn student!" She took a wooden spoon from a drawer and stirred the soup pot. "We start talking about the exercise—arguing, really—and the next thing I know, Johann's knocking on my door. He tells me the secretary says I've got an emergency call. I immediately thought of the Buford twins and that something terrible had happened, that they were pulling out or something. Then I realized Johann was faking it, rescuing me. His office is right across the hall, and he must have heard us arguing. So I chase the student out and get back to Susumo and we're back in business. The only problem is, when I finished the call and stepped out in the hall, the shit was standing there with a smirk on his face. He says, 'Are you done with your emergency?' It made me realize I'd been talking loudly and laughing—hell, I was enjoying the call, *as I had a right to*. So he comes back into the office and we're at each other's throats for half an hour. That was fun, I'll tell you." She set her jaw. "I didn't give an inch. I refuse to coddle. Through four years of college and five years of graduate school, no one coddled me. I didn't have it easy, so why should they? He threatened to go over my head and file a grievance. Let him, the shit. I'll take him on." She looked at Cook for the first time. "So, tell me about your day."

Cook turned away. In hearing this tale, he had identified completely with the student. He hung up his coat, then returned to the kitchen. Paula was setting out soup bowls on the table.

"'I didn't have it easy, so why should they?'" he said. "Is this humane social policy? Why not 'I didn't have it easy, and no one else should suffer the way I did'?"

"Please don't start on that theme again. Ooh, you'll want to read this." She picked up a newspaper from the counter next to the stove. "It's about Ted's brother-in-law. His secretary stole a quarter of a million dollars from the business. The Nut King of St. Louis has had his nuts cut off."

# 20

Cook called that night and again the next day, but all he got was Karen's sweet greeting on the answering machine. He left no message. Finally, in the afternoon, while Paula was off romping on some indoor court with Sherry, he tried again.

Susan answered. Cook had no idea how she would take his calling. Who was he, after all? Where did he rank in their circle? Down low, certainly. Nonetheless, he offered his condolences. It felt strange to do it—to treat the loss of money like a death. He had never engaged in this particular speech act.

Susan thanked him with surprising warmth. "It's changed everything, to put it mildly," she said.

"How?" said Cook.

"I hate everybody. That's quite a change. I'm sick of people saying, 'Oh, Susan, I don't know what to say!' Am I supposed to comfort them because words fail them?" She said all this with accelerating tempo. More slowly, she said, "They're enjoying it, Jeremy."

"No."

"Some of them. They're getting off on it. People like having victims around—for entertainment, for something to talk about. At dinner last night, Karen asked Ben out of the blue why he'd had so much cash in the business. *Cash*. She doesn't know what cash is, in that sense. She got it from some fourth-grade friend, who got it from her parents. People are pricks."

"I agree."

"Pam's furious. She's not talking to Ben at all. It's hardest for her, because of her age. She has no consciousness *except* self-conciousness. The attention is torture to her."

"How about Andrea?"

"Well, first she felt terrible for Ben and furious at Roberta. That's Ben's secretary, the bitch who stole our money. I've had her under this roof hundreds of times. Don't get me going on her."

"I won't."

"She had a thing for Ben. She's crazy. Don't get me started."

"Okay."

"Anyway, once she got over her anger—Andrea, I mean—she told us she was worried about college. We assured her we'd do whatever it takes to see she can go where she wants to."

"I'm sure you will."

"Since then she's been strangely calm. I can't figure out what she's thinking."

"Is there anything I can do?" Cook said.

"Actually, for a while I thought there might be. I told Ben I would jump back into work with him. I helped him years ago. I thought we could schedule you when Ben needed me. I'm not being very clear. What I mean is—"

"I baby-sit Molly while I observe her. Sure. It sounds great."

"Ben wouldn't hear of it. He gave me all sorts of reasons. He said he wants Molly to be with me. It's nothing against you. He just says I'm the best for her. He says the business has changed too much for me to be useful at work, and he doesn't want to take the time to train me. It's easier for him to take everything on—so he says. He's there all the time now. Last night he didn't get home till two in the morning. He's punishing himself. He's wearing himself out, and he's had some dizzy spells. He had one last night and had to pull the car over until it passed. I'm making him go see a doctor. He says it's just worry—right after he tells me not to worry. He keeps saying we'll be okay as long as nothing goes wrong. Nothing else, that is. He's applied for another loan—he already got one, but it's just sustaining us. We've still got no cushion. He'll feel better when that's settled." She made an odd noise. "It's funny. Here I am talking about money to you. I guess I feel our finances are public property or something. The sad thing for Ben is the way it's set him back just when he was about to leap forward."

"The cashew venture?"

"That's one of the things, one of the leaps. It's out of the question now. He really wanted to do something new." Susan paused. "Actually, me too."

"You're very supportive."

"I mean *I* want to do something new. I just sent my manuscript out." She laughed almost devilishly.

"Really? That's exciting."

"I thought I was a ways from completing it, but I was just over-polishing it. Polishing the polish. So it's out in the world."

"Good luck." Cook asked after Molly and the other children, then realized she had already talked about them. They said goodbye. He hung up feeling pretty good about the call, but less good about his access to Molly. The household, still sore from its injury,

209

seemed to be resisting intrusion of any kind. He would have to wait, even though Molly's rules could change overnight.

～

Three days later, notebook in hand, Cook watched a congressional committee discuss banking. He watched a call-in show and listened to deeply layered questions from Norman in Novato and Hattie in Tallahassee. He watched conferences open, build, climax, taper off, and adjourn. The last was the best part, for the camera at the rear of the room would remain rigidly fixed on the departing audience, as if its operator had long before slumped to the floor, while, to the strains of Vivaldi, women straightened their skirts and men shook their parts free. It was experimental cinema, surely.

Yes, he was hooked up! And yes, conservatives spoke, but no, they produced nothing useful for his paper, not yet anyway. He did notice something new though. Conservatives were never funny. Their material was bad, their delivery as lame as Quasimodo. It was pulpit humor, only worse—they were ministers on a bad day. He hoped this would make it into his paper, which Paula, his partner in all things, had scheduled for twelve-thirty P.M. on the first day of the conference.

He was a little nervous about it. The analysis he had in mind didn't belong to any recognized field of linguistics, and linguists never cut anyone any slack. At the last conference he had attended, he had heard one presenter declare that while there were many languages in which two negatives made a positive, there were no languages anywhere in the world in which two positives made a negative—a statement immediately met by a derisive "Yeah, yeah" from the rear of the audience. The auditorium rocked with laughter.

The cable installer had done the deed that morning, one day

after Cook had hand-delivered his request for installation with Delong's signature forged—and the "Box required?" question answered "yes," but Cook had gotten back at them by pressing really hard with his pen and tearing the form. The installer, who clomped in his boots and jingle-jangled in his tool belt like a modern-day cowboy, arrived early enough to avoid discovery by Delong, just as Cook had requested. But then he recklessly aimed his drill right next to the rear door to Delong's office, where the electric and phone lines entered the building. Delong often used this door and would have spotted the penetration immediately. Cook called a halt. The installer, bushy of beard and sallow of skin, rested his horror-movie drill on his shoulder and eyed Cook closely, some would say cruelly. Cook urged him around the corner to a less visible spot; the man grunted but went along with Cook's wishes. When he was done, Cook checked for telltale signs and picked up a few scraps of cable from the ground. He would have eaten the sawdust, if necessary.

This installation was a briefly vivifying event in the melancholy days following Cook's discovery of Paula's murder plot—now unfolding, evidently. He had seen the envelope addressed to her father on the kitchen counter on Monday morning—the first document in her paper trail. Cook had asked if she had said anything particular to her father, since they usually talked on the phone instead of corresponding. Her "no" sounded as if it had been expelled by the Heimlich maneuver. She went on to say she felt letter writing was a dying art, and she, for one, would fight that trend—another blow struck for excellence in all things, no doubt. In another week or two, her father's "answer" to her "question" about the suspected "irregularities" in the certificate would arrive, ending their "marriage." Significantly, neither Paula's decision to go ahead with this plot nor his secret knowledge of it had had the slightest effect on the way they talked to each other.

As for why he stayed on, why he silently endured her company, why he didn't do something wonderful like barge into her class-room and tell her students that she called them "shits": he needed her. Not for sex, although that continued, oddly enough. It was now such a purely physical act that Cook easily constructed an imaginary scenario to explain it: an accident had put them both in a coma, in the same wing of a hospital, and a sympathetic nurs-ing staff secretly brought them together after hours and steered their sexual intercourse.

No, it wasn't for sex that he stayed on. She had her secrets, but he had his too.

A week and a half later, shortly before noon, amid the lackluster mail that plopped through Cook's letter slot came an envelope containing two tickets to the high school production of *Our Town*, along with a short note from Andrea saying she hoped he could come. The performance was scheduled for a Saturday two weeks distant, the same day as Paula's conference. The two P.M. curtain time was just late enough for Cook to make it after giving his twelve-thirty paper. Paula, who did not love life, would not be attending.

When the mail came, Cook was watching C-SPAN, as he had been doing all morning, with Paula frequently yelling from her study for him to turn it down while he yelled "Sorry" with-out moving from the couch. Now he turned it off to go get a haircut in order to look his best in two weeks. Where he went, he needed a generous recovery period. At the Nifty Barber College, haircuts were free and often painful. He liked subjecting his ap-pearance to the unknown every two or three months. It was always a new face, a new pair of trembling hands. Some time ago, well before Paula hatched her murder plot and such things were still worth talking about, she addressed the issue of their empty social life by saying, "You don't like anybody or anything—all you like is bad haircuts and empty restaurants." A bit unfair, that. Sometimes the haircuts weren't too bad at all.

He went to the hall closet, grabbed his parka—the cranberry one that Paula hated and often asked him to throw out—and went down the stairs. He would have to pass Delong's front door, which made him a little nervous. Earlier in the week, when Cook had been at the library, Paula had bumped into Delong on the sidewalk and thoughtlessly asked him to step into the apartment to appraise her grandmother's necklace. He immediately spotted the cable hookup in the living room and, in Paula's words, "turned ashen." Delong said nothing, but to Paula his expression suggested something more than anger at Cook for flouting his wishes. She wasn't sure what, though.

On the sidewalk, Cook was pleased to see a man trying the door of Delong's store and not having any luck—pleased not just because it meant Cook was safe, but also because the customer's wishes were being thwarted. Anyone who wore what this guy was wearing—a black leather jacket with sleeves that looked inflated—deserved bad luck. The guy turned and their eyes met. It was Ben.

Cook privately retracted his curse and publicly said hello. Ben took a second to recognize him. When he did, he raised a hand and gave a fleeting smile.

"He keeps strange hours," Cook said, stepping closer.

Ben stepped back from the door and swept his eyes over the facade. "I wonder if he carries china."

Cook said that he did. Ben gave him a curious look. His thoughts seemed to be coming slowly. "You live around here?"

"Above the store."

"Oh, yeah," Ben said, apparently remembering. He looked up at the apartment windows. "What's that like?"

Cook pondered this spacy question. "We rent from Delong. I hate him."

"How does he get away with these hours? I can't stand people who prosper mysteriously."

Cook laughed. His response seemed to invigorate Ben a little.

"You stopped coming to see Molly. Did you wrap up that project?"

Another odd question, Cook thought. It was the kind of thing one says who is out of touch with what goes on under his own roof. Given recent circumstances, Ben had probably become such a man. Cook would not make him feel worse. He would not say, "I never got invited back." He just said yes, he was finished. It pained him to realize that he probably was.

Cook mentioned the tickets he had just received from Andrea. Then, conscious of speaking carefully, he said, "I guess things have been kind of crazy for you."

Ben nodded several times. "Have been, are, will be."

"I'm very sorry about your troubles."

"Which ones?" Ben asked sharply.

Cook didn't know what to do with this. "I meant the money that was stolen. But Susan also mentioned you were working too hard and having some dizzy spells."

Ben's face darkened as he looked away, toward the grassy hill and the seminary buildings beyond it. He looked back at Cook. "You going somewhere?"

"The Nifty Barber College on Clayton. They're free."

"I'll probably be going there soon," Ben said. "Were you walking? I'll give you a ride." He pointed to his Saab parked at the curb. Cook noticed the license plate for the first time: "4 GIRLZ."

As he got in, he felt awkward, and not just because of Ben's situation. He hadn't ridden in a car with someone other than Paula driving in several years.

"Buckle up," Ben commanded. Then he laughed. "Sorry. I'm in the habit of saying that to the kids." He started the engine and executed a U-turn. Some boxes jostled on the backseat, and what sounded like dishes clinked inside them. Cook's heart sank: Ben was hocking the china.

"Habits are odd things," Ben went on. "Here's a story about one." His tone was toastmaster-like. He seemed to want to fill the car with words. "I taught Andrea to drive, and when she turned sixteen and soloed for the first time, she was so used to me being in the car beside her that she talked to me out loud. But I wasn't even there!"

"A presence," Cook said. "That's nice."

"I don't know about a presence. It was a habit." Ben asked Cook about his Thanksgiving plans. Cook had none. He didn't even know when Thanksgiving was. He didn't like days that were supposed to be different from other days.

"What are you going to do?" Cook said.

"For Thanksgiving?"

"No."

Ben didn't respond right away. He stopped at a red light and tapped at the steering wheel. "I just got turned down for a loan. It's never happened to me before." Ben took a deep breath. "I got one from the same bank earlier, right after I found out about the embezzlement but before anyone else knew. I didn't mention it to the banker. How could I? When he found out, he felt tricked. He enjoyed fucking me over on the second loan. Art Talbot. It's an ugly name, isn't it?" The light changed. Ben drove on.

"I'd like to help," Cook said.

Ben said nothing.

"With your money problem," Cook said. "I'd like to help."

Ben was busy with traffic. He changed lanes, then slowed to let a car in ahead of him, signaling with a wave to the driver. He clearly meant to use this preoccupation as an excuse to ignore the subject.

"I'm in a position to help," Cook said. "And you put me there. It's only right that I help."

"*I* did? What did I do?"

"You told me about Archway International. I bought six thousand dollars' worth of their stock right after you told me about their merger plans. I made a bundle."

"I don't recall telling you about any merger plans."

"You did. And I made a killing. I got out last week after I talked with Susan. She told me your cashew deal was dead, and I thought that might have a negative effect on Archway, so I—"

"My cashew deal?" Ben laughed. "It's small potatoes to an outfit that size. I wasn't sure about using them anyway. You got it all wrong."

"Really? Well, anyway, I called my broker and sold the stock. It climbed like a champ in the short time I owned it." Cook waited for Ben to ask him about the numbers. When he didn't, Cook was puzzled, but he went ahead on his own. "When I called my broker, he told me I was a savvy guy for not calling and bothering him all the time. The truth is I'd had other things on my mind and forgotten all about it. Then he said that unfortunately things had gotten a little soft. That word 'soft' threw me, but I knew what 'unfortunately' meant, and I thought, shit, maybe my six thousand is down to five thousand, maybe even four. He says, 'Your total is about thirty-one now.' And I say 'Fuck!' and start yelling at him. He apologizes all over the place and says most people would be happy with that kind of appreciation, and I'm thinking what the hell? He says it had been up to thirty-five a couple days earlier, but how could he know it was going to drop to thirty-one? And I suddenly realize he's saying thirty-one *thousand*, not thirty-one hundred. From six thousand to thirty-one thousand. Isn't that amazing?" Cook shook his own head in amazement, to make up for Ben's failure to. "I spent three years writing a book that earned me just fifteen hundred dollars. Compare that with making two phone calls, one to buy and one to sell, a total of about three *minutes* of work, and earning twenty-five thousand dollars." Cook laughed. "It was such a rush, let me tell you. But I didn't let on to my broker that I'd misunderstood him. After all, he had already apologized, which told me my reaction couldn't have been totally out of line. I guess there are people out there who invest six thousand, get back thirty-one thousand lickety-split, and then bitch up their broker because it could have been thirty-five. And my broker thinks I'm one of those people." This made Cook laugh harder than ever. Then he shook his head in renewed amazement. "Christ, if I knew making money was this easy, I would have done it a long time ago."

"Here we are." Ben pulled to the curb in front of the barber college.

"Oh yeah." Cook had lost himself in his tale. "What about my offer?"

"Keep it," Ben said curtly. "You've earned it." His face was unreadable.

"But I didn't earn it at all. That's the point."

"Keep it."

"I want to help with a loan. I don't need it."

"Nope."

"It means nothing to me."

Ben's face went hard. He revved the engine. Cook searched for the door handle. The car was strange to him, and he couldn't find it. Ben reached across, yanked the handle, and gave the door a shove.

Cook got out but leaned back in to speak. "Really, it means nothing to me."

"I can tell," Ben said coldly. He signaled for Cook to close the door.

# 21

Ben pulled his Saab into the lot next to the Windermere Day School athletic field. He was late for the first end-of-season Districts game. From his car he could see Andrea's field hockey team taking a half-time rest, huddling and tugging on their water bottles. The scoreboard read one-one.

He phoned the warehouse from his car and learned that a delayed shipment of nuts had still not arrived. Four packers were idle, with hundreds of incomplete orders in front of them. Ben told them to go on home.

He stared out his windshield. If the nuts didn't come tomorrow, it would be too late for Thanksgiving orders to arrive by regular ground shipping. Crunch guaranteed on-time delivery, and he didn't want to have to eat UPS Blue Label shipping costs because of a supplier's screwup.

He was debating his next move when Susan pulled into the lot. Her mouth was pulled down at the corners in a way he hated to see. He got out but left his coat in the car. St. Louis had been enjoying a warm interlude, a common November occurrence before the plunge into winter.

Molly looked happier to see him than Susan. He slid the side door of the van open and scooped her out of her car seat. When he tried to stand her on her feet, she went jelly-legged.

"Shoulders," she said.

"Why don't you walk a little ways first?"

"Shoulders."

"Walk to that fence. Then shoulders."

"Shoulders."

Ben lifted her over his head to his shoulders. At least she was past the stage where she flopped like a noodle up there, always making him afraid she might lurch backward without warning.

When he joined Susan, he said, "On her wedding day, when it's time for me to walk her down the aisle, she'll say, 'Shoulders.'" He searched Susan's face. "Nothing? Nothing for me?" She walked off toward the field.

He was at her mercy. For the past three weeks her anger had defined their relationship. When it was churned up, he groveled. Recently, though, he had begun to address it. It was the only way he could think of to keep some dignity. She had a right to be furious. But he had a right to go on living in the world.

"It'll always be there," she liked to say, and she was right. What chafed him was how his sexual and financial bungling had become entangled. Susan's response to the loss of the money had had just a few seconds of purity before the Marlins waltzed into the picture. Those seconds had been pretty good, compared with the present. Yes, she had yelled at him about the loss—who wouldn't have?—but then they had begun to move on. They had set their faces to the future, side-by-side. But then came the Marlins, and Susan withdrew all charity, even on notes already forgiven.

He bore Molly from the lot, trudging after his wife. They reached the fence behind one of the goals as the teams took their positions for the second half. Ben and Susan hesitated at the fence. The bleachers were to the right, on a narrow strip of grass between the sideline and a wooded area. The Aberdeen parents were there, people they knew, friends and acquaintances whose smiles had become tinged with condolence. Susan was looking the other way, to the empty hillside above the field.

"Molly can roll on the hill," he said. "She can play in the leaves."

Susan led him that way. They found a good spot atop a grassy embankment near the Aberdeen goal, which it was Andrea's job to protect. Ben gave a little two-tone whistle, and, with the ball far upfield, Andrea could take the time to wave her big glove at them. She was unrecognizable in her goalie gear—helmet, face mask, and huge pads that misshaped her long body into comical lumpiness.

Susan sat down on the hillside and watched the game while Ben followed a roaming Molly through a small stand of pines above the field. He kept one eye on her and one on the game. He became aware of loud shouts of encouragement from the Windermere parents leaning against the white rail fence behind their goal. The fence made Ben think of horses. Windermere's campus, deep in the reach of the western suburbs, had the feel of country gentry. The shouts had extra meaning to him. "Go!" and "Pass it!" and "Clear it!" struck him as variations on a single command: "Strive!" Ben had been on this campus several times, had seen these well-heeled people before, had seen the women's blond hair glinting in the sunlight and had heard the men's shouts. But he had never seen them as he did now—as objects of curiosity.

Molly found some pinecones and began piling them near

Susan. The Windermere team moved, in fits and starts, on Andrea. They took a couple of weak shots at her, and she blocked the ball easily. Ben was happy for her, but then a scrappy Windermere forward, a child no doubt destined for greatness, took a hard shot. Andrea's dive was late, and the ball banged into the board at the back of the goal. The Windermere people erupted in cheers.

"Oh," Susan moaned.

Andrea slowly got up. A few teammates commiserated with her before heading upfield for the pass-back. Alone in the goal, she banged her stick angrily on the ground—a sudden, violent gesture that puzzled Ben. In all that protective gear, her emotions were masked. She could have maintained outward calm even while grimacing and swearing. Watching her, he assumed she *was* calm. But that flare with the stick ruined it.

"This is her last game," Susan said.

"Well—"

"She's been playing field hockey for four years. She'll never play again. This is the last game of her life."

"Only if they lose."

"They'll lose."

Molly had climbed onto a small rock outcrop, and Ben hurried to her. He held out his arms, and she jumped into them. He carried her back to where Susan sat at the top of the bank and suggested she roll down the hill. He looked at Susan to see if she would object because of grass stains. She was crying.

"Honey?"

She shook her head.

"We'll get through it. Really."

"It's not that."

"Is it Andrea? She'll play soccer in the spring."

She shook her head again in quick little jerks. "It's my book. It's *terrible*."

"Your book? Did you have a bad morning?"

She stared at the ground in front of her. "Will you please stop saying stupid things?"

He stood in silence while she collected herself. Molly, unable to figure out how to roll, began to fuss, so he straightened her out and gave her a nudge. After a few turns she went crooked and came to a stop with her feet pointing downhill. She grunted.

"I've been freaked out about money," Susan said. "I'd been thinking it was time to show the manuscript to someone anyway, so I sent it to the editor I've been in touch with. I must have reached her at a good time because she got right to it. I couldn't believe it when I got it in the mail, already coming back. She wrote, 'Doesn't quite work for me.' That's it. After two years of writing."

"That's just one opinion. That's—"

"I asked you to shut up, okay? I *know* it's just one opinion, and I wanted to get another one right away. I was desperate for one. I sure wasn't going to ask you for it. I won't be asking you for anything for a long time. So I—I can't believe I did this—I showed it to Andrea. She read it last night. She hated it."

"No."

"She's such a dear. She's just too good." Susan started to cry again, then stopped. "It was awful of me to put that kind of pressure on her. She knew the situation. She knew I was desperate." Susan took a deep breath. "When I went to bed she was still reading it. She'd gone to school by the time I came downstairs this morning. No note. I knew the verdict. She came home for lunch. She never does that. It just shows how good she is, what a great girl. She knew I was waiting to hear from her."

"What did she say?"

"That it failed completely."

"She couldn't have said that."

"*I'm* saying it, based on what she said, which was all nice and supportive. I know my daughter. I know what she felt."

"I'll talk to her. I'm sure you misunderstood her."

Susan closed her eyes. "You have no reason for saying that."

"Sure I do. Your first book. It was terrific."

"I had one story to tell, and I told it." She turned to him. "I'm done writing."

"No. I'm sure—"

"Shut up! Can't you hear me? I'm done." She looked away from him to the field. "It's a relief. It's sad too. In fact, it's a nightmare. But I'm done. You don't have to get up every morning with Molly now."

At the sound of her name, Molly looked up, curious. Then she tried to roll down the hill again, failed, and squirmed unhappily. Ben repositioned her and she rolled all the way to the bottom, where she lay on her back and stared at the sky.

"This is the wrong time to make a decision like that," he said to Susan. "Put it on hold. But it was good of you to try to scrape up some money."

"Don't patronize me," Susan said, her face turning ugly. "I know I don't bring in the money you do, but don't treat me like a little girl with a part-time job."

"I didn't mean to patronize you. I'm just saying it was good of you."

Susan stood up and brushed herself off. "It wasn't *good* of me at all. I did it because I have to start looking out for myself. I can't count on you anymore." She stared across the field. Her face hardened at something she saw. "Perfect. There she is. She'll always be there. Always."

Ben didn't bother pretending not to know what Susan was talking about. He had already seen her. "Sarah's on the J-V team," he said reasonably. "They play next. She's here to watch her. Okay?"

"I've never seen her at a game before. Why is she here today?"

"I don't know. Susan, I haven't talked to her in eleven years."

"I can't take this." Susan stalked off, at first along the hillside, then down to the flat ground next to the sideline. Ben kept expecting her to stop and come back, or at least stop. Then, when she reached the van, he expected her just to sit in it. He didn't expect her to roar out of the parking lot like that.

Molly was still lying on her back. The Aberdeen team was trying to score, leaving Andrea alone at the near end of the field. He wondered how much she had seen. When he looked at her, she turned away from him in her heavy armor and faced upfield again.

Aberdeen lost, but through no fault of Andrea's. Her team just couldn't move the ball past midfield in the final quarter, and no goalie can withstand shot after shot. He would tell her that when he saw her back home.

Her team huddled for a farewell talk among themselves. Ben lifted Molly onto his shoulders and waited for Andrea to look up across the field at them. When she did, he waved good-bye and told Molly to do the same. Andrea returned his wave, holding her hand up for a long time until she knew Molly had located it, and then she flapped it wildly.

Susan must have thought, if she thought about it at all, that he had planned to come right home after the game. In fact he had a number of things still to do at the office, but only one of them was urgent, a phone call to his dilatory supplier. He figured Molly could put up with one phone call.

As he drove to the office, the words of one of the fathers calling to the team stuck in his mind. It was an Aberdeen father, not a Windermere one. "You've got to want it!" he cried. What he said was both true and ridiculous. They did have to want it to win it. But what if they didn't want it? You couldn't *make* them want it. Someone like himself, he couldn't help wanting it. So he worked, and strived, and hoped. Even in the midst of the mess he was in, he squared his shoulders and kept at it. What else could he do?

Sighing wasn't the answer, sighing and spinning. He hadn't realized what a fragile thing the body was, and how easily the mind could ruin it. His dizziness had sent him to the doctor, who was not a good friend and was clearly not up on local news. "You worried about something, Ben?" he said. Ben could only laugh. The doctor sat him down and proposed an exercise. Ben was to breathe in deeply when the doctor's hand went up, then blow the air out when his hand went down. The doctor matched him breath for breath. After three or four blows, Ben had to stop because the room had taken off with him as a passenger. The doctor, a cocky guy, kept at it, showing Ben what was possible—hell, what was normal, provided you weren't hyperventilated like Ben. Apparently he had been sighing so much he had screwed up the oxygen level in his blood. Over the next several days, he caught himself taking huge gulps of air. He conquered the habit, and his environment stopped giving him rides.

But he had other struggles. His desk at home had become a disaster. Before, when bills came, he would pay them instantly. "Never let a paper hit your desk twice"—that had been his creed. Now his desk was a cooking pot, and all he did was stir. His hands shook when he wrote checks. The money was there, for now, but the knowledge that it was dwindling unmanned him. He couldn't abide anything having to do with money. But everything had to do with money.

As for Susan, she wasn't sleeping. She was up a lot, wandering at night, often ending up on the daybed in her study. She was snapping at people too—something she hadn't done since their fighting days, which the kids, all but Andrea, were too young to remember. A few days earlier, after dinner, Pam had asked Susan where her purse was. Susan had blown up, saying she couldn't be giving Pam money every time she asked for it. Things had changed, she yelled. Pam, in the moral right for the first time since her breasts had budded, said she had just wanted to get some gum out of the purse. Everyone in the house had listened with the same thought: things had changed indeed.

He pulled into the parking lot. He hadn't had Molly to his office for some time—half a year, maybe. In the utility closet he found an old, broken-strapped busy box and set her up with it. She seemed sufficiently perplexed with the toy to allow him a few minutes of peace, and he hustled to his Rolodex.

He was in luck on two counts. It was after hours but he still connected with Zender Nut Co., and he got Bill Zender, Jr., not the old man.

"How are you, Ben?" Zender said. "Hang on. Let me close the door. There's a horrible racket out there."

Ben listened. Molly had carried the busy box up to the leather couch with her. Other than its squeaks and rattles and the sound of Zender's door closing in New Jersey, he heard no racket at all.

"That's better," Zender said. Ben expected him to say more. When he didn't, he spoke himself:

"I'd like you to check your records and see when my Brazils and cashews were shipped, Bill. I haven't gotten them, and I'm up against a deadline."

After a long pause, Zender said, "Dad was supposed to call you."

"Nobody's called. I've left four messages in the past two days."

"I didn't know that. Dad must have pitched them. But he was supposed to call you anyway."

"What do you mean? Why?"

227

"I'll be blunt, Ben. My father said he doesn't want to do business with you anymore."

Ben sat bolt upright. Had old Bill Zender found out about the embezzlement? Did he see Ben as a credit risk? "What are you saying?"

"The way you brought up that issue of the Brazilian workers—he's not gonna stand for that, Ben."

"Jesus Christ," said Ben. *"That?"* This was better—but also worse—than he had feared. "All I did was *ask*. I asked if he could get Brazil nuts from Peru."

"Well, you did a bit more than that, from what I understand. But I don't want to get into that. You've just got to understand that he's touchy as hell on the subject. It's come up before. We get it from reporters and bleeding hearts, but we've never gotten it from someone *inside*, for God's sake. He was storming around for days afterward." Zender paused. "I'm sorry. That's the way it is."

"Whoa," Ben said. "I feel like you're about to say good-bye."

"Well, there's not much I can do."

"Yes, there is. You can send me the shipment I had every reason to expect you'd send me."

"That would be very hard for me to do, Ben."

"You guys changed the rules and didn't tell me."

"Yeah, but—"

"You'd be mad as hell if one of your suppliers did that to you."

Zender was silent.

"Wouldn't you?" Ben said.

Zender was silent for an eternity. "He'll kill me if he finds out. What is it that you want?"

"You've got the order. Call it up."

"It's gone. If Dad makes a decision like that, he wipes out the account."

"Christ. Hang on. Let me get it. *Don't go away.*"

Ben put him on hold. He had some trouble getting the order on his screen. He couldn't seem to hit the right keys, and he kept making the same mistakes. He finally got it and read it to Zender.

"Why so many?" Zender said. "This isn't for Christmas, is it?"

"Thanksgiving. An ad agency in L.A. had a huge order for client gifts."

Zender sighed. "This is a big order, Ben."

Ben sat forward in his chair. "I know it's big. Don't you like big orders? What are you saying?"

"It's just going to be tough to slip this by the old man. I'll have to tell him it was spoilage. Of course, that's gonna piss him off too. . . . Don't worry. I'll take care of it."

"I want it overnighted."

"Well—"

"You pitched my order and didn't tell me. I've been dealing with you for six years."

"Yeah, and you never got on your high horse all that time either."

"What—*you're* mad too? I thought he was the mad one."

Zender was silent.

"You'll overnight it?"

"Yeah. But don't count on Christmas, Ben. I'll give you fair warning."

"*What?*"

"I can't keep fooling Dad. I can't do business behind his back."

Ben wanted to scream at him to grow up. "I'm two days away from sending you my Christmas order. You know what Christmas means in this business. My gift boxes are going to be half empty."

"Sorry, Ben. I'm saying no. I'm saying yes for Thanksgiving, and I'm saying no for Christmas."

"And I'm saying fuck you for New Year's."

Zender absorbed this quietly. "That's the way it is, Ben. Good-bye."

Ben slammed the phone down. Air seemed to rush in his ears. It settled down, and between the squeaks and rattles from Molly's busy box on the floor, he heard a different sound, an exhalation. It came from the long leather couch Molly had just vacated. The cushions were sighing as they pressed themselves back into shape.

He went to the shelf along the wall near the window, where his directory of brokers and catalogs were. He could probably fill the gap. But he would have to scramble.

# 22

"My talk today, 'Lexical Hiding Places,' treats deep-seated emotions masked by language. My methodology is impressionistic, anecdotal, and circular. I hope you like it."

Some surprised chuckles rippled forward toward Cook.

"I begin with the word 'thug.'"

He had to begin with "thug." The brutal little gem, the starting point of his research, occupied a fond place in his heart. As the small audience settled in, Cook traced the word's etymology from Sanskrit to Hindi, thence into English (first documented occurrence, 1810), where it originally referred to one of a band of Hindi robbers and assassins partial to strangulation. His words, like his haircut, felt out of place here in the Louis XIV Room of the Ritz-Carlton Hotel in downtown Aberdeen. Paula had gone first-class in choosing a conference venue.

"'Thug,' ladies and gentlemen, is third world in origin. More important, it is third world in current reference. One hears 'that thug Amin/Quaddafi/Noriega' much more often than one hears 'that thug Stalin/Brezhnev/Ceausescu.'" He laid some numbers on them. Working from the Nexis newspaper and magazine database, he had found thirty-one co-occurrences of "Amin" and "thug"; using identical search criteria, he had found only seven co-occurrences of "Brezhnev" and "thug."

"More stories have been written about Brezhnev," Cook said, "because of his longer reign and greater importance in world affairs. Thus 'thug' actually had more chances to occur with 'Brezhnev' than with 'Amin,' but in fact it occurred fewer times." Cook loved it when his sample was distorted against his hypothesis and nonetheless supported it. It was like sneaking up on his enemies and cutting them down at the knees.

After giving some more comparative numbers, he said, "If two groups of leaders exhibit the same bad behavior, why would someone apply a pejorative label with higher frequency to one group than to the other? Because of an additional feature distinguishing that group: its dark skin. I submit that 'thug' is a racist word. And what political constituency uses 'thug' more than any other? The one most concerned with 'getting tough'—conservatives."

Cook congratulated himself for the way his paper glided into the actual focus of his paper: the hidden hate that drives conservatives. No doubt some in the audience thought he was making an aside. But it was more than that. The camel's nose was in the tent.

"Example number two. What do conservatives say about the money spent on social programs? Do they say 'invest money in'? No. They say 'throw money at.'" This was Cook's most fun example. He liked it for its vitriol. It was an angry splash of acid on the canvas, sketching liberals as wild-eyed spendthrifts hell-bent on papering the world with currency. He said all this in the rollicking spirit in which he appreciated it himself.

But alas, that was all he had to say about it. He sensed a coolness from the audience. Some of the thirty or so scholars in attendance, dispersed haphazardly throughout the unfortunately large lecture hall, were perhaps wondering where this unaffiliated renegade was taking them. But he was of good cheer. There was no name for the school of linguistics whose bell he was wildly ringing, and he couldn't expect everyone to respond to it.

He hurried on. "Let's look at the construction 'happen to,' as in 'I happen to believe in a citizen's right to bear arms.' It is normally used to describe chance events, as in 'I happened to run into Lulu at the store.' Why would one use a construction associated with chance to state a deeply held conviction? To hide his rage. 'Happen to' is a signal flare for repressed rage. There is a humbleness to it, an engaging modesty, as if the speaker is saying, 'Look, I don't want to preach, and I'm not saying you should share this belief, but, for what it's worth, I happen to believe in a citizen's right to bear arms.' Those two words perform all that semantic and interactional work."

Cook paused a moment before delivering four more examples of this construction, all rather recent: "I happen to believe that tenure should go to those who deserve it/that grading standards have gotten too lax/that you make your own breaks in this life/that a nation of crybabies gets exactly what it deserves." He quoted them without attribution, and he could only wonder if Paula, seated in the second row, recognized any of these chickens as they waddled homeward.

He moved on to an item he had picked up at the Nifty Barber College from the pig-faced apprentice who had mangled his hair. Predicting an American utopia after the next election, the man had said, "The American people aren't stupid." Cook invited the audience to think about the sentence in light of the type of government Americans choose. "How do Americans vote over the long haul?" he said, trying to enliven things by involving the crowd. Paula looked unhappy with the strategy. "Conservative, moderate, or liberal? Moderate, right? If they swing rightward, they hurry up and swing back to the center in the next election, almost as if it scared them. They just won't take that full plunge into the sea of conservatism. Now, I ask you, how do conservatives feel about this reluctance? It drives them crazy, doesn't it? They think the American people *are* stupid. They want them to die—or at least stop voting. They say the exact opposite of what they feel. They hide their rage. *Quod erat demonstrandum.*"

A brief cackle of laughter from the rear of the hall confirmed Cook's sense that he had lost some of the crowd, not for political reasons—most linguists were liberal to radical—but on methodological grounds. He wasn't really on the cutting edge. He was *off* the edge. And he liked it there.

It was time for "bleeding heart." This one fascinated Cook. When conservatives made fun of "bleeding hearts," they were making fun of people who felt sorry for other people. He couldn't understand this. He wanted the audience to join him in his confusion.

"How can someone ridicule sympathy?" he asked after introducing them to the construction. "But I can hear some of you saying, 'Hold on now. Nobody's ridiculing sympathy. They're ridiculing *excessive* sympathy.' I can hear you saying that." Cook eyed the crowd indulgently, like a parent watching a straying youngster. "But what is excessive sympathy? Did Jesus teach us to be wary of caring too much for others? Hold on, some of you are saying again, and I can practically see this couple in the front row saying it. Don't deny it, you two—none of that. You're saying that 'bleeding heart' makes fun of reckless spending for social programs prompted by sympathy. Fine. But why does conservative language single out sympathy for opprobrium? Because they find sympathy ridiculous. In the rough-and-tumble Darwinian world of conservatism, it *is* ridiculous. But they would never admit they feel that way. They hide it. But not very well."

Cook sensed a new level of awkwardness in the room, which puzzled him. This example seemed no weaker than any of his previous ones.

"To wrap up my discussion of 'bleeding heart,'" he said, "I shall quote two more occurrences from recent experience, both spoken by the same informant. The first concerns an escalating grade dispute: 'Some bleeding heart in the dean's office took the little shit's side and tried to pressure me to raise the grade.' The second was uttered in response to the doorbell ringing at the dinner hour— presumably a footsore solicitor for some charitable cause: 'Jesus Christ, Jeremy, if it's another fucking bleeding heart with a tin cup, I'm going to scream.'"

At this point, his unwitting informant no doubt became witting, if she wasn't already. Yes, he had to admit it: he had married a right-winger. Or rather, he had married a woman who had become one when he wasn't looking. How did these things happen? How could she choose to be *that*?

Cook pressed on. His next example also came from an informant in his building, but downstairs this time. As Cook was passing by the entrance to Delong's store just two days earlier, he had heard the antiquarian chatting with a fellow aristocrat in the doorway. Delong said, "I'll tell you, Harvey, there's one group that's not going to be happy about it and that's the shareholders." The sentence rang in Cook's ears like the Tibetan Gong ($599) displayed in the front window. It suggested, on the surface, that conservatives were not entirely full of hate. There was one group they cared about, little people of their own, whom they cradled in their arms: the shareholders.

But it was a sham display, as Cook now pointed out. "The word 'shareholders' suggests small investors with hard-earned savings entrusted to corporations. In imagining such people, we often think of elderly investors, who are particularly vulnerable." Cook inadvertently threw a glance at the front-row couple he had singled out for mention earlier and felt a twinge. They were late-middle-aged, and they may have felt he was referring to them. He hurried on. "There *are* such investors, of course, but they hold a small fraction of shares. Big shots hold the most. Sixty percent of stocks are held by the wealthiest one percent of the population. All this ostensible solicitude for shareholders is just a plutocratic euphemism for maximizing profit."

Cook paused for a drink from his water glass. It wasn't going too badly now. The back-row cackler had been silent for some time. The entire group was hushed. As for Paula, a glance her way revealed that her face was entirely flat, her lips thinner than he had ever seen them.

"I invite you to consider the word 'darling,'" Cook said. "Is it a good word or a bad word? Wouldn't you like to be someone's 'darling'? I certainly would. Now, hold that thought, please. I shall return to it.

"A fundamental principle of conservatism is that everyone is responsible for his own fate, good or bad. When it comes to bad fates, conservatives say things like 'He fouled his own nest,' and 'He made his bed, so he'll have to sleep in it,' and 'If you lie down with dogs, you get up with fleas.' A curious feature of these expressions is their common concern with bedding. What happens in bed, ladies and gentlemen? People sleep, yes, but they also make love. The conservative selection of bedding as the semantic domain of negative preference leads me to believe that conservatives are opposed to sexual intercourse. They make no secret, of course, of their opposition to homosexual intercourse—this despite the fact that, unless I am overlooking something, all of its forms can and do occur heterosexually as well. I submit that conservatives equally abhor heterosexual sex, but they try to disguise their abhorrence. They try, and they fail.

"Now, I have talked about sympathy. They hate it. I have talked about sex. They hate it. Pathos is no good, and neither is eros. Whither am I tending? I submit, ladies and gentlemen, that conservatives hate love. Now we may return to 'darling.' Consider: 'He's a darling of the liberal establishment'; 'she's a well-known darling of the left'; and a real-life example uttered, as it happens, in bed, 'The dean is a darling of the vice-chancellor's, Jeremy, so I can't expect any support from that overpaid cretin.'" Cook pressed his lips together, for he was genuinely moved. "It's a sad day in the history of civilization when it is bad to be a darling."

Cook swept an unfocused gaze across the group. It was time for his valediction. "It has been my pleasure, up until recently, to have had the company of a very special informant in my life, a lady who means more to me than anyone in the world." Cook paused and looked at Paula. She sat stone-faced, as rigid as an ironing board. "This informant's name is Molly, and she is two and a half years old. Molly likes to play hide-and-seek, but she is a most incompetent hider. When I seek her, I talk to myself out loud. I say, 'Where's Molly? Where is that girl?' Failing to recognize that I am engaging in self-speech, she yells, 'Ovuh heah!' I discover her facedown in the middle of the carpet, hiding her eyes, with her butt sticking up. She considers that a hiding place.

"Similarly, our conservative brethren think they have found clever hiding places. But their butts are sticking way out. It is not a pleasant sight across the land, and we must do our best to expose them and make them ashamed of their nakedness. I thank you."

The applause did not follow Cook down from the stage. Later, he couldn't remember if there had actually been any. He was too aware of the cackler at the back, who had started in again, and of Paula, talking earnestly to the couple in the front row. He had expected her to leave the room, or walk up to him and snarl something. He hadn't expected her to talk with people. She was hard at it, along with a man Cook recognized as Chairman Sam. Cook heard the fragments "juvenile" and "not at all representative of the kinds of things we—" The couple didn't have much to say. They looked like a pair of midwestern farmers whose crops had gone bad. The image reminded Cook of something. But what?

Cook stood at the front of the room by the stage, making himself available for Q and A (no takers as of yet). He grabbed his cranberry parka from a chair and put it on. Paula disengaged herself from the group and took some long strides to him.

"You did it, Jeremy."

"All facts. All of them. Facts."

"You killed any chance we had of getting funded. You've queered the whole center."

"What do you mean?"

Without turning around, she jerked her head in a gesture. "Those are the Buford twins—the ones you called 'a couple,' which I'm sure they also enjoyed." The twins had begun to make their way, under Chairman Sam's guidance, to the exit at the rear of the room. The woman threw a nervous glance at Cook, as if fearful he might come after her. "Didn't it occur to you that they would be here? Didn't I tell you they're conservative? I know you hate me, but you didn't have to do this to me."

"I had no idea," Cook said, but not with distress. "I was just pursuing an interest of mine."

"Christ," she said. She looked after the departing twins.

"It serves you right anyway," Cook said. "Here you talk about enterprise and honest labor, and you've presented a false front to these moneybags from the beginning. You're sucking at the money tit just like the slackers you despise. And while I'm at it, look at how you treated Ted. Look at how you treat your students. This pursuit of 'excellence' has killed all your other values. You're a confused woman."

Paula huffed through her nose. "Apart from the damage you've done, your paper was idiotic. I want to say that, for the record."

"For the record, eh? Is this it?"

"That's right. I want out, Jeremy."

"Oh, you're out, Paula. You were out when you were in."

"You were the same way. We were never married, really."

"With the scheme you've cooked up, that'll be literally true, won't it? Don't worry, I won't fight it. I'll let you restore your perfect record."

He enjoyed the way she stiffened at his knowledge. But he didn't enjoy her next words: "At least I had the balls to do something about it." She turned away and hurried after the others.

⌒

Cook left the Ritz-Carlton and walked into the forest of aloneness. It was a dark place full of strange voices. These mingled with his own, freely talking to himself. It was a sadly comfortable place. He connected it with Europe—the Europe of history, which he saw as a stage of suffering, and the Europe he had hitchhiked through alone, always alone. The tall office buildings surrounding him were a shadowy *Schwarzwald*. Cold Europe had come to Aberdeen.

On the other side of the small business district he found the high school, then the auditorium. It rang with noise. Big men grinned and pumped one another's hands while women threw their heads back in horsey laughter. Cook had thought of trying to locate Ben and Susan and sitting with them, but the wall of noise sent him into a rear corner seat. With some effort, from his seat he spied Susan and two of her daughters, Pam and Karen. He kept expecting Ben to appear from somewhere and join them, but he didn't.

The play, of course, was about Cook. It was about what he wasn't. It was about the fabric of society: *Our* (plural pronoun) *Town* (collective noun). A comparable play about Cook's life would have to be called *My Town*—no, not *Town*. *My House.* No, a house could be near other houses. *My Cabin.*

And of course the production was wonderful. It was Andrea's production, and *she* was wonderful. The play was about her, about being active, not reactive, like Cook. Philosophically, he knew that all action was a reaction, yet the distinction was still useful. Active people had far-reaching reactions; reactive people reacted tinily, with a quivering eye on the immediate threat at hand. He had never reached far in his life.

When the graveyard scene came, he had to leave. But he didn't get away in time. The familiar words rained down on him accusingly. The newly dead in the play ached because they were not fully "weaned from the living." When his time came, there would be no such problem. He was already weaned.

He trudged the full length of Aberdeen, from the high school at the extreme western end through the downtown steel forest, along the edge of Ben and Susan's neighborhood, through Buford U. to Demun. Near the seminary, a gathering of humanity blocked his progress. It felt like a larger version of the graveyard scene he had just fled. He worked his way around the rear of the crowd, which was most dense across the street from his apartment building, and with good reason: his building was no longer standing there.

"What happened?" Cook cried out to anybody who would answer. A woman in front of him half turned and said there had been a huge explosion. She pointed to the shattered windows in the building across the side street. A foul smell hung in the air, like popcorn that had burned for hours.

He asked another question, privately. What had perished? He

looked at his watch. Paula would be safe at the Ritz-Carlton. Conference papers had been scheduled all the way to five o'clock, and it was just four-fifteen. As for property, the only thing that came to his mind was the slingshot that his father had bought him at the Monterey Hobby Shop. That was gone now. So were his notes, his files, his work-in-progress. But none of these interested him.

Cook imagined Delong's ashes mingling with those of his antique furniture, and he asked another bystander when the explosion had occurred. "About two hours ago," he said. "Burned hot and fast." Cook wondered if the rubble was being searched. The crowd obscured his view. Behind him, the seminary grounds rose after a slight dip. He hurried up for a better look.

If a search had been conducted in the charred ruins, it was now over. Up the street, two policemen and a fireman were laughing. One of the policemen poked at the fireman's long rubber boots, making fun of them. Farther up the street, an ambulance sat idle. Cook's eye went back to the ruins. He was struck by how little was left. The rear and side brick walls stood no higher than ten feet now, and nothing remained of the front wall. Two cars in front of the building had burned. One was crushed by bricks.

Cook looked around in a wild search for meaning. He settled on a pale, clean-looking young man standing alone on the grassy slope. "Are you a student at the seminary?" he called out.

The student said yes, he was.

"Can you tell me why these things happen?"

The student looked at the scene below and thoughtfully put a finger to his lips.

"Too slow," Cook snapped. He climbed up the hill away from there.

# 23

"Tuna or peanut butter?"

"Olive."

"Tuna or peanut butter?"

"Olive."

"You can't just have olives for lunch. Tuna or peanut butter?"

"Black olive."

Ben hung his head over the kitchen table in profound weariness. He took an olive from the can and held it like a gem between thumb and forefinger, out of Molly's reach. Her eyes widened. She squirmed in her booster seat. "Peanut butter or tuna?" he said, reversing the order because she always picked the last-named option, and tuna was healthier.

"Peanut butter," she said.

Ben laughed and set four olives on her plastic plate. "You're growing up," he said. He took a jar of peanut butter from the pantry and began to make a sandwich.

Karen came into the kitchen. She wore a new wool Christmas-tree sweater with a pleated green skirt and red leggings. She was pressing her lips together to hide her pleasure in her appearance.

Ben gasped. "You look gorgeous."

She beamed with delight. "That's what Mom said. Can you make me one of those?"

"Sure. Let Molly introduce you to her olive family."

Karen joined her sister, who was wiggling the olives on the tips of her fingers. "Is Andrea going to be in the play?" Karen said.

"No. She's the director. She picked the actors and helped them learn how to act their parts. It's the most important job."

"Does she get to take a bow at the end?"

"I don't think so."

"You don't think so about what?" Susan said as she came in, fastening her watch band. This was new behavior—entering a room and an ongoing conversation at the same time, demanding an update. The habit sprang, no doubt, from an understandable fear of surprises. Before Ben could answer, Susan said, "She needs to eat something besides olives."

"I know. I'm making her a sandwich."

"You should eat too, Karen," Susan said.

"Dad's making me one," Karen said.

Susan did not commend him for being on top of things.

"I phoned Pam," Ben said. "She's all dressed and ready." Pam had spent the night at Dawn's house in their former neighborhood, near where the baby-sitter lived—Cindy, a childhood playmate of Andrea's now in her first year of junior college.

Susan struggled with her watch band. "We'll go as soon as I get back with them. I want to get a good seat." She finally succeeded with the clasp and grabbed her purse and coat from the hall closet. She called to Molly, "Cindy will baby-sit you when I get back, okay?"

"I told her already," Ben said. He followed Susan to the front door. "That guy Jack called. He asked if he could pick up the piano earlier than we agreed."

"What did you say?" Susan asked sharply.

"From your tone, probably the wrong thing. I said as long as he brought the check."

"Jesus," Susan said. "I want it here while we're showing the house. Call him back."

"He's kind of on his way with a crew."

"Then *kind of* say no when they get here." She put on her coat with a grumble. "I can't believe you did that. There isn't even time right now for them to get it out of here. What's the rush? We don't need the money today, unless there's something else you haven't told me."

"Don't."

"The point is, the piano looks good in the living room. It'll help get us top dollar for the house." He felt the expression "top dollar" like a blow to the head. Susan seemed to use it every time she referred to the imminent sale of the house. It was her way of declaring that she would now play a role in all household money management.

Susan left. Ben asked Karen to watch Molly for a minute and hurried to his study to try to reach Jack, whom he hadn't actually met, but who had managed to impress Susan when he came to look at the piano. He could tell this from the way she speculated afterward about what he did and where he lived. There was no answer at Jack's. Ben glared at the baby grand on his way back to the kitchen as if it were the root of his problems. They would get seven thousand dollars for it, which seemed like a fortune right now. They had bought it for that same amount eight years earlier and had barely noticed the expense.

Karen had Molly well in hand, so Ben went upstairs and put on a clean shirt. His tie took four attacks before he got it right. He found himself hoping he could escape to the play before Jack and his crew showed up. Then he angrily chased the idea away. By his reckoning, he would have to face, in the months immediately ahead, one rotten moment after another. He had never slinked, never dodged anything. He wouldn't start now.

He reviewed the day ahead of him. First, the *Our Town* matinee at two. There would be a whole new layer of people to deal with—second- and third-tier friends. They would congratulate him on Andrea's achievement. Then, as if his life were a cop show and they had missed a few episodes, they would ask him about the progress of the investigation. He would tell them bluntly that it had stalled.

After that, Karen and Pam would baby-sit Molly while he and Susan put in a couple hours at the warehouse, packing orders. They were short-staffed for the season, but he was in no position to hire new help. Between these two events, Ben and Susan would sit the kids down and inform them that they were going to sell the house and move across town to a less expensive Aberdeen neighborhood. Ben and Susan had chosen the house and put down earnest money. Andrea already knew: they had told her as soon as they knew. She said two things: "That bitch of all bitches," meaning Roberta, and "They'll cry," meaning her sisters.

All along, he had told Susan they would be fine as long as nothing else went wrong. Thanks to Zender Nut Co., that premise had collapsed. After losing his Brazil nut and cashew supplier, Ben was able to track down four alternative sources, but he was astonished to find they all demanded up-front payment. The climate had changed in the six years he had been with Zender. Cashews were the heart and soul of his Christmas trade. Without cashews, there would be no Christmas, which meant almost certainly there would be no Crunch.

He had just one source of cash: the house they had lived in for nearly twelve years, financed too heavily for a second mortgage, but not so heavily that they wouldn't come away with sixty-five or seventy thousand after taxes. Thirty-four thousand of that would be the 20 percent down payment for their new house. (In his publicly distressed position, he would certainly have to put down 20 percent to get financing.) The balance would see the business through Christmas, which they would celebrate in a house that, in dollar value, was one-quarter the house they were used to.

The sound of doors slamming at the front curb announced the next immediate challenge. Ben looked out the window and hurried down the stairs. Karen was lying on her back on the living room carpet while Molly knelt beside her and set colorful fruit candies—little ornaments—on the Christmas tree embroidered on Karen's sweater.

Ben went out and headed straight for the flatbed truck. Two brawny young men were readying it for the piano, throwing tarps and ropes around, while an older man directed them. Another man was getting out of a sky-blue Jaguar at the curb near the driveway, some distance from the truck. Handsome Jack. He was tall and had a sharp jaw that looked like it could dig dirt. A bored-looking boy about Karen's age remained in the car.

Jack gestured to the house as he approached. "Lovely house," he called out. "Lovely. We almost bought in this neighborhood." He wore his argyle sweater like a flag on his chest. When he reached Ben, he shook his hand warmly.

"I'm afraid I spoke out of turn," Ben said. "My wife wants to keep the piano until next month, as we originally agreed."

"Whoa," Jack said, raising his hands in controlled surprise.

"I'm sorry. I'll pay for your crew's time."

"Let me explain what I've got going here," Jack said. "I want to surprise my wife with the piano for Christmas. She surprised

246

me with this toy last year." He snapped his head toward the Jaguar. The boy inside was staring at them and ardently picking his nose. "I mean she surprised me by going to the dealer's and choosing the model. We both know who wrote the check." Handsome Jack laughed.

"I'm sorry. We're putting the house up for sale, and the piano makes a good impression. I overlooked that this morning."

Jack grinned and shook his head. "That's not acceptable, Ben."

"Well, it's the way it is." Ben, in the midst of this, found himself fascinated by Jack's sweater.

"You don't understand. I've come for the piano. As agreed."

"Sorry. Send me a copy of your crew's bill, and we'll deduct it from the price. Or I'll pay them right now." Ben turned to await the crew, now approaching across the lawn.

"They're my men, and you'll say nothing to them," Jack said sharply. "Now, listen to me. We have a question of nonperformance here. You don't want to get into that. I've come for the piano."

"No."

Jack laughed. "You have no choice! A deal's a deal. I'm not leaving without that piano."

Ben looked at the men, now on hand, and smiled at them, inviting them to join him in marveling at Jack. While they didn't visibly accept his invitation, Ben felt a kinship. He looked back at Jack and said, "No."

"I don't do business this way. I don't know how you do business, but I don't do it this way."

"I don't either, usually," Ben said. He wondered what Jack knew. Had he read of the embezzlement or seen a story on a newscast? One of the TV reports had shown their house, their lovely house, as if it were part of the story. He looked at Jack's sweater again and finally placed it. It was a cashmere argyle sweater that

247

Susan had shown him in a Saks catalog earlier in the week during an argument. She had grabbed the catalog and thumbed through it in a fury until she found the page, and then she had shoved it in his face. She said she had planned on getting him that sweater for Christmas—Ben read the price: $415—but she wouldn't be ordering it now, for lots of reasons. Lots and lots of reasons, she said.

"I'm going back to my car," Jack said with a little puff of his chest, "and I'm going to call my lawyer. I think you'll be relinquishing that piano after all."

"Oh, grow up," Ben snapped, suddenly tired of it all. "Hasn't anyone ever said no to you before? I'm saying no. Now get out of here." Ben turned to the foreman. "What do I owe you for your time today?"

The foreman looked at his watch and silently moved his lips, calculating the amount. This sent Handsome Jack over the top. He let loose with variations on what he had said thus far, and Ben took the foreman by the arm so that they could step away from the noise. Jack finally stormed off. Ben paid the foreman and apologized to him.

He was about to go back into the house when he spotted another assault in progress. A blue-suited man had just pounded a For Sale sign into the lawn near the front walk. He saluted Ben with a wooden mallet. "Welcome to the Ewell-Myers family!" he called out.

Ben stalked across the lawn and yanked the sign out of the ground. It had this man's cheerful mug on it, along with that of the woman Ben had spoken with the week before.

"No signs until tomorrow. I told Doreen."

"I thought we'd get a jump on things, Ben. A nice Saturday like this, a lot of folks'll be out window-shopping."

"We haven't told the kids yet. Go away. Take this with you."

But it was too late. Susan was pulling up to the curb with Pam and the baby-sitter. Ben tried to hide the sign with his body. But

Pam was an expert at interpreting the world when it conspired against her. She ran into the house, screaming a simple message at Ben as she passed by: "You've ruined my life!"

The real estate agent slipped away quietly. The piano movers were gone. The Jaguar now pulled away. Ben closed his eyes a moment, gathered his strength, and walked to the front door. He heard Pam's bedroom door slam. Karen was sitting up on the floor, her spilled candy ornaments sending Molly into a confused rage.

"Dad, it's not true, is it?" Karen said. Her face pleaded. His words were going to be blows against that face.

"I'm sorry, honey. We'll stay in Aberdeen, and you'll go to the same school, but we can't afford to live in this house anymore."

"Oh God!" she cried, and she ran up the stairs.

Susan and the baby-sitter came into the house. Molly was crying because Karen had left. Susan silently walked to the stairs and climbed them to be with Karen and Pam. Ben picked Molly up, comforted her, and said something to the baby-sitter about their lives being in transition. He carried Molly into the kitchen, stroking her hair and kissing the side of her head, for his own comfort as much as hers. She suddenly wriggled from his arms and hurried back into the living room for her candy. He followed her and watched her collect it and put it in a front pocket of her dress. Then she reached for him to be picked up again.

He did so differently this time. He put his thumbs in her palms, lapped his fingers over the top of her wrists, and pulled her in a high arc up to his shoulder. She immediately burst out crying. He set her down and knelt to her. She clutched her right forearm in an odd way, an adult way. He carried her to the couch and tried to comfort her, wondering what he had done to hurt her. He thought each cry would be the last. But she just wouldn't stop. "It not getting better," she wailed. She knew that her body should have stopped hurting by now.

Susan, Pam, and Karen—three grim faces—came down the

stairs. The girls went right out the door. Susan sat down next to Molly on the couch, and Molly raised her one good arm and put it around her mother's neck.

"I picked her up wrong," Ben lamely explained. "I don't know what I did, if I broke something or what. I've got to take her to the doctor." He went to the kitchen for his keys and wallet. When he came back he said, "You go ahead with the girls. Cindy can stay here. If we're lucky and it's something simple, maybe I can bring Molly home and make it to the play." He looked at Cindy. She nodded and said whatever they wanted was fine with her—she just hoped Molly was okay.

"It not getting better," Molly cried to her mother. Susan hugged her and looked at Ben.

"I've picked her up like that a hundred times." He moved his hands helplessly. "I'm making all my girls cry."

"You did nothing wrong," Susan said, so softly he barely heard her. She told Molly what was going to happen and gave her a kiss. Then she left.

⌒

"Nursemaid's elbow," the pediatrician said. "Picture a nursemaid yanking on a child's arm, pulling her straight up. That's how it got the name." He said it was a common dislocation, repairable by the slightest manipulation, which he performed so quickly that afterward Ben couldn't recall what he had actually done. A little touch, and Molly's radius was back where it belonged. It was like a laying on of hands. Ben picked her up—carefully—and thrilled to feel both her arms go around his neck.

"This is the most satisfying medical experience I've ever had," Ben said, full of feeling. The doctor burst out laughing.

When he drove away from the doctor's office, he suddenly

didn't want to rush anywhere. He didn't want to dash back home, dump poor Molly, and hurry into the play late and hunt for Susan in the audience. He just didn't want to do all that. There would be another performance tomorrow. Andrea would understand when she saw he wasn't in the audience. With luck, she wouldn't cry.

"Molly," he said, "let's go get some candy."

"I like candy," she said.

He laughed. She said this as if it were unique and newsworthy. He drove to a nearby Walgreen's. There he guided her through the candy options. He steered her away from hard candies and finally convinced her to try a small package of Sugar Babies. At the last moment, he grabbed a Milky Way too, in case she didn't like the Sugar Babies.

As they walked to the cashier, he glanced up the seasonal aisle, where he had seen Halloween turn to Thanksgiving and now to Christmas. Wendy Marlin was there, halfway down the aisle, looking over a Christmas candle. He passed unseen. But this too, he felt, was a dodge. He took Molly's hand and led her back to the aisle, and, a little short of breath, he called out, "Wendy."

It was the first time they had been alone—or this close to it, anyway—in eleven years, and it was the first time one had gone out of the way to talk to the other. Wendy had several quick reactions to his greeting, one right after another, and he watched them until her face settled down.

"Hi, Ben," she said with a small smile. She knelt to Molly as they neared. "I haven't seen you in a while, Molly. You got some Sugar Babies?" Molly clutched her package with one hand, her father's leg with the other. Wendy's youngest child was a year older than Pam. As she rose, she seemed to look at Molly wistfully.

"I'm sorry we couldn't talk when you and George came by last month," Ben said. "It was good of you."

"Bad timing, though. I could tell." Wendy looked him squarely in the face, and he felt a wave of desire. How could he feel such a thing now, after all that had happened?

"There's something I've been meaning to say," he said.

She folded her arms and cocked her head slightly. "This should be interesting."

"I'm sorry about the way I ended it. I handled it badly." He waved a hand vaguely. "I was scared. Threatened. My way of life." He stopped because she frowned and gave a quick shake of her head. "Just one more thing. I went through Roberta's desk after she skipped town. I found the letter you wrote. I never got it."

Wendy looked away, up a bit, then back at him. "I don't remember writing a letter."

"You don't?" Ben wasn't prepared for this. Nor was he prepared to refresh her memory by summarizing its contents: I love you and know you love me, nothing else matters, to end it now is to choose half a life over a whole one . . .

"You did the right thing," she said simply. She smiled at his reaction. "Don't look so surprised. Hasn't what's happened since then convinced you of that? Eleven years of happiness? You're happy, aren't you?"

"Yeah," he said. She had missed his point. He had just wanted to set the record straight.

"*I'm* not happy," Wendy said with a laugh, "but I wouldn't be anyway. It's something I've learned about myself." He frowned. She shook her head again. Her gaze dropped to Molly, who was fussing with her candy bag. Ben knelt, opened it, and shook a piece into her palm.

When he stood up, he said, "Susan knows. I told her. I wanted you to know that."

Wendy widened her eyes. "I wondered. I'm glad to know. One

would want to know. If I ever tell George, I'll advise you of it." A smile flickered.

"Have you been okay?" he said. "You look okay. I mean, you look good."

She stood there. The silence lengthened, and it became clear she had no intention of answering. He almost reached out for her—almost stepped away from Molly, who was no longer clutching his leg but was leaning against it. It was a familiar feeling, this desire to have her. It involved pressing her head into his neck and stroking her hair. This was part of his feeling for her. But then, why sleep with her? Why did he want to even now, eleven years later, when she was a little plumper, but with those same burning eyes?

"Hey, why aren't you at the play?" she said. "I deliberately didn't go this afternoon because you'd be there."

"I'm going tomorrow." He didn't want to get into nursemaid's elbow. "I'll be happy to escape the house anyway. We're putting it up for sale."

She nodded knowingly, which irked him until she explained. "George told me you'd probably have to. He has a nose for these things. Twenty years of business journalism." She looked sympathetic. "It'll be tough on the kids. But they'll bounce back. They're strong. You're strong."

"Susan's strong," Ben added—thoughtlessly, he saw, for it made her frown. She seemed to size him up.

"Your wish came true," she said.

"What wish?"

"You always told me how you didn't belong in that house. I figured you had a secret wish to get out."

"I've never thought that for a minute. It's our dream house."

Wendy took a step closer to him. "When I heard those words, I'm pretty sure it was you in the bed beside me. It was either you or George, and he's always wanted more than he has, not less."

He felt it again—desire in the purest form. He felt it for no other woman, not this way. It was a need to leave the world he was in and enter hers, even though he had no idea what that world was like, day in and day out.

"I miss you," Wendy said.

"I know. It's awful."

She reached up to give him a pat on the cheek. At first he didn't know what she had in mind, but he drew a quick, incorrect conclusion and began to respond right away. He wrapped an arm low around her waist and was about to pull her into him when her little pat-pat landed, and he stopped himself—but too late. She drew back, then gave a little cry, and with a world of pain on her face she turned and hurried away from him.

He stood and watched her go. He had no idea why he did half the things he did. Now, he thought bitterly, there would be this moment to regret in addition to everything else.

On his way home, he made a decision. He would accept Jeremy's offer of help. If he could get at least twenty thousand dollars, he would have enough to get the business through the Christmas season. His pride had made him refuse Jeremy's offer earlier. His pride was forcing him to sell the house. His pride was making his children cry.

At home, having established that Molly would rather play with the baby-sitter for a while than have him take her home, he tracked down Jeremy's phone number in Susan's address book. Molly and Cindy went upstairs, so he made the call from the kitchen, hoping he didn't get that Paula woman. No one was home. He left a message asking Jeremy to give him a call as soon as possible.

As he hung up, he remembered that Andrea had sent Jeremy

tickets to *Our Town*. He looked at his watch. It was just after two. He picked up his keys. He could make it. The school was just a ten-minute drive. He could tell Cindy and Molly and take off and see all but the first few minutes of the play.

He stood there a moment, then set his keys down. Molly was still pretty shaky. He probably shouldn't leave her right now.

# 24

"Come, come, now, Mr. Cook. What do you take me for? When you looked on the ruins of your building, you knew that people would assume the worst."

"I knew."

"And you knew that police, at taxpayers' expense, would launch a full-scale search for you."

"Well, I didn't imagine helicopters or anything."

"Did I say helicopters? Did I say helicopters?"

"No, but—"

"Instead of identifying yourself at the scene, you skulked away. Tell me, did you have a good time hiding out at the Tucker Inn?"

"Oh, yes. They have cable."

"Ha! An authorized installation, I take it. But what about your poor wife? You let her think she had become a widow. That was a lie."

"Not really."

"What do you mean?"

"She killed me already."

"Ah. So you said. The 'bungled' Italian wedding. That *was* bitchy. By the by, that's a lovely parka. An unusual color."

"It's cranberry. Listen, are you the good cop or the bad cop?"

"Both. We're short-staffed."

Cook had this interesting conversation with himself while he lay in bed and waited for dawn to poke its rosy fingers between the heavy curtains of Room 408 of the Tucker Inn. He had a plan. He hoped it didn't end like this, in the Aberdeen Police Station.

He got up, still in his clothes—the only clothes he owned—and went to the window. What he saw made his lips part. The world he looked on was soft and at rest. Well over a foot of snow had fallen, and big, carefree flakes were still coming down. He poignantly imagined them covering his rubbly grave. The snow would probably delay the search. That was good.

He found a newsstand around the corner and bought a Sunday paper. Its contents would determine whether or not he carried out his plan. He wedged the paper under his arm and crossed the street to McDonald's for breakfast. He would be safe there. The social world he moved in, such as it was, did not breakfast at McDonald's. He settled in with his coffee. The front-page headline confused him, but he plunged into the story, hoping for the best:

FIRE DESTROYS ABERDEEN BUILDING

POLICE INVESTIGATE LINK TO POWER THEFT

A large explosion rocked the east end of Aberdeen Saturday at 2:20 P.M., destroying a building at 302 Demun. Firefighters were unable to put out the blaze before it leveled the two-story structure. No injuries were confirmed, although the building's owner and one tenant in the second-floor apartment are as yet unaccounted for.

257

Police are seeking the owner of the building, Arthur Delong, for questioning about the fire as well as about a possibly related matter, electric utility theft. Delong owned and operated an antiques store in the building, and the fire occurred during business hours. A preliminary search, cut short by darkness, revealed no human remains.

Another possible victim is Jeremy Cook, one of two tenants in the apartment above Delong's Antiques. Cook, an unemployed linguist, inhabited the apartment "pretty much around the clock," according to the woman who shared it with him, Paula Nouvelles. Nouvelles, who describes Cook as an ex-boyfriend, was not in the building at the time of the fire.

The cause of the explosion is not known. Sal Mercato, a St. Louis County Fire Investigator, stated that the large concentration of wood in the first-floor store—what fire experts call a "heavy fire load"—contributed to the ferocity of the blaze.

Earlier in the day, a warrant was issued for Delong's arrest on charges that authorities suspect may be linked to the fire. Since early last month, police have been investigating electric meters at Delong's many rental properties and at an electroplating plant in south St. Louis operated by Delong's brother, Matthew Delong, who is presently in police custody. Authorities believe the Delongs may have diverted tens of thousands of dollars' worth of electricity over a period of several years.

St. Louis County Prosecuting Attorney Carl Musgrave said that a variety of devices for power theft were discovered at seventeen rental properties owned by the Delong brothers and at the Elite Electroplating plant at 4815 Thaw St. At some locations, investigators found a metal strap installed behind the meter, which allowed the current to "jump" and bypass the meter. Some of the meters had been turned upside down, causing them to run backward and subtract billable energy.

The most common method at the rental properties was to drill a small hole into the side of the glass meter cover and insert a wire to create a drag on the meter wheel. Such tampering is often spotted by meter readers because of the projecting wire, but without the wire it is hard to detect. Musgrave stated that power thieves often remove the wire just prior to readings and reinsert it afterward. It is believed that the Delongs operated this way.

The operation was allegedly conceived by Arthur Delong and an older brother, Willie, who was involved until his accidental death by electrocution in 1989. After Willie's death, "Arthur became kind of obsessed with power theft," said Musgrave. "He would take time out from his antiques store to go snake a wire out of a meter clear across the county." Musgrave said Delong kept detailed organizational charts of meter reading schedules, along with meticulous records of the readings, apparently to avoid a common mistake of power thieves—reducing the consumption record so greatly that the utility company becomes suspicious.

Indeed, the Delong operation would probably have gone undetected were it not for the sharp eyes of a cablevision installer. Under a mutual agreement between Show-Me Cablevision and Union Electric, cable installers are rewarded for reporting electrical power theft, and electric line workers are rewarded for spotting illegal cable hookups. On November 7, an installer for Show-Me Cablevision noticed a small piece of coat hanger wire projecting from the meter at the rear of the Demun building. His report triggered an immediate full-scale investigation into all of the Delong properties.

On Saturday afternoon, even as the fire raged at the Aberdeen property, the St. Louis Power Theft Strike Force, under the direction of St. Louis County Detective Stan Phillips, arrested Matthew Delong in his office at Elite Electroplating.

Police were unable to locate Arthur Delong to serve a warrant against him. When asked if Delong may have planted a bomb or set the fire in retaliation against his tenant, Jeremy Cook, for ordering cable installation—the first step in the unraveling of the complex power theft scheme—Phillips told reporters, "We'll see what we find tomorrow. It's a real mess in there. We might find nothing, or we might find one unlucky son of a gun."

Cook found much to ejaculate over in this text, but he kept things pretty much under control, burning his mouth and hands just a few times on his coffee. Delong had tried to kill him! For pure offensiveness, this ranked well above materialism, hauteur, and fondness for jazz. Cook had rented from, lived above, and talked to—a murderer!

Mixed with his rage was a certain delight. Balzac was right. Behind every fortune there *was* a great crime. And Cook had tried to apply this aphorism to Ben. What had he been thinking?

His plan would make up for it. His plan would make up for everything—for an entire lifetime of sterile inaction. But he needed someone to help him with it, and he had been beating his fists against his brain all night in search of that someone. Whom did he know in town? Ted? A good guy, but their relationship consisted of one elevator ride together. Besides, Ted was too much in Paula's neighborhood, and he might slip up.

There was just one other possibility. He was hardly a friend, but he would have to do.

~

Duckwall drummed his fingers on his desk. It was the neatest desk Cook had ever seen. The Error Institute was housed in a former gas station, still identifiable as such despite some architect's desperate ingenuity. By Cook's calculations, Duckwall's desk was smack in the middle of a service bay.

Duckwall stopped drumming. "It's quite a tale, both yours and your friend's, insofar as I understand them. It is rich in the couldn't-have-seen, the could-have-seen, and the should-have-seen. Without fail, mistakes were made—not surprising when such a quantity of energy is discharged. To strive is to err, as they say. But I have a question. How does your plan get around the obstacle of his pride?"

"If I'm dead, he can't return the money," said Cook. "It's that simple."

"But there's your widow. He would want her to have it."

"My widow, my ass," Cook snarled. "But I'm glad you brought that up." He leaned over Duckwall's desk and added a postscript to the letter he had just scribbled. "How does this sound? 'A pre-monition haunts me, Ben. I want you to enjoy the use of the en-closed for your children's sake if my fear, which is as vague as it is disturbing, is borne out. Yours, Jeremy. P.S. Paula and I, after try-ing our darnedest to save our marriage, are calling it quits.'"

Duckwall swayed back and forth in his swivel chair and fiddled distractedly with a cuff link. Although it was a Sunday morning and Cook had summoned him from his home with a barely co-herent phone call, Duckwall had arrived at his office as crisply at-tired as if he were to address the Board of Directors. "Aren't you afraid he'll be sad?" he said.

"Nah. I don't mean a thing to them."

Duckwall pressed his fingertips together. "Sketch the idea once again. I'll search for further error opportunities."

"I send a check for twenty-one thousand to Ben. That leaves ten thousand in my account. I need it to travel on, but I can't get it from the bank because I'm dead. I write a check to you and pop it in the mailbox near my apartment, along with the check for twenty-one thou to Ben. Both checks will have yesterday's date on them. I was still alive then. The mailbox has a Monday-through-Saturday eleven A.M. pickup. If I mail the checks tonight, people will assume I mailed them after eleven yesterday, which is actually very plausible because I was on my way to a con-ference. Ben gets his twenty-one thou and it saves his ass, I hope. You get my ten thou and distribute it to me as I need it."

"It's going to look fishy, you suddenly divesting yourself of all your money."

"I've thought about that. Paula doesn't know about this new money. The bank does, but people write checks and empty ac-counts all the time. If someone at the bank happens to notice the coincidence that I died the same day I wrote the checks, well, that's what it is—a coincidence. There's no fraud here. There's no

261

life insurance. What's my crime? I let people think I was dead when I wasn't. So what?"

"They're going to search for you in the ruins, and they're not going to find you."

"I've done some reading on this. If a fire is hot enough, it burns the bones. It also superheats your blood and brain, which can produce enough steam to blow your skull open. That's what I'm hoping happened to me. The teeth wouldn't have burned, but they turn black in a fire, and it's hard to tell them from charred wood. If my skull blew every which-a-way, it would take them weeks to find my teeth. The important thing is not certainty on this point. It's that with every passing day, my gift to Ben becomes more and more his own."

"In essence, you're asking me to launder your money," Duckwall said.

"Hey," said Cook, delighted. "I've never understood money laundering. Now I do. That's right."

"Do you plan to come back to life?"

"Hell yes! You think I want to be an underground man forever? I figure three or four months. I want to be sure Ben has made the money *his*, psychologically. I want him to have spent it, or at least to have committed it. When I reappear, he'll insist on paying me back as soon as he can, which will be nice. He really just needs a loan. I plan to knock on his door some morning in the spring and surprise the hell out of him."

"Tell me, thus far have you significantly affected the course of this fellow's life?"

Cook shrugged. "I have no idea."

"Has he significantly affected the course of *your* life?"

"I don't know," Cook said impatiently. "Who can say? Why does it matter?"

Duckwall looked hard at Cook. "People enter another's life

and have a permanent effect. That's what I'm facing right now with you. You entered my life briefly before, but you didn't affect it. Now you will. I am sitting here seeing it coming, and I don't know if it's a mistake or not. That is the great terror of life."

Duckwall's long, oval face had taken on a lugubrious cast. Cook was listening respectfully. He had no idea what the man was talking about.

"Look at this." Duckwall picked up a model of a car from his desk and turned it so that it faced Cook. "It's an Edsel. Do you know why the Edsel failed?"

Cook said that he did not.

"Because the grille looks like a vagina." Duckwall pointed to the vertical grille on the model, achieving slight penetration with his index finger. "The Edsel was targeted for 'the young executive on his way up.' In 1958, that would have been a man. But no man wants to drive a vagina. He wants to drive a penis. Correct?"

Cook said he agreed.

"All those years of design and planning, and no one at Ford saw what is now obvious to the eye—that they were producing a rolling vagina. All error is visual error, Jeremy. With study, my vision has improved over the years. But I still haven't learned to see into the future." He set down the Edsel rather firmly. "I accept your plan. How can I not? It is humane, and it is interesting. But I am afraid."

While Cook waited for the fear to be further identified, Duckwall reached into his desk and took out two envelopes. He wrote on one of them, affixed a stamp to both, and extended them one at a time to Cook. "This one comes to me. This one you address to your friend. Please be on guard against the very mundane error of putting the checks in the wrong envelopes. You have your checkbook with you?"

"I always carry a couple of blank checks."

Duckwall seemed impressed. "Backups. Very important. One can never have enough. Three Mile Island resulted from the failure of a backup to a backup to a backup to a backup."

Cook put a highly interested look on his face even as he changed the subject. "Is there a gas furnace or hot water heater in this building that I can have access to? I need to scorch the bejesus out of my wedding band."

"Of course you do," Duckwall said, rising. "Of course you do."

⌒

Cook holed up in the Tucker Inn the rest of the day, hunched over maps of Europe, Asia, and Africa that he had bought at a nearby bookstore. He was planning a unique global tour, a linguistic tour. It was time to taste life, and he would dine on phenomena he had thus far only read about in the library. He would start in the Pacific Northwest, site of the only language family in the world that had no nasal consonants: he would track down a Nootka and inhale his unique orality. He had read that in Burmese, a tonal language, one could say a sentence consisting solely of *ma* spoken with five different tones, and it would carry this meaning: "Help the horse; a mad dog comes!" He would love to meet the challenge of designing a context to elicit such a sentence from a native speaker. Then on to Bali so that he could participate in the eerie national day of silence. He had always wanted to hear Turkish vowel harmony, not to mention Dravidian retroflexion. In Sweden, he would feign an injury in public to see if Swedes in fact said "uffda"—the "ouch" of sympathy. He would have a jolly time.

At ten o'clock he watched a local newscast, a friendly program that united the weekend community with tips about the health hazards of snow shoveling, warm-beverage suggestions to keep you toasty, and dead-linguist updates. The Delong fire was the lead story. Apparently word of Delong's jewelry collection had reached the subculture of looters, and several had descended on the ruin during the overnight snowstorm. They were eventually chased away, according to the reporter live on the dead scene, but their rummaging would complicate the search for the remains of Jeremy Cook, "the as-yet-unaccounted-for resident of the building." The camera had an opinion, though: it panned his final resting place as the reporter spoke. In a further development, Arthur Delong had been nabbed in the Central West End on a tip by a disgruntled former tenant, who had spotted him making a call from a phone booth. Justice was gently falling upon the earth. The broadcast showed a mug shot of Delong. One eyebrow, Cook noted, was slightly elevated.

Near midnight, Cook set out across Aberdeen—a two-mile trek. There was not much traffic, and in some neighborhoods he walked down the middle of the street, which was more clear than the sidewalk. The snow had stopped earlier, but now it was back, small flakes falling hard in a rush of stillness. He skirted wide of his old address and came to the mailbox at the end of his street. He knocked the snow from the lid and divested himself.

He walked along the edge of the seminary grounds. At the site, snow covered everything but the vertical faces of the rear and side walls. The street and sidewalk had been cleared of debris. If it weren't for the yellow tape around the site, one would think the building had been bombed out a decade ago. A police car idled in front, its exhaust puffing into the falling snowflakes. The windows were steamed up, but Cook could see one policeman inside, presumably guarding against looters.

Cook walked farther up the street, thinking and patting his coat pocket. Inside it was a plastic baggie containing his blackened wedding band, on which was engraved part of a verse from

Dante about love moving the sun and the other stars: *"L'amor che muove il sole e l'altre stelle."* This sentiment, which Cook now saw as erroneous in more than its cosmology, united his band with Paula's. They had had them engraved in Siena after the wedding by an excitable man given to frequent exclamations as he worked. *"Bene?"* the engraver had asked when he had engraved Paula's band with *"L'amor che muove."* *"Bene,"* they had said. They traded *Bene's* again when he completed the phrase inside Cook's band.

Some teenage boys and girls were sledding down the long slope of the seminary grounds. They had set candles up along their route. Cook watched a plastic toboggan careen down the hill and skid to a stop at his feet. Two boys laughed and struggled to their feet. One was trying not to spill beer from a can. He was quite young, and when he saw Cook he hid the can behind him. Cook greeted them pleasantly and asked them to do him a favor. He wanted to play a practical joke on the cop in the car down the street—his kid brother, he said. Could the boys go back up the hill and ask everyone up there to start screaming for help at the top of their lungs?

"Cool," the beer drinker said.

Their screams from the hilltop were so good that they almost fooled Cook. The cop jumped from his car and took off to the rescue. Cook emerged from the shadows, a mere shadow himself now, leaned in from the sidewalk, and planted the ring two feet down, under one foot of snow and one foot of rubble. *"Bene,"* he said.

He hurried up the sidewalk, staying on the side of the street away from the seminary. He didn't look back until he was well up Demun. The policeman, no doubt miffed, was returning to his post. Meanwhile, a car had pulled up to the curb at the bottom of the slope. The driver got out and yelled something. The kids scattered in all directions across the snowy expanse—all but one, who stood in place for a moment, then silently walked down the hill and got into the car.

Cook turned and resumed walking. When the car passed him, he started at the sight of it. It was Ben's Saab. Ben was on the job, tracking down one of his "4 GIRLZ," probably Pam, and taking her back into the fold of the family.

# 25

"Okay, you sonofabitch. It's springtime. Out you go."

Ben wrestled the chicken-wire cage from the storeroom to the basement door. The animal inside scurried in protest, making the cage rock and sway like a gyroscope in his hands. The odor of ammonia, unearthed from newspaper strata by the scampering paws, socked Ben full in the face.

He set the cage down at the door and unlocked the deadbolt. He fought the door until it became unstuck. It hadn't been opened in three months, since January, when they had used this entrance to move Pam's bedroom furniture in from the Ryder truck. He hauled the cage up the narrow concrete stairwell, banging it against the crumbling mortar of the limestone wall, accidentally at first, then, when he saw how it maddened the bunny, deliberately.

Ben carried the cage across the lawn to the decade-old Wolmanized wood climber, a ladder-and-fort structure they had inherited from the previous owner, whom Ben imagined moving up in the world, probably to custom-built cedar. He set the bunny's cage down on the moldy wood chips under the fort floor, which was about five feet above ground level and would protect the bunny from the elements.

"You'll like it," he said, "once you get used to the traffic. I'm almost used to it." A cyclone fence ran the length of the yard. Beyond it, and beyond a clump of riotous trees of heaven, but not quite far enough beyond either, was Highway 40.

Boone Street—how the kids mocked the hickness of that name—ran directly under the highway, and theirs was the last house on the north side of the highway bridge spanning the street. The bunker of sloping concrete from the bridge abutment to the street was a new retreat for Pam and Karen, easily reached through a hole in the fence and a worn path through the trees. Ben had initially forbidden it as a hangout, but he relented in the end. "Under the Boardwalk," "Up on the Roof." Why not "Under the Interstate"? He would have to police it, though. Make sure it was safe, stay on top of things, take care.

When he came back into the basement from the yard, he heard Molly yelling from overhead. She had an uncanny sense of even the briefest abandonment. He went to the bottom of the basement stairs and yelled, "What?"

"Apple juice."

"Just a minute." He waited for a moment. She was watching *Sesame Street*. He had another few minutes before she would bellow again. The girls had already left for school, and Susan was writing in the bedroom. A new idea had struck, and a new book was in progress. The family had lost its third floor, so Susan had lost her study, but she still had her writing time. She worked in the kitchen in the early morning, and when Ben brought Molly down, she threw them distracted greetings and hurried to her desk in the bedroom.

Ben got some rags from the rag bin, wetted several of them, and squatted and mopped up bunny overflow on the concrete floor in the storeroom, holding his breath against the smell. He threw the rags in the washer and started the machine. Then he locked the outside door and returned the deadbolt key to its nail in a joist over the furnace—a hiding place known only to him and Susan.

The northeast corner of the basement was Pam's bedroom. The house had four standard bedrooms, one short of what they needed without doubling up any of the kids—something Susan, a bedroom-sharer with her younger sister until she went to college, had strong feelings about, not to mention the kids themselves. When the family discussed the bedroom assignments, there was no question about who would get the basement. Pam didn't even pretend not to want it, thereby muffing an opportunity to fake a concession that she could have cashed in later. But the basement had an outside door. Susan likened it to the wardrobe passage in the Narnia books: Pam could go anywhere through that door. Ben installed a double-cylinder deadbolt before they moved in.

So Pam got the basement. Karen got her bunny. Molly didn't get anything special but was too young to know. And Andrea? A curious case. At one point in their downward slide, in the nail-biting hell between contingent purchase and back-to-back closings, she plopped down on the couch in the den next to him. He was watching the tail end of an NFL playoff game in a rare moment of rest, and she watched a few plays with him. When a car commercial came on, she made an unhappy noise and said she hated ads in a way she never did before. Ben said he just hated the ones with happy families in them. "Why?" she said, sitting up. She grabbed the remote and turned the TV off. "You don't think we're unhappy, do you? We're all exactly as happy as we were before. *Exactly.* I mean it." Susan entered at that moment and said, "Mean what?" Andrea clammed up and left the room shortly afterward. It was a thing between the two of them.

On his way to the stairs, he paused at a wadded-up pair of jeans on the floor. Pam's assigned corner, still lacking a wall to define it, often threatened to take over the rest of the basement, especially the path from the laundry room to the stairs. Susan used to complain frequently about the mess. Every time she did, Ben, the ultimate cause of it all, felt rebuked. Either because she sensed this or because she decided Pam was incorrigible, Susan cut back her complaints to explosions every two or three weeks.

Ben usually kicked Pam's clothes back into her corner, using the point of his shoe like a placekicker and watching blouses and bras come to rest on her desk and lamp. Now, because he felt he owed Pam something extra on this day, he picked up her encroaching garments and actually folded a few. They seemed to pulse with her energy. He untangled her phone cord. He straightened her bed a little. He wouldn't make it, but he did straighten it. Then he trotted up the stairs and joined Molly in the den.

"Apple juice," she said without looking at him, her eyes fixed to the TV screen.

"You can't have apple juice," he said.

"Apple juice."

"You can't have it. You've been sick." Molly had just gotten over a viral diarrhea that had kept him or Susan up with her a couple of nights. "You can have 7-UP or ginger ale."

"Orange juice."

"You can't have orange juice either. 7-UP or ginger ale."

"I want *Care Bears*."

"We don't get *Care Bears* in the new house." Because Daddy had to cancel the premium channels. "Do you want a Popsicle?"

A long pause. He decided that all of his future happiness would rest on her answer.

"Popsicle," she said.

He grinned. Then he remembered they were out of Popsicles.

He didn't despair but went right to the candy cabinet and grabbed a string of red licorice. He dropped it in Molly's lap. She had never eaten candy at this hour of the day in her life. She lifted one end of it to her mouth slowly, to avoid attracting attention in case it was all a mistake.

The phone rang. He answered it in the kitchen.

"Ben? Stan Phillips."

"Stan!" Ben said heartily. His tone matched the speaker's, though he didn't place him immediately.

"It's been a while. I have some news."

"Ah," said Ben. Recognition gave way to itchy, unpleasant hope. "News?"

"About Orson and Roberta."

"Did you find them?"

Phillips took a long breath. "Pieces. They were in a plane crash in Africa last week. In Tanzania. They were on a plane going from Nairobi to—"

"Dar es Salaam?"

"Yeah. The FBI has been monitoring the area because it was one of the remote spots you said she had been to before."

"Yes. The cashew farms near the coast. What happened? Are they dead?"

"Oh, yeah. No one survived. They were listed as Olive and Robert Nussgeld. A guy here tells me 'Nussgeld' is German for 'nut money.' They were a fun-loving couple, all right, at least until they crashed into Mount Kilimanjaro. I know what your next question's going to be, and the answer is no, we didn't find it. One of Roberta's suitcases was pretty much intact, but it didn't give a hint about where it's stashed. There was about four hundred and fifty in American dollars in there. That'll make its way to you, eventually."

"Well, that's something."

"They might have already blown it all. There was a bunch of busted-up camera equipment in the wreckage. Expensive stuff, apparently, like they'd been on a spree. Oh, she was still writing those love letters, Ben. There were some in her suitcase."

Ben said nothing.

"They were getting better. Her style improved."

"Great."

"I've got an odd question for you. I'm not even sure you can answer it." Phillips's tone was puzzled, scholarly. "There was one other American on board. I don't have any information on him, besides his name. Jeremy Cook. Is that a St. Louis name? Why is it familiar to me?"

It pained Ben to hear the name like that, so unexpectedly. "I had a friend with that name. He died in that fire on Demun over the winter. He lived above the antiques store."

"Oh, yeah!" Phillips said. "The Delong case. That guy was a friend of yours?"

"Yes. Not a good friend." Ben hesitated. He wasn't sure what kind of friend Jeremy had been. He didn't fit any category.

"So this passenger just had the same name. I'm glad that's settled. A coincidence. It was really bugging me. That's all for now, Ben. If we get any better news, I'll call. But don't hope."

"I won't. I don't. Thanks."

Ben hung up and stared vacantly at the phone. He wandered to the kitchen window—a leaky aluminum jalousie window from the 1950s. He watched the traffic up on Highway 40, one whoosh after another. He wondered if a new, tightly caulked, double-pane thermal window would block the noise. Four hundred and fifty might cover the cost. He could put a plaque on it—"The Roberta and Orson Memorial Window"—to remind him always to stay on course, never to run off the rails.

Ben had a sudden, strong desire to see Jeremy to thank him for his clumsy attempts to help. Of course, Ben had been clumsy too, saying no, then trying to say yes but just getting an answering machine—which, by his calculations, must have blown up shortly after he had left his message. Ben was still puzzled that Jeremy hadn't picked up the phone when he called. For a while he had even seen it as a reason for hope that Jeremy hadn't been home at the time of the explosion. But then a few days later they found Jeremy's wedding band in the ashes, and that settled it.

The check came that same day, too late to be useful. The house had been too good, too desirable, and they had gotten a "top dollar" contract on the very first day they had shown it. They were legally obliged to go forward with the sale. When it was all over, their downgrading generated a cash cushion, as planned, and Jeremy's loan became irrelevant. The twenty-one thousand was rightfully Paula's. Ben felt this despite the brush-off she had given Susan when she called to offer her condolences. It had taken Susan weeks to get over that. He never deposited Jeremy's check. He just tore it up. The money would stay in Jeremy's account and eventually go to Paula. She could buy etiquette lessons with it.

Jeremy's donation still puzzled him because he didn't really know the donor. He knew Jeremy for a twitcher, a blurter, a sudden brooder. Kind of a mess, really, but a likeable mess. He seemed miscast, but then Ben couldn't think of a suitable role to cast him in.

There had been no memorial service. Paula told Susan no one would have come. But she was wrong. Ben's family would have come, all of them. Andrea, Pam, and Karen all cried when they learned what had happened to him.

Ben imagined performing his own little service for Jeremy. He would use a box of cashews. The guy sure went for them, no doubt about that. He would take a nice gift box down to the Mississippi and let the nuts stand in for the bones that were never found in the ruins. He would cast them across the water and have some nice thoughts. He could imagine doing that.

And he could imagine saying a few words to Jeremy as he did it. He would bring him up to date.

He'd tell him that Karen had gotten her goddamn bunny.

He'd tell him that Andrea had gotten a good financial aid package that would allow her to go to Swarthmore.

He'd tell him that Molly now said "tomato" instead of "pomato."

And he'd tell him that Pam, as she left for school this morning, paused at the front door—paused for no reason at all—and said, "Bye, Dad."

Printed in the United States
127248LV00002B/108/A